JACINTHA

JACINTHA

DUNDURN
TORONTO

Publisher: Scott Fraser | Editor: Dominic Farrell
Cover designer: Laura Boyle
Cover image: istock.com/jozefmicic
Printer: Webcom, a division of Marquis Book Printing Inc.

Library and Archives Canada Cataloguing in Publication

Title: Jacintha / Lorraine Davies.
Names: Davies, Lorraine (Lorraine E.) author.
Identifiers: Canadiana (print) 20190075775 | Canadiana (ebook) 20190075783 | ISBN 9781459744554 (softcover) | ISBN 9781459744561 (PDF) | ISBN 9781459744578 (EPUB)
Classification: LCC PS8607.A923 J33 2019 | DDC C813/.6—dc23

We acknowledge the support of the Canada Council for the Arts and the Ontario Arts Council for our publishing program. We also acknowledge the financial support of the Government of Ontario, through the Ontario Book Publishing Tax Credit and Ontario Creates, and the Government of Canada.

Care has been taken to trace the ownership of copyright material used in this book. The author and the publisher welcome any information enabling them to rectify any references or credits in subsequent editions.

The publisher is not responsible for websites or their content unless they are owned by the publisher.

Printed and bound in Canada.

VISIT US AT

dundurn.com | @dundurnpress | dundurnpress | dundurnpress

Dundurn
3 Church Street, Suite 500
Toronto, Ontario, Canada
M5E 1M2

For my beloved daughters, Carrie and Budge

PREFACE

THIS IS A TRUE STORY, written in the form of a novel, about my relationship with a woman I've called Jacintha. It was completed seven years after the events.

I could have written a memoir, but I believe the truth, in this case, can be more richly and deeply expressed in fiction. I've used pseudonyms for everyone in the story. Were our real names known, Jacintha and my family would almost certainly suffer.

I've changed the location, too, as a further barrier to discovery.

I showed my ex-wife, Carol, a few chapters at a time while polishing a final draft, and included our email exchanges in the book.

Richard Wilson
September 2012

SHE WOKE UP *with a cry. Her childhood nightmare again. The man she called The Dirty Man loomed over her, huge as a bear. He pushed her to the floor, held her down with his knee as he unzipped his pants, put his paw over her mouth when she screamed.*

He smelled like fish and beer and pee. She could see his horrible thing, like a purply sausage, coming closer.

She had seen him with her mother more than once and had opened the door when he knocked, even though her mother was out. Stupid. Stupid. Didn't Mummy tell me never to open the door?

Her tears were mixing with the sweat on his fingers, wetting her lips. She gagged and he said a bad word and pressed down harder. She tasted blood.

She woke up as always, screaming, before he could push the ugly thing into her, hurting her terribly, the way he had in real life.

The nightmare had recurred often in the past, well into her teen years, usually after she had seen a man on the street who looked like him. There were altogether too many bald men with fat paunches and noses red veined from drink. Too many ugly men.

After she had turned twenty, five years ago, the nightmare hap-pened rarely.

She would tell Richard what had happened to her, of course. It was part of the whole plan.

But not yet.

ONE

January 2005

RICHARD DREAMED HE was lying half-drowned on a beach while a group of women and children pointed and laughed at him. He heard faint music, but it wasn't sweet. It was menacing. Water gurgled sporadically from his mouth, as though he were a damaged fountain gargoyle. Carol was there, dressed in rags, but he didn't recognize anyone else. He was guilty of something, but what? Racked with guilt. Wracked. Wrack was seaweed washed up on shore. Washed up. His legs were covered with small, sharp things that pricked his skin and felt like needles entering his bones to their aching marrow. He tried to brush the tormentors away and a few small crabs fled, but the other blue-black things clung. The colour of barnacles, but not barnacles. Creatures with teeth and claws.

He woke with a cry of fear, and Carol reached out and stroked his forehead, saying, "It's all right, Richard, you're safe."

Both his legs were in casts. His concussion had turned out to be mild, thanks to plaster rather than timbers or toilets striking his head. Carol, her left arm in a cast and her ribs taped, had been released from hospital. She was visiting Richard before she went to meet the parents of their boarder, Jenny, at a funeral parlour. They had flown in from Montreal to take her body home.

"Bad dream," Richard said. "I'm all right." *What a hollow phrase*, he thought. *More often than not a lie, a glib social lie.*

When his head cleared enough to understand Carol's mission, he asked her if she'd bought a card of condolence, and when she said she hadn't yet, he told her his requirements for the card, so particular that he could tell it was all Carol could do not to lose patience with him.

"Not one of those white lily things, you know — embossed. They're so gloomy. Dire. Sorry, odd word. It is dire, after all. Not too much colour, of course, but maybe a little — a pale-yellow rose, maybe, although Jenny was such a red rose, if she were a flower, wasn't she? And no verse; no soppy verse. I'll write something. Oh God, what will I write?"

"Write that she was a wonderful girl and you were very fond of her and so glad to have known her — something like that," Carol said.

"Very fond. It seems too lukewarm. It was more than that, but I can't presume to say I loved her, can I? After knowing her such a short time? Not to her parents."

"Say something conventional. Write a letter to them later, when you've had some time. You'll think of the right things to say."

"No, you write in the card, from both of us. Say I'll write later. Or I'll phone them. We can talk on the phone. I wish I could have been the one to tell them. I feel it was my duty. It shouldn't have happened. We shouldn't have let it happen."

"Look at me, Richard. And listen. We didn't *let it happen*. It was an accident. An accident."

Richard said nothing, looked away.

Carol took his chin in her hand and turned his face toward her, as though he were a pouting child. "Say it."

"An accident," he said flatly.

It had happened less than forty-eight hours earlier. He had heard the roar first; an unearthly, apocalyptic sound. He'd thought absurdly of gods hurling boulders, thundering, throwing down lightning bolts. He should run, but which way? When the river of mud crashed through the living room ceiling, he was thrown to the floor. Something fell across his legs and he screamed in pain. Things were still falling, and he put his arms up to shield his head. When he dared to look, he saw all around him chairs, lamps, bureau drawers, clothes. Jesus! He lay perfectly still in the cold mud, most of which had rushed past him, smashing the French doors on the way out. He was held somewhere between panic and numbness, each vying for supremacy. After a while, a terrible stillness fell.

Carol. Where is she? He tried to call her but his voice broke, rasping like an animal's. He tried again.

"Carol!" A croaking sound. *Not loud enough. Try again.* "Carol!"

"Here, Richard. I'm here. In the dining room."

"Are you okay? Are you hurt? Christ, Carol, what the hell happened?" Panic was winning.

"I think I'm all right. Are you?" Her voice was weak, but he thought she was trying to sound brave.

Brave, Richard thought, and then the word floated away.

"I'm okay," he said. With an effort he tried to push himself up, but his hands slipped and he fell down again. His back was wet and cold. The oak bookcase was across his shins and books lay everywhere in the swamp of mud. *My books are drowning. Why that phrase?*

Oh, yes. He'd been reading by the fireplace, which was gone now. Its tiles lay in shards. Bathroom sink from upstairs on the floor. Furniture upside down. Floorboards hanging. Chunks of plaster. The cliff above must have tried to bury them. Not tried. No. Pathetic fallacy. Act of God. No God. Act of nature. Fuck! Completely random fucking catastrophe.

Yes. By the fireplace. He had been reading *The Tempest*, because of Jenny, thinking of Jenny, beginnings of an erection. A pleasurable guilt. No. Shouldn't.

"Richard. What are you doing?" Fear in Carol's voice. "Can you come to me?"

His heart thumped. A moan escaped him. "No, I'm trapped. Can you move?"

"I'm squashed up against the wall. Our mattress fell on me."

"Mattress? In the dining room?" *Why not? The toilet is now in the living room.*

"I thought it might smother me, but it's leaning on something. A chair is pressing me into the corner."

"Oh, Jesus. Carol, I'm going to try to get free, come to you." He managed this time to sit up.

It was awful now. Timbers creaked. The whoosh of heavy rain lashed the house. Plaster and dust and water fell in sudden flurries. Something more was going to come down. Maybe the whole upper floor would fall on him. On Carol.

And Jenny! Oh god. Was she here? "Jenny! Jenny! Answer me, please, Jenny!"

Nothing.

"I think Jenny's gone to class," Carol called.

He could hear she was suffering, but fear overcame his sympathy. "You think? You think? Shit. Has she or hasn't she?"

"Richard, please calm down. Don't panic. Please."

"Don't panic? The house has fallen on us and I don't know where Jenny is. I'm trying to lift the bookcase off my legs." He tightened his arm muscles, willed them to be steel-like, lifted the case an inch or two, but it dropped back down and he yelled.

"Richard?"

He steadied his voice. "I'm all right."

On his next try, he lifted the bookcase high enough and long enough to free his right leg. With his arms straight out and straining, it was going to require a terrible twist of his body to push the bookcase to the left and shift his left leg to the right. He couldn't get any traction and his shoulders were giving out. He lost his grip and the bookcase dropped the last inch and thudded onto his leg again and he fell back and began to cry and then everything went dark.

He woke to see black rubber boots and yellow rubber pants. A man looking at him.

"Can you hear me, sir?"

Richard tried to sit up, but the man squatted, put his arms around Richard's shoulders, and gently eased him down. "Don't move now," he said. "We're bringing a stretcher in. You're going to be all right."

"I feel dizzy."

"Probably a concussion. Some of the ceiling seems to have fallen on you."

There were things he should remember. What were they? Carol, yes. "My wife?"

"She's all right. She's in the ambulance. You'll see her soon."

"Is she badly hurt?"

"No, a broken arm. Maybe a cracked rib."

And then he remembered. "Jenny," he said. "Where's Jenny?" He called her name, once, twice, his voice rising to a wail.

"Sir, sir, please stay calm. Is there someone else in the house?"

"Yes, Jenny. She boards here. I don't know if she left for class. She has an afternoon class."

"Okay. Just a minute. I'll check." He went away. Came back after what seemed like a long time. "Yes, your wife told us about her. We've looked around already. But we'll look again. Don't worry."

"Don't worry! Who the fuck are you people? Can't you do a proper search?" He began to whimper like a child and was crying uncontrollably as they loaded him into the ambulance.

They found Jenny's body in her bedroom. The roof had fallen on her and she'd been crushed and buried under the debris. Richard, concussed and in shock, wasn't told about her until the following day.

"I think it would lift your spirits a little if you heard from Imogen," Carol said. "I left a message for her telling her you've been injured but you are going to be all right. Have you heard from her?"

Imogen was Richard's daughter from his first marriage. She'd lived in England with her mother ever since the divorce thirteen years ago, when Imogen was seven years old.

"No, I called last week and Grace said Imogen was travelling in Europe with her boyfriend."

"Well, I hope she gets in touch soon."

"Yes, well." Richard looked out the window and didn't speak for a moment. The droop of his mouth reminded Carol of the way he had looked on visits with Imogen — a look of pain and regret and longing.

"I guess no flowers for the Walkers," Richard said. "If they're flying home right away. It seems a shame, no flowers." He started to cry.
"Yes, get flowers. They can take them or not, but get flowers. Roses."

Carol bought a blank card with a yellow rose on it and wrote
exactly what she'd suggested Richard write. She bought a bouquet
of pale-yellow roses as well. She had been fond of Jenny, but the
word, now that she thought about it, did seem lukewarm. How
could anyone not love a young woman as bright and pretty as
Jenny? So pretty she'd made Carol, who usually believed she looked
young for her age, feel old and rumpled, especially in the morn-
ings when Jenny was dewy and Carol's face was lined with pillow
creases and she'd yet to put on her eyeliner and mascara.

She found Jenny's parents, Gordon and Amanda Walker, in a
stuffy little reception room lit by a lamp and a trickle of daylight
from a small, high window. It smelled of stale perfume and some
kind of chemical. Carpet cleaner? Embalming fluid?

Codeine was making Carol woozy.

Amanda Walker looked like she didn't know whose clothes she
was wearing. The fur coat seemed massive on her — more like a fur
blanket, or a bearskin with its limp arms around her. (The weather
would have been icy when they left Montreal.) Her black fur hat
was at a strange angle, maybe knocked askew without her noticing.
Or caring. Only the salt-stained suede boots seemed to be hers.
She bent down for a moment and traced the salt lines with a finger
as though the lines were part of a map to a place she'd lost, a place
Jenny might be. Carol drew in her breath sharply, as sadness hit
her, and the woman looked up at her.

Carol introduced herself and thrust the roses toward Amanda,
who took them with a vague glance and put them in her lap.

"Thank you," she said.

She looked down at her boots again and mumbled something.

"What's that, Amanda dear?" Gordon Walker asked. He
was about sixty-five, tall, with very short, grey hair. He wore an

impeccable dark suit and a navy-blue overcoat of heavy wool. Expensive. Jenny had told them he was the president of a chain of supermarkets — twenty years older than her mother, whom he'd met while she was working in one of his stores. Her mother had since made a career as a charity fundraiser; a "lady who lunches," Jenny had said with a mixture of amusement and disdain.

Gordon Walker's expression was stern, perhaps in an effort to keep his emotions from bursting forth. His taut and shiny skin seemed to be holding it all in. He put his hand on his wife's shoulder, which drooped under the pressure. She looked up at him, puzzled.

"Never mind," he said.

"No, no. It's all right. I said the salt on the sidewalks always ruins suede boots. That's what I said. I don't know why I buy them." She was as beautiful as her daughter, even with her swollen eyes. Dark curls like Jenny's spilled from her hat. She was crying silently, her tears running over her high cheekbones and down to the corners of her lips.

Carol said, "Jenny was lovely to have around. We feel so terrible about what happened. A lovely, lovely young woman. It shouldn't have happened. Our house, you know, it shouldn't … it shouldn't have …" She began to cry, too.

"Please, it wasn't your fault," Gordon Walker said.

Husband and wife sat and listened to Carol cry. Amanda's eyes were dryer now. Nearer to the deserts of grief they would become.

When Carol could speak again, she asked, "Will you have a funeral in Montreal?"

"In our church, yes," Gordon said.

"*It is your fault*," Amanda said, every icy word precisely separate.

"Amanda!"

"No, Gordon, I will say it." Again she mouthed the carefully separated words, then went on. "You and your husband should have had the risk assessed, living at the bottom of a cliff like that. What kind of fools are you?" Her voice became high pitched. "It was criminally careless. Criminally. Oh, yes. But I can't make a criminal charge against you. Or even a civil one. My lawyer advised me neither would hold."

"Amanda! When did you talk to our lawyer?"

"I thought about it on the flight and this morning I phoned him and told him the house must have been unsafe, that these people should have known, and he said it would be too hard to prosecute successfully." She stopped to suck in air, a drowning woman. "And anyway, it won't bring Jenny back. But I want you to know. I blame you. I want you to suffer, knowing that it's your fault. And that I'll always blame you."

Carol was unable to speak.

Gordon raised his wife out of her chair and held her close. "Amanda, Amanda," he crooned, and kissed her eyes, wet again with slow tears.

After a minute, she pushed him away and left the room, a room now seeming to be emptied of whatever air and light there had been.

Carol continued to sit in stunned silence.

"I apologize for my wife," Gordon said. "Grief can make savages of us all. Did someone say that? Is it a quote? Anyway, it's true. I know I seem to be bearing up all right, but if I break down now, I won't be able to help my wife."

"Yes, it's all right. I understand," Carol said. *I can't tell Richard this*, she thought. *He already blames himself. I can never tell him this.*

Dear Mr. and Mrs. Walker,

I've phoned you several times to offer my condolences but haven't been able to reach you. I can understand you wanting to be quiet in your grief.

I'm grieving, too, very much. Jenny was a bright light in what seems to me a world growing darker and darker. A shining girl.

I know from our conversations that she had an excellent mind and was very insightful. We sometimes discussed her courses and I was particularly pleased with her love of Shakespeare's plays, which I have taught for many years.

I won't make this too long — please call me sometime when you want to talk about Jenny. I'd like to share some memories with you. You can reach me in the hospital at 555-233-9495. I'll give you my home number when I know where I'll be living.

With my heartfelt sympathy for your great loss,
Richard Wilson

A week later he phoned again and got the Walkers' answering machine. He left his name and number again. Another week went by without a reply.

"Maybe they don't want to talk to me," he said to Carol. "Maybe ..." The truth hit him suddenly, a hammer to his gut. "Maybe they blame me for her death."

"Don't read too much into not hearing from them, Richard. It's only been three weeks and they're devastated and probably are talking only to friends and relatives."

"No, no. They blame me. Oh god, they do, don't they? They blame me." *It should have been obvious to me*, he thought, *had I not been wrapped in my cloak of self-pity.* "Did they say something to you about this?"

"First of all, if they blamed anyone, they'd blame both of us, not just you. But they said they blamed no one, that it was a tragic accident."

"Oh, Carol, is that true?"

"Yes. It's true."

TWO

THEY'D LOST EVERYTHING. Everything had been buried in mud and rubble or was too water damaged to salvage, and even if it had been salvageable, they couldn't have got to it. The house had been declared out of bounds, yellow-taped like a crime scene, waiting for the bulldozer.

Carol had done the tedious job of replacing their social insurance, health insurance, and Visa cards, as well as other necessary papers and cards. They both bought new laptops. They'd had no cellphones, having agreed that such devices were great for herding teenaged off-spring, of which they had none, but highly unnecessary for phoning to say that you were ten minutes from home, unless someone ill was waiting for you, or, as Carol joked, "someone was pining for you as strongly as a Norwegian blue parrot pines for the fjords."

They both taught at the University of British Columbia — Richard, English literature, and Carol, art history — and their lesson plans and lecture notes had been lost with the computers. Since they'd both been teaching their courses for many years, though, it wasn't difficult to replace them.

Carol felt now like she'd lost her anchors, that she was floating dangerously without her collection of art books (nice and heavy), her antique sideboard (nice and heavy, too), her vintage velvet coat, the elegant shoes she had bought in Venice. All of these, and more, held precious memories and had the gravity of beauty. But her biggest loss was Richard. He was there and not there. She hadn't thought she owned him (had she?), but he had in some essential way been hers, she *knew* him, and now he too was floating away into some darkness of his own, becoming a stranger.

Richard took a long time to recover physically. He was in casts for two months, on crutches for a month, and then reliant on a cane. Now, except for a slight limp, he seemed all right.

The big thing, the worrying thing for Carol, was that they hadn't made love since the landslide, and to make matters worse, her desire had increased greatly. She often had almost electrical surges of desire that took minutes to subside and left her aching for sex, sometimes for hours, even after masturbating. In the first months she hadn't said anything about her frustration, realizing Richard was often in pain, and depressed and tired, but lately she'd been begging him to make love with her. She'd told him about her "surges," but he hadn't seemed to really grasp what she was saying; hadn't understood the intensity of her need.

One night he finally said yes, but without much enthusiasm. He lay on his back and she leaned over and kissed him. There was no heat in his response. She stroked him, but he remained soft and continued to lie passively, except for making a few limp passes of his hand across her back. She decided to tell him one of her stories, an occasional variation in their foreplay. She started with one that she knew he liked, about one of her first lovers, when she was eighteen, in which she'd kept pretending she didn't want him as things got more and more intense, and Richard would be aroused and ask questions. This time he said nothing, but she went on. "I kept resisting until he was frantic, and so was I." Still no response.

Carol lay back, discouraged, and noticed how musty the room smelled, probably from the old floorboards. Her mother, Frances, was renting them this house in East Vancouver that she had bought years earlier as an investment. It was all they could afford, having had no landslide insurance. One of the best things about it was that there were no cliffs anywhere near.

Carol missed their airy North Vancouver bedroom. In the winter a witch hazel tree had perfumed the room, and in the summer the intense sweetness of pear blossoms took over. The curtains were never closed there, and moonlight streamed in every night, it seemed to her now, although in rainy winters that couldn't have been possible.

Too dark. She turned on a bedside lamp so she could see Richard. And be seen. Her breasts were bare, and they were beautiful, maybe less beautiful now than when she was younger, but still fine — full curves underneath and lovely indentations above from the gentle pull of their weight. One lover had said upon their parting, "It's your breasts I'll miss," and she knew he had meant it. Richard had never made such a fuss over them. That was all right. She didn't want to be reduced to body parts.

He glanced at her now, but didn't reach out.

"I was tight, aching, getting so wet," Carol said, having decided to keep trying.

Here, in the past, Richard would say something like, "You're wet now, aren't you? You'll let me in, won't you?"

"No," she'd say, and Richard would say, "Yes," and she'd resist until Richard pushed her legs apart, saying he must have her, and it was wonderful after that. This time he didn't respond.

She slid down, kissed his nipples, his belly, but when she tried to go further, he said, "No," loudly, grabbed her by her shoulders and pushed her up.

Stunned, she said, "Shit, Richard. What the hell's wrong? I'm so frustrated. Tell me, please. Are your legs still hurting? You've been saying you're feeling all right. Are you in pain?"

"No."

"Well, then, tell me what's wrong. Why don't you want me anymore?"

"That's putting it too strongly. It's not … I don't know … not that definite. Sorry, Carol, sorry. I don't know. I don't know."

"I know you're still grieving and still healing, and so am I, but you've gone so far into yourself, you seem to be falling into a full-blown depression. I don't know why you refuse to go to a therapist. Please, Richard, it's time. Medications …"

He had been avoiding eye contact, but looked at her now and shook his head impatiently. "No. I need to feel … all of it. A therapist would just tell me … dull me with drugs."

"You don't know that. He might help. Drugs might help. Just for a while." She felt a bit hypocritical, remembering that she had refused tranquilizers when she went to her doctor about her sexual overdrive. But depression was different — more serious, surely. "Anyway, I don't know … don't know if I can go on this way."

Fear widened Richard's eyes. "You're not leaving me?"

"No, no. I love you, but I need … the way it used to be." She was leaning over him, willing him to keep looking into her eyes, but he touched her arm, looked at the ceiling as though there might be an answer there.

"Who said, 'You must change your life'?" he asked finally.

"Oh, Richard. Rilke, I think."

"That's how I feel," he said. "Must. Something else entirely."

She looked with stupid fascination at a strand of her hair, curled like an offering on his chest, red-gold against his pale skin. He swept it off, absently, with the flat of his hand.

"I feel half-crazy," she said, and he seemed then to really see her for the first time since they'd gone to bed, and he smiled at her ruefully.

She lay down, arm across his chest, hot cheek against his cool shoulder. "Don't stop loving me. When you change."

"No, I won't. Be patient. Please. Will you?"

She kissed the damp hollow of his neck.

"Let's sleep now," he said, gently moving her arm and turning onto his side.

She lay looking at his back, moved closer to smell his skin. He had three moles, brown and velvety, in a triangular pattern on his neck. She resisted the impulse to touch them one by one. His slim waist and nicely rounded butt were covered now, but she knew them by heart and turned away with a groan.

In the living room, she lay down on the couch and brought herself to orgasm, thinking of him.

THREE

RICHARD GOT UP at ten o'clock, after Carol was safely away to UBC. She'd chosen to teach a summer course, which was just ending. Richard's course was due to start next week. He hadn't wanted to face Carol after his failure to make love to her. He couldn't stand the prospect of her sadness, and anger, too, at what seemed to her to be pigheadedness in not getting help as he drifted further and further away from her. God knew he needed her. If only she could stand by like a nurse who feeds and bathes her patient, smiles sympathetically, never makes judgments, never expects anything in return. He laughed at the unreasonableness, the infantile nature of his vision. If only Carol would wait until he'd sorted himself out. If only she'd wait.

He'd had his recurring dream about Jenny. They walked into the ocean together, the warm water climbing from ankles to knees to thighs, to chests and mouths, until they embraced and kissed underwater and came up laughing. And then she was floating away, staring at him, frightened, one arm reaching out. He started swimming to her frantically, but he could get no closer, no matter how hard he tried, and then she disappeared and he woke crying out. And his first thought, when he'd calmed down, was, as always, that he should have asked her to leave, made up some excuse, anything — a relative needed her room — as soon as his feelings for her, even occasionally, became inappropriate.

He'd never touched her, was appalled by the idea, and had been ashamed of the stirrings he felt for her when she sat at the breakfast table across from him, her dark curls a bit wild after her shower and smelling of lemons, her brown eyes lively, her skin damp and glowing. She'd made him think of a beach after rain, the sun's sudden heat.

If I'd asked her to leave, she'd still be alive.

But how would he have explained asking her to leave to Carol? He could have said that Jenny had become flirtatious, but if Carol had confronted her, Jenny would have felt hurt, betrayed. *But she'd still be alive.*

What he had said to Carol, after the disaster, was that they should never have rented to Jenny, that by renting to her they'd killed her. They'd assumed (why, oh why, had they assumed?) that the cliff above them had been checked for stability before houses were allowed to be built below, and that the cliff had been inspected periodically after that. Carol stared at him, hesitated as though she were about to agree with him, but finally replied that he was thinking crazily, suffering from survivor's guilt, and that he should go for therapy. And he'd said, "Maybe you're right," but hadn't meant it. Survivor's guilt implied one wasn't guilty of anything.

He'd stopped trying to reach Jenny's parents. They didn't know him and didn't want to know him. Better to let them grieve in peace.

The only course he had this coming semester was his third-year Shakespeare seminar. He'd asked Gabe, the head of the English department, to excuse him from his other classes on health grounds, with a vague promise — a lie, in fact — that he'd go back to his full load in the new year.

He was going to teach *The Tempest* as an homage to Jenny, who'd told him she was planning to write a version of the play set in present time, with an environmentalism theme.

Richard greatly regretted that he hadn't learned more about Jenny's vision for the play. She'd said, as best as he could remember, "I love *The Tempest*. It's a wonderful story of forgiveness. And I'd respect that in the rewrite. But Prospero does take over the island and makes a native of the island his slave. Prospero doesn't harm the island, it's true, but his sort of colonialism was and is guilty of destroying or degrading many parts of the world."

And then she had said, "Of course, there is the love story of Miranda and Ferdinand, which is important. And there is also the love between Prospero and his daughter, whom he has raised and protected. Love is as central as forgiveness."

Richard had said, "I'd like to hear a lot more about what you've planned, it sounds wonderful, but I have to rush off to an appointment." But he never had another chance.

He would give his class the task that she hadn't lived to fulfill. Jenny had had a sweet earnestness about her, and like so many of her generation, believed she should help to save the planet, and that her play would be a small contribution to the cause. He hoped his new students would have a similar belief.

A note from Carol on the fridge said: *Don't forget we're invited to Mum's for dinner tonight, 6:30. Hope you have a good day, darling.*

Richard was grateful to Frances for providing them with a place to live. The landslide had left them with a ruin of a house, a pile of rubble they'd had to pay to have cleared away. Underneath was a piece of property that was going to be very hard to sell, and would probably not sell for much if they did manage to find a buyer. They were going to have to start saving money in earnest if they ever wanted to buy a house again. Richard wasn't sure he cared but he knew Carol did.

What to do with the day? He found it hard to read anymore. His attention tended to wander now, and books made him feel claustrophobic, as though he were trapped in their airless world. Just being in the house too long made him claustrophobic, too, maybe because of the fear he'd experienced during the landslide when he was pinned down, not knowing if he'd live or die. Well, no "maybe" about it, but it was more than that. His mind went round and round, never settling peacefully anywhere, trying to convince himself that Jenny's death was an accident — only that — but it was remarkably hard to reason himself out of irrationality. And the pressing need to radically change his life? Was that irrational, too?

Anyway, he needed fresh air. He needed to walk.

One day he'd taken a bus to Stanley Park and walked for hours, until his legs became painful. This despite the fact that he was taking more painkillers than Carol knew about. But parks were beginning to make him feel anxious — all that beauty giving itself to him, and him giving nothing but his sadness and restlessness.

It was a hot beginning to September. He dressed in cotton khaki pants, a short-sleeved white shirt, socks and sneakers, and set off. He'd decided to walk down Powell Street, all the way to Main, several miles. The street was an industrial one, and its grubbiness and starkness suited his mood.

For the first six blocks or so after Nanaimo Street, bland, boxy apartment buildings lined the streets, their wrought-iron-railed balconies holding bikes, boxes, and green garbage bags stuffed with who-knew-what.

A man who looked a bit like Richard walked toward him. He wore clothes like Richard's, too, except the man's white shirt, khaki pants, and running shoes were stained and dirty. As they passed each other, the man nodded, smiled a gap-toothed smile, and tipped an imaginary hat.

"Watch out," he said. "It'll bite you in the ass."

Christ, he's like me, if I sink to my lowest. Or he's me now, a physical representation of my soul.

That phrase. Grace had used a similar one when Imogen was a newborn. She'd told Richard she'd been on the bus, sitting across from a woman with a terrible pallor — almost chalk white. Jet-black hair and scarlet lipstick.

"I felt frightened, Richard," Grace had said. "I had a mad moment when I thought she was *being shown to me*, a picture of the state of my soul."

Richard had hotly denied there was anything wrong with Grace's soul and said she must be overtired from all her sleepless nights with the baby, and he'd do more to help. He realized now that she was probably suffering from postpartum depression, and he hadn't taken her to a doctor, hadn't helped with Imogen nearly enough. Grace had got through it, but had his insensitivity removed the first brick in the foundation of their marriage?

A hot wave of shame suffused his body, and his head hurt. In a daze, he stepped off a curb and a car honked at him, brakes squealed, and someone yelled. He saw that the light was red and he'd nearly been run over.

He walked on, trying to pay more attention to his surroundings. To his right was the massive pile of a grain elevator, its walls made up of gigantic, grey-concrete columns with no spaces between, like an ancient Greek temple squeezed and compacted between the hands of an angry god. Railway tracks ran in front of it and the North Shore Mountains were its backdrop.

A few blocks along, he saw a young woman standing on a corner. She was wearing white vinyl boots with six-inch heels, a leopard-print miniskirt that barely covered her crotch, and a red tank top stretched tightly across her small breasts. Her hair was messily gathered into a high ponytail. She was painfully thin and pale. A wraith. *The ghost of a sixties go-go dancer*, Richard thought. She was smoking with an elegantly casual flair, taking a drag and then letting her arm float sideways, a Bette Davis gesture. *Has she even heard of Bette Davis? She can't be more than eighteen.*

He felt tears in his eyes and he found he was standing still, watching her.

"Hey, honey!" she called. "Whyn't you come over here and talk to me."

Richard crossed the street. (Much later, when he tried to understand why he had done so, he wasn't sure, although his sudden onset of pity seemed to be the most plausible explanation.)

"Wanna blow job?" she said. "Only twenty bucks."

"No."

"Fucking's a lot more expensive."

Oh, hell. He looked away toward the mountains for a moment, then turned and said, "No. No. I don't want anything." He took twenty dollars from his wallet. "Get something to eat," he said and turned to go.

"Do you want to feed me? Be my daddy? Change my diapers?"

Then she gave a sudden raucous laugh, and Richard's body jerked, the way a body, when it's drifting asleep and thinks it's falling, jerks awake. A pain stabbed his chest and a phrase came to him suddenly. It seemed to come from outside him, a whisper in his ear: *All the lost daughters.*

He walked away quickly and didn't look back.

When he came to the No5 Orange on Main Street, he heard someone call his name. An acquaintance he hadn't seen for more than two years was exiting the pub — Nick Wallinsky, a painter whose work was admired in the local art scene, but not by Richard. Carol had met Nick at one of his openings and she'd invited him over for dinner a couple of times. Richard hadn't liked him much.

Jesus, this walk was proving bizarre. Had he entered some intro-
ductory plane of hell, some Buddhist *bardo* where one is given an
inkling of worse things to come?

"Richard, you old fart. Come into the pub and I'll buy you a
beer."

Richard looked at the sign advertising strippers, and said, "No,
it's too early to look at strippers." Never would be too early.

"Oh, hell, don't worry about that. They don't start until twelve
thirty. That's a whole hour away. It's not too early for a drink,
though, eh?"

FOUR

"OF COURSE HE SHOULD follow his dream," Carol's mother said. The two women were sitting in Frances's garden, drinking wine. Freshly cut grass perfumed the air, and a few late-blooming yellow roses dotted a trellis near them. They were waiting for Richard, who was late arriving for dinner. Although it was almost seven o'clock, it was still warm.

"The trouble is, he doesn't really have a dream. He's just fed up with everything, apparently. He wants to do something *useful.*" Carol knew she had made the idea sound distasteful.

Frances stood up and pinched some discoloured leaves from a rose bush.

"I had a friend once," she said, "who dreamed of being a filmmaker. Angel was her name, appropriately enough — she was more than a little unattached to the earth. In the clouds. Anyway, she kept phoning Steven Spielberg. How she got his number, I don't know. She phoned him so often, getting through to his assistant several times, that they finally threatened to get a restraining order if she persisted. She wanted to start at the top. Funny, I never thought of this before: her film was about a woman walking across a city on rooftops — already at the top, you might say. Why she was doing it, or how she got from build-ing to building, Angel didn't say. Maybe the woman could fly. That was as far as Angel got with the plot. To be developed later with Spielberg, no doubt."

Carol had been tapping her fingernails on her wineglass and swinging one leg nervously. Now she said, "Mum, why do you always go off on tangents like that? What's it got to do with Richard?"

"Don't be so quick to dismiss it as irrelevant. Think about it."

"I don't … I can't think right now. My head hurts and I'm tired and I don't feel like deciphering some sort of parable."

"It's not a parable. It's true." She took a sip of wine, looked into Carol's eyes. "All right, what I mean is this: Richard doesn't have to start at the top — doesn't have to change all at once. He can take small steps, climb the stairs. He can start with one useful thing. I, for example, have joined the civic party that I think will do the most to solve our homelessness crisis. Of course, I think gardening and meditating are useful activities, too, but probably at this point, Richard wouldn't agree. From what you've told me."

"I think he's seriously depressed. Stuck. I don't know if he can find one useful thing."

"Suggest one to him."

"He's rejecting my most important suggestion: to get counselling."

"Well, give him a little more time." Frances stood up. "I'm going to make a pot of herbal tea for us. We'll be drunk by the time Richard gets here if we don't stop drinking wine."

"You have tea, I'll have more wine," Carol said.

She was hot. She'd come straight from shopping at the Bay. She removed her linen suit jacket. Her T-shirt was wet under the arms and sweat had gathered in the band of her bra, which she took off without removing her shirt, down one arm and then the other; then she removed her pumps and, lifting her skirt, pulled off her pantyhose. The grass was deliciously cool on her bare feet. She found a hair elastic in her purse and pulled her hair into it, up off her neck.

She looked in one of the shopping bags on the lawn beside her and pulled out the towels she'd bought, one coral and one aquamarine, to add some colour to the boring beige of the bathroom. In another bag were silk cushions of shell-pink and silver to put on the old, dull-mauve couch. And she'd found the perfect cashmere V-neck pullover for Richard — aquamarine like the towels, a colour that always made his eyes look bluer. She'd splurged when she should be saving money, but she didn't care. She needed to boost her spirits, and hopefully Richard's, too.

She poured herself another glass of wine, took a large gulp, and stood up and stuck her nose into a blown yellow rose, narrowly missing a fat bumblebee that was just flying out of it. The flower's sweet perfume made her dizzy. She sat down again.

Frances returned with a mug of tea.

"Where has Richard got to, I wonder?" Carol said. "It isn't like him to be late."

"We don't have to worry about dinner getting ruined, anyway," Frances said. "It's a vegetable casserole with cheese, easy to warm up. Have you noticed in movies how dinners are always getting ruined? At least they used to be, as though cooks were unaware that almost everything can be successfully reheated, and chicken and roast beef, for example, are very good lukewarm. Is that happening less now in movies, in the microwave era?"

Carol said nothing.

"Have you noticed?" Frances asked.

"Noticed what? Look, Mum, I'm not worried about dinner, I'm worried about Richard."

"I know, dear — I'm sorry." She stood up and pulled Carol's head gently against her, murmuring, "I know, I know."

Carol started to cry.

F I V E

WHEN RICHARD AWAKENED he found himself sitting in an armchair, facing a huge abstract painting. Where was he? Then he remembered. He'd come to Nick's work-live studio on Alexander Street, just a few blocks from the No5 Orange.

He'd felt depressed the moment he'd walked into the pub. It smelled of the stale smoke that permeated the hideous carpeting. He'd sat with his back to the stage, so there'd be no chance of seeing any dancers by accident if they came on early.

Nick had started in by saying, "Still pushing literature on people, Richard?"

Richard remembered then the conversation he'd had with Nick a few years before, the one that had pissed him off so much. Over dinner, Nick had said that literature was just an entertainment and probably did more harm than good. "Stories plant ideas in people's heads — lies, fantasies."

What an asshole, Richard had thought. He'd given the standard line back: stories teach us about ourselves and others in a way it would otherwise take lifetimes to learn. And then there was the beauty of language and the reaching for transcendence, and so on. Richard didn't remember exactly what he'd said, but he remembered getting angry at Nick's smirking and head shaking and had become more and more heated in his defence of literature. Now, though, he wasn't the least bit angry. He was interested.

Nick had gone on, saying again what he'd said at that long-ago dinner. "Painting," he said, "is less harmful. The female form. How can we go wrong, contemplating it day and night?"

"I'm not very keen on teaching right now, as it happens," Richard said over his second bottle of beer. "I don't see my work as harmful, but it's becoming irrelevant to me, not meaningful enough."

"Well, I don't know about meaningful," Nick said. "Life's a crock."

"How existential of you," Richard said.

Over a third beer, Richard, beginning to feel tearful, told Nick about the landslide and Jenny's death and his depression. Nick listened, giving a few sympathetic nods and hmms from time to time.

When the music for the strippers started, Nick said, "How about lunch at a Chinese restaurant? It's just a short walk to one of my favourite places."

After lunch, washed down by two bottles of Chinese beer each, they'd come to the studio, where they started drinking Scotch. *What time is it?* He looked at his watch. *Shit, almost seven.*

Richard looked around the room. Nick was sleeping on a couch, his slim frame stretched out, his chin jutting up — arrogant even in sleep.

The painting on the wall behind the couch seemed to be of a human being floating in cobalt-blue water. A few pale shapes near the bottom looked to Richard like bones and skulls. When he'd first seen it, he said, "It needs a couple of pearls." He'd immediately regretted it because Nick said, "Ah, yes. *Full fathom five thy father lies*, something, something, something. *Those are pearls that were his eyes.* Two of the few lines of Shakespeare I remember."

The words seemed to Richard irreverent in Nick's mouth.

"Shakespeare I can stomach," Nick went on. "Plays are the best things in literature, I think, because you can see people behaving badly toward one another right before your eyes. There's an honesty to it. I haven't read Shakespeare since school, but I go to stage productions now and then."

"Do you think people behaving badly toward each other is the norm?" Richard had asked.

"I do indeed," Nick had replied.

Richard stood up, and Nick opened his eyes.

"Can I make some coffee for you?" Nick asked.

"No, I have to be going," Richard said. He'd be late for dinner with Frances, and Carol would be angry, but it would be minor compared with the anger that was building up in her about his inability to make love.

"Shall I call you a cab?"

"Thanks."

As Richard was leaving, Nick said, "Right, well, I'll see you around sometime. Hope you find what you're looking for." And he lay back down and closed his eyes.

Reluctant at first, Carol eventually consented to read my MS and to comment and/or criticize whenever she was moved to do so. The following is her first email.

September 2012

Richard,

I have a feeling guilt will come up quite a lot in this story. But regarding Jenny, I think the degree of guilt you felt was unwarranted. I was aware that you found her attractive, but I never believed you would have seduced her.

I wish I'd known the extent of your suffering over what you perceived as your part in her death. I tried to convince you that you were in no way at fault in the days and weeks after, as you have written, but maybe I could have done more, would have done more if I'd known. Oh dear. Guilt seems to be infectious.

Our "sex scene" is pretty much as I remember it and you handled it delicately.

I'm reacting well so far, aren't I? But that might change.

Carol

Dear Carol,

I don't know if the outcome would have been any different in the long run. Jenny's death, combined with the trauma of my own near escape from death, were, I think, enough to cause a kind of breakdown, guilt or no guilt. Still, I kept my deepest feelings from you and that points to the corrosive effects secrets can have, how they can engender mistrust between people, especially sexual secrets.

Gratefully,

Richard

S I X

"I PRESUME YOU'VE all read *The Tempest* at least once," Richard said to the eleven faces in front of him, some mildly expectant, some almost eager, one or two unreadable. The students sat at various angles in the wooden, desk-armed chairs. One of the young men was mainly horizontal, so far were his legs extended into the space between him and Richard. Richard had asked for a regular classroom, rather than a seminar room with a large, central table, because he wanted space for movement and separate groups.

"Have any of you seen the play performed?"

A few raised their hands.

"Good — that's good. If you haven't read it, please do so before the next class. Will someone please briefly outline what the play is about?"

A hand went up.

"And you are …?"

"John Garven."

"Okay. Go ahead."

"Well, Prospero's a magician who's been living with his daughter, Miranda, on an island for about ten years. There's also a rough, beastie sort of guy called Caliban, and a spirit called Ariel, and both of them are kind of servants to Prospero."

John's delivery was rapid-fire; he barely paused for breath.

"Prospero causes a storm to shipwreck his brother … Antonio, who sent him and Miranda out in a boat to die, and then usurped his title, Duke of Milan. This duke is with a king and various other cronies. Anyway, all of them survive the wreck, but Prospero separates them into small groups so they think the others have drowned. The son of the duke, Ferdinand I think his name is, meets Miranda and they fall in love. Prospero puts his enemies through all kinds of shit and then they all — well, almost all — live happily ever after."

"Yay!" someone called out, and the class laughed and clapped.

John stood up and took a bow.

"Yes, quite well done," Richard said. "Now, what is the main theme of the play? Anyone? Yes, you are …?"

"Anna Giovanni. Revenge."

"Is that all?"

"And forgiveness, I guess."

"Good. Reconciliation is one of Prospero's aims throughout. He makes sure, for example, that no physical harm comes to anyone in the shipwreck."

"But he kind of tortures them, you know, psychologically," a student said, but before Richard could learn his name or respond, the door to the classroom opened and everyone turned to see a young woman with long, blond hair and long legs high-booted in green suede.

A violet, wide-collared jacket billowed out around her. She stood stock still like some exotic flower and smiled at Richard. "Sorry I'm late. What did I miss?"

"Thanks for not asking *if* you missed anything. Drives teachers crazy. Name?"

"Jacintha Peters."

"We were just speaking of the theme of reconciliation in *The Tempest*," Richard said.

"Ah!" Jacintha took off her jacket, revealing a sweater moulded to her very round breasts, and sat down. "But it takes the whole play to get there, doesn't it? There's all that satisfying revenge on the way."

"Okay," Richard said, and waited as everyone's eyes turned slowly back to him. "Here's what I propose: during this semester we write, together, an environmentally themed play based on *The Tempest*."

Stunned silence.

"Bear with me. It seems to me it will be an excellent way to get to know the play inside out and at the same time do something timely, something relevant."

More silence, until Anna said softly, "It seems to me Shakespeare is always relevant, without any updating, or bells and whistles. I dislike most of those modern-dress versions."

"Yes, I agree," Richard said. "He's always relevant in his eternal themes, but some modern treatments have been very successful. And there's an urgency for us now, with climate change. I propose the island in our play be up the BC coast, home to a small community with ecological and perhaps spiritual interests."

Richard wasn't going to tell them that his project was an homage to Jenny, and that it gave him a sense of "usefulness," which he no longer felt about ordinary teaching, because they might ask him why he didn't write it himself, if it was so important to him and so personal. The truth was he didn't think he could do it well, having never written a play. And also, he could believe he was doing his students a favour by giving them an innovative way of approaching the play and a heightened awareness of environmental concerns at the same time.

He'd wanted to be a short-story writer, had been especially inspired, indeed bowled over, by the work of Norman Levine when he first encountered it. (The only regret he had about not teaching Canadian literature was that he hadn't had the opportunity to turn students on to Norman Levine.) Levine's style was understated, lean, yet revealed so much; was so surprisingly deep. He wanted to write like that. For three years he wrote stories in which he strove to leave out just enough, include just enough, create a fine balance, and sent them to almost every little magazine in North America. He was rejected every time. Sometimes editors offered opinions that contradicted those offered by other editors about the same story. Some wanted to know more: What is Henry's motivation for leaving Henrietta? Some wanted to know less: "You explicate too much. It's obvious that Henry resents Henrietta's success."

He stopped writing short stories.

"You gave up too soon," Carol had said when he pulled the stories out of a drawer a few years later. She read them and liked them, but said they didn't quite sound like Richard. "Forget your idol, your Mr. Levine," she said. "Find your own voice."

She was right, of course, but he was afraid he didn't have a voice, not a compelling or original one.

"Do we get to vote on this?" a student asked. "Because this is an English literature course, not creative writing. Not Ecology 101, either."

"And you are?" Richard asked.

"Jordan Olafson."

"No, Jordan. No vote. Here's the deal. I won't mark you on your creative writing ability, but on the amount of thought you put into the project and your level of participation. Some of you are probably better writers than others, but you can all contribute."

Another student immediately announced he was transferring out of the class.

"Fine." Richard asked his name, crossed him off his list, and the young man left. "All right. Let's get this started. Any comments? Ideas?"

"I have a problem with the theme of reconciliation as it has to do with males and females in the play, since there's such a power imbalance," Jacintha said. "Miranda has to obey her father and she has to remain a virgin and is then *handed over* to Ferdinand. And doesn't Prospero say early on that he created the shipwreck just for her benefit? Is the 'benefit' a husband, whether she wants one or not?"

"Yes, at least partly that," Richard said. "He says, 'I have done nothing but in care of thee.' We could take that as evidence that the marriage of male and female is an important theme in the play."

"Maybe," Jacintha said. "But I propose our rewrite give some power to Miranda. And she doesn't have to be the only woman in our play. If we're going to unite male and female, let's have equal numbers."

"Someone's been reading feminist critiques," Jordan said, and everyone laughed.

"I have," Jacintha said, glaring at him. "There's nothing funny about it. I'm surprised you've even heard of a feminist critique." Her voice was harsh and sarcastic.

Richard was a bit alarmed by the ferocity of her reply. He hoped she wasn't going to be that "one in every class" who caused discord.

"I agree with Jacintha," Anna said. "We definitely need some more women in our version."

"Yeah, and let's sex it up," Jordan said, apparently undaunted.

"Enough now. I've split you into three groups, at random. I want you to choose a scene or part of one, and rewrite it in modern dress, so to speak, keeping in mind especially the environmental theme. We'll read the scenes in our next class. You can start now but will no doubt have to meet again to finish them."

He read out their names and they dragged their chairs to separate corners of the room.

Christ! Richard hadn't thought this was going to be easy, but he now saw the unlikelihood of successfully herding his woolly little flock into Shakespeare's shining enclosure.

SEVEN

JACINTHA, HER BOYFRIEND, Skitch, and his friend, Greg, were sitting in a red leatherette booth in Helen's Grill, a café that looked like it was straight out of the 1950s, with lots of Formica and chrome and small jukebox song selectors mounted on the wall at each table.

The middle-aged waitress arrived with Skitch and Greg's orders. Her greying hair was neatly curled, her expression reminiscent of an overworked but loving mother.

"How's your little pet today?" she asked, referring to the tattoo on Skitch's neck, a green snake twisting around a paler-green vine. His only other adornment was a gold eyebrow stud.

"Fine, thanks, Betty. He's glad you care."

Her smile in response was warm. "Can I get you anything else, Skitch, honey?"

"No, thanks, Betty. This looks great."

Betty took Jacintha's order for coffee and a club sandwich, and after she left, Greg said, "Jesus, why do women go for you like that — all ages. You're not that good-looking."

"Oh, but he is," Jacintha said, and puckered up and smacked her lips in a mock kiss.

"Thanks, babe," Skitch said.

He had told her that he'd been picked on at school for being skinny and "girlie," and that, to change how he was being treated, he'd shaved his head and started working out in a gym. Now, at twenty-two, he had carved biceps and washboard abs to go with his pretty mouth and innocent brown eyes. *Yes*, Jacintha thought, *he really is good-looking.* And he was remarkably good-natured, too. He certainly had been with her, considering that she had been refusing to have sex with him ever since they'd met three weeks earlier.

"Skitch told me you've gone back to school," Greg said. "What's that about?"

"I don't know — I was beginning to feel a bit ghostlike," Jacintha said. "I needed a shot of Shakespeare to perk me up."

"Let me know how that works out," Greg said. "I get a bit wispy myself sometimes."

Skitch took a large bite of his hamburger, and mayonnaise ran down his chin. He brushed it up with the back of his hand and smeared it down the leg of his jeans. Greg was eating an avocado and cheese sandwich, being careful not to drip anything on his Indian shirt of gauzy white cotton.

"I wish avocados could be grown locally," Greg said. "I really should try to eat only local stuff. And we shouldn't be drinking this shit," he added, picking up his coffee cup. "We should drink fair-trade coffee."

"Try not to bore us to death," Skitch said. "Just eat your damn food." He finished his hamburger, scooped mayonnaise and meat juice from his plate with a finger, which he then sucked.

"Manners!" Jacintha said, reaching across the table to dab at his mouth with a napkin.

Skitch burped discreetly into his fist. "There, see, I've got manners. I know how to act. You're the one who wants to cause trouble. You're the one who wants us to create a cell."

"Like terrorists?" Greg asked.

"Yeah, but no bombs or guns. We'll be the Gaia Collective. We'll organize protests," Jacintha said. "Against the Olympics, a stupid waste of money. And for the environment and affordable housing. We have to stop being passive. I want you and Tanya and Brian to join me and Skitch and my old friend Beth in a core group."

"The Olympics are still more than four years away," Greg said.

"Yes, but that gives us lots of time to make a big noise about it. The Olympic organizers are using the time to plan their shit. For one thing, they intend to do massive clear-cutting on Eagleridge Bluffs, above Horseshoe Bay, to 'improve' the highway to Whistler so that people can drive like maniacs to the slopes for seventeen days."

"We probably can't stop the fuckers," Greg said, "but we can generate bad publicity at the very least. Yeah. Beautiful. I'm in."

"I'll call a meeting soon," Jacintha said.

Jacintha had heard about the Shakespeare seminar accidentally, although now she thought of it as fatefully. She'd run into Beth, who had lived on the same street as her several years earlier. When she'd asked Beth what she'd been up to, Beth had told her she was excited about the seminar and the professor, Richard Wilson. "I've heard he's very good," she'd said. "I've seen him around, of course. He's kind of hot, and I've always wanted to be in one of his classes."

Richard Wilson. Jesus. Remain calm. It's only a name. Probably not the man I'm looking for. "Hot how?" Jacintha had asked.

"Oh, you know, just generally sexy. Kind of blond. Blue eyes."

"Young?"

"I don't know — forty-five, maybe a bit older."

Jacintha's heart had started to pound, but her expression remained neutral. She prided herself on revealing only those emotions she chose to. Someone had once complimented her on her poise, and she liked the word. Poised, yes. *Now*, she thought, smiling to herself, *its other meaning might apply.*

"I've been thinking about going back to school," she'd said to Beth. "I'll see if I can get into that seminar." She'd almost completed her third year at Simon Fraser University as an English major when she'd dropped out three years earlier. Transferring to UBC would be no problem.

"That was a very quick decision," Beth had said, her eyes wide.

"My favourite kind," Jacintha said, smiling. She remembered how easy it had always been to impress Beth. "See you in class."

When Jacintha had arrived home, she'd done a tarot reading about the possibility that she had found the man she was looking for. Her thoughts buzzed, her body buzzed, as though she'd had too much caffeine. She had mixed feelings about tarot divination and usually did it just for fun, but this time the message could be important.

She used the High Priestess as the signifier, and the card she turned up for the past was the Knight of Swords, and for the future, the lightning-struck Tower. Two supporting cards were the Fool and the Magician. She'd laughed at that. A Shakespeare seminar. Caliban and Prospero. Perfect. And swords and lightning predicted trouble; someone brought crashing down.

"You're playing in the major leagues now," she remembered a friend and fellow tarot reader saying when a similarly large number of Major Arcana cards had appeared in a reading. In this present reading, the Tower was reversed, meaning things could backfire, but Jacintha never credited reversals. The ancient images and symbols were what mattered. They had a power that, even at her most skeptical, she found hard to dismiss.

Her mother, Catherine, had taught her tarot, starting when Jacintha was six years old. They'd sit on the big bed and take out the deck and play in the short but blissful time between when Catherine finished work and when she fell asleep from exhaustion and alcohol. Catherine, wearing only her lilac-coloured silk robe, embroidered with butterflies, would be fresh out of the shower, smelling of perfume. The perfume was called Poison.

"That's not a very nice name," Jacintha said, the first time she heard it.

"But it smells nice, doesn't it?"

Beside Catherine on the bedside table would sit a bottle of whisky and a full glass already poured. Jacintha would sit close and stroke the silk and the soft skin of her mother's leg where the robe fell away.

"Pay attention now. Here's the Fool. How silly. He's about to step off the cliff."

"But he looks happy. Will he be all right?"

"Maybe. Some fools are protected by angels. And here's the High Priestess. Magical. She's an old soul who can get whatever she wants. Now, here's Death."

"He scares me."

"Don't be scared. This card means only that a big change is coming. Changes can be very good. Remember when the teacher you didn't like left your school and you got a teacher you liked better? A good change, wasn't it?"

The biggest, most awful change came when Jacintha was taken away from her mother.

That was after she was raped by a "client" of her mother's, a john, and Social Services deemed Catherine an unfit parent.

Sometimes Jacintha thought she shouldn't have run crying to the neighbours, but she was only seven years old and the man had hurt her so much and she was so scared.

She was fostered by a kind, middle-class couple, Edith and Charles Bennett, who looked after her until Catherine died and adopted her when she was twelve. They let her keep her mother's surname, Peters.

Catherine had given her an exciting history, which Jacintha had believed for a long time. She had realized its falseness when she was thirteen, but even now she carried it in her body and attitudes and strategies. It still served her. She had her mother's beauty: the carved cheekbones that could have been Slavic, eyes the cold blue of a northern sky, the heavy inner fold of the eyelids suggestive of the farthest steppes, and the dignified posture of the Russian royal ancestry her mother had claimed for them.

"My great-grandmother was a cousin of the Duchess Catherine, named after Catherine the Great," she'd told Jacintha. "Her last name was Petrov, but later the family changed it to Peters. She fled to Canada in 1916, just before the revolution that killed the royal family. She lived in obscurity from then on, as we do now. But we know who we are."

"My little Tsarina," she'd coo as she braided Jacintha's hair and pinned it crown-like to the top of her head, and Jacintha had felt the pomp and ceremony — although she didn't have those words — strengthening her spine and tingling her skin. "Important" was a word she had.

"Your great-grandma was important, wasn't she?" she'd ask.

"Yes, and so are you."

Living in the endless present of their two small rooms, full of clutter, empty of hope, Catherine had needed a history more uplifting than her real one.

After the tarot lesson, Catherine would say, "Get yourself a cup of milk now, before bed," and Jacintha would lift a cup from the grubby sideboard beside the stained sink and see a cockroach scuttle away.

But sometimes when Catherine was drunk she ranted, and a recurring name in her tirades was Richard. "He hurt me the most," she would say. "Richard, Dick, prick. I could have loved him. I would have loved him. He should be punished for hurting me."

And then, still babbling, with "Richard" the only clear word, she would pass out.

Jacintha asked once or twice how this Richard had hurt her — had he hit her, pinched her? She had seen bruises on her mother's arms, and once a black eye. But her mother said it was nothing like that, and not to worry about it, so it became relatively minor in the things she did worry about, like the frightening men she sometimes saw her mother with on the street.

After Catherine died, Jacintha was given a small box of her meagre possessions: a few pieces of cheap jewellery, photos of Jacintha as a baby and small child, a red hair ribbon that Jacintha remembered wearing, an old theatre program, a ticket stub from a rock concert, and other odds and ends. And among all these was a photo of Catherine with some other people. On the back she had written "Richard and me at the Driftwood Pub on his 23rd birthday," and under that the date, including the year. She would have just turned nineteen. She is smiling, raising a glass of beer to the camera. Two men in the dim background appear to be talking to each other. Their features are unclear.

The photo was tucked into a book of poems, William Blake's *Songs of Innocence*, the first part of *Songs of Innocence and of Experience*. "Richard Wilson" was written inside the cover.

As a teenager, Jacintha had been interested in the photo and book, but she hadn't dwelled on them, hadn't wondered too long about who Richard was.

But then, last month, something had changed. Her adoptive mother, Edith, had relayed the story Catherine had told her about Richard Wilson. Why Edith had waited so long, Jacintha didn't know. Perhaps she hadn't thought Jacintha was ready to hear it any sooner. And Edith was probably right. It was upsetting, but she was old enough now to deal with it.

So she had begun to look for him.

She phoned all eleven of the Richard Wilsons in the Vancouver phone book and said, "I'm looking for an old school friend named Richard Wilson. He'd be forty-eight by now." Most were polite, one slammed the phone down, and two were flirtatious. The men eager to tell their ages were between twenty-nine and eighty-five. One said, "Well, I'm pushing forty-nine," and when she asked if he'd ever lost a book of Blake's poetry, he said proudly that he had never once owned a book of "pomes" in his life.

She googled the name and found one elderly British actor, two British artists, an internationally known lawyer, and a famous Shakespearean scholar, all to no avail. Anyway, although it was not impossible, it was unlikely that "her" Richard had become famous.

Two dozen Richard Wilsons were lined up on Facebook in a very un-roguish gallery, but most, not surprisingly, were a lot younger. The one who was forty-eight informed anyone who might be interested that he was a loyal Torontonian who had lived there all his life.

She realized she'd have to start looking further afield — across Canada, for a start — and use more sophisticated methods, but she felt out of her depth and was considering hiring a private detective.

Then the universe, the gods, the angels, maybe just coincidence (was anything ever just coincidental?) had lain the information she wanted, like a ripe peach, into her waiting lap. This Richard Wilson was an English literature professor who could easily love Blake as much as Shakespeare.

She would think of a plausible reason to ask him his age, and she would do it so nicely that he would be pleased to tell her.

But she wouldn't show him the Blake book. She had a firm plan now, and if he was the right man, her having the book might tip her hand.

February 2012

Richard,

I was surprised that you portrayed Skitch almost tenderly — the pretty boy who had to learn to be tough. Surprised considering what he ultimately did to you. At least, I'm presuming he was the one, since, this being a novel, it would probably complicate the plot too much to give Jacintha a second boyfriend.

I have no quarrel with your depiction of Jacintha. I can well believe she had a terrible childhood. You told me some of it, of course, but never in so much detail. I presume she told you most of that at some point. Anyway, I've never been able to completely excuse her for what she did, however hard her life had been. Nor have I been able to excuse you, a different thing from forgiving you, which I have mostly done.

Carol

Dear Carol,

I don't want you to excuse me. Nor do I want you to blame Jacintha. I take all the blame, as I hope you will see.

As for Skitch, he was my saviour. If he hadn't done what he did, I might have plummeted into the pit. I was wobbling on the edge, leaning dangerously, and his was the restraining hand. Ironic, I know.

Best wishes,

Richard

E I G H T

AFTER GABE EXTRICATED himself from underneath her, Carol rolled onto her back. Now her thighs and bum were sticking to the leather of the couch and for a moment she was seventeen again, in the back seat of a car, sticking to hot vinyl with a boy pungent with sweat grunting against her and then rolling off and turning away as if she were an embarrassment. She'd been disgusted and ashamed.

Gabe, of course, was nothing like that boy. Gabe had been her friend for years and she'd gone to him for sympathy and ended up getting comforted in a more thorough way than she'd intended. In fact, his lovemaking was surprisingly comforting. She liked his thick body, the stiff, dark hair on his chest, even his ridiculous moustache. He was so unlike Richard; maybe that was part of his appeal. She thought of it, fleetingly, as so different from sex with

Richard that it was more of a friendly coupling than cheating, and then she saw how crazy that was.

Gabe, even though he was head of the English department at UBC, was her friend, not Richard's. Richard had never liked him. (She couldn't have stooped so low as to have sex with one of his friends.) Richard considered Gabe a bit of a buffoon, but although he was given to rather silly jokes, he was intelligent and very knowledgeable about Carol's field: art history. She had once told Richard that Gabe was like an erudite bear, and Richard had replied that he was more like a bear snuffling and snorting out of hibernation.

The first time she and Gabe were together, his weight had frightened her, and as he propped himself above her, ready to press in, she'd panicked, reliving the moment when the mattress had almost smothered her in the landslide. After that she was never under him.

They were in Gabe's office, his door locked. They'd been meeting there a couple of times a week for a month.

Gabe finished doing up his belt buckle, knelt down beside her, and took her hand in his large and warm ones. "Carol, I feel lucky you wanted me, but I don't think this is making you any happier."

"Do affairs ever make people happy?"

"I don't know. I haven't had any affairs, really. A few encounters, you might say; none that my ex-wife found out about. It was she who found someone else."

"Anyway, you're right," Carol said. "I'm not happy about this. I feel driven."

The warmth and lightness of satiety went away so quickly after sex now, and her body became as heavy as her mind until the next time the craving electrified her, made her jumpy and horribly needy.

"Things aren't getting any better with Richard, I gather."

"No." She'd told Gabe only that she and Richard had become estranged since the landslide. "And he still won't go to counselling with me."

"Have you considered seeing a counsellor alone?"

"I should see someone, I know." She sat up and Gabe sat beside her and pulled her to him. When she looked into his eyes, she saw with a jolt that he was feeling a lot more than friendship. Too much longing. Oh, hell, she didn't want him to fall in love with her. She wasn't being fair to him.

"I should leave you alone, not drag you into this," she said.

"No, please don't leave me alone," Gabe said.

"I do have to go now." She retrieved her pants, pantyhose, bra, blouse, scarf — all scattered around the couch and floor — and dressed quickly. She took out her compact, removed mascara smudges from under her eyes, reapplied her lipstick. These everyday acts made her feel suddenly deeply lonely. The small death, indeed, and the return to life was a walk out into a hot, uncaring world. The campus, for all its beauty, seemed airless and bleak today.

Gabe opened the door, peered out to make sure no one was in the hallway, and ushered her out with a peck on the cheek. "Remember, I care very much," he whispered, but his words did not comfort her.

That evening Carol made a meal of deli lasagna and prewashed salad greens with a vinaigrette, and called Richard to dinner, for the first time that week. They had got out of the habit of eating together, a time in which they had always shared their day and grown closer for it.

Richard noticed that Carol seemed nervous, chirpily describing how she'd chosen the lasagna and used cider vinegar instead of balsamic in the dressing.

As she sat down at the table, she exhaled loudly and smiled tentatively. After two mouthfuls of salad, she asked, "Are you happy to be back teaching?"

"Yes, fairly," Richard said. "I'm having my students write a version of *The Tempest*. With an environmental theme. In honour of Jenny, you know. She talked about doing it herself. We've started it in class and it's going pretty well." He hadn't told Carol about it earlier because it had seemed too private, just between him and Jenny, but now, since at least twelve others knew about it, it was obviously foolish not to tell.

"Oh." Carol's face clouded.

"I should have told you sooner," Richard said.

"No, it's all right," Carol said, but she was still frowning. She shook her head as if to banish hurt or resentment, Richard wasn't sure which.

After another forkful of salad, she said, "Anyway, I like it. It's a lovely way to remember Jenny. And even if you don't get something stageable out of it, it's a way for your students to become intimate with the play. You can always take what they come up with — they're bound to have a few good ideas — and make it into something viable yourself."

"Not exactly unconditional support. Sorry I mentioned it," Richard said. He'd heard mainly "even if" and "a few ideas," as opposed to "enough ideas."

"I *am* giving you unconditional support! No need to get defensive. I'm saying I have faith in you as a teacher no matter what happens, and just as importantly, I have faith in you as a writer. I believe you could write it yourself, and no doubt you'll have a lot of input about both content and style. It might be the spur you need to get back into writing."

"What makes you think I want to get back into writing?"

"Richard. Calm down."

"Sorry. I'm probably too close to this because of Jenny."

"I know." She stood up, leaned down, and put her arms around him. "I know, I know," she said, her breath on his cheek.

Suddenly she pulled away, and smiled too brightly, Richard thought, like a mother who is promising ice cream to a boy with a scraped and bloody knee.

She said, "When it's finished, you can send a copy of the play, with a dedication, to Jenny's parents."

"But no pressure," Richard said.

"No pressure," Carol said and laughed.

Richard moved to the living room to read *The Tempest* again, starting where he'd left off the last time, at one of the most beautiful of all the speeches, by Caliban: *Be not afeard; the isle is full of noises, / Sounds and sweet airs that give delight and hurt not.* When he read Stephano's reply, he realized he'd never before seen the full significance of it: *This will prove a brave kingdom to me, where I shall have my music for nothing.* Wasn't that what he, Richard, had been assuming all his life? Didn't most privileged people expect to have all the good things in life, without making any sacrifices? Wasn't that why he needed to make a profound change?

When he'd told Carol, a few weeks earlier, that he might like to work with AIDS orphans in Africa, she'd said, "Coming from you, that sounds more like a death wish. You don't even like camping. Mosquitoes drive you crazy, and then there's the risk of malaria. And you're paranoid about getting bitten by a tick. Your idea of an ideal vacation is a five-star hotel in New York City."

"But I can change," he'd said. "I *have* changed. Everything I do now seems trivial."

"You're simply depressed," Carol had said. "You should see a doctor."

"Don't start that again," had been his conversation-ending reply.

February 2012

Richard,

It must have cost you something to imagine me with "Gabe" (of course, I know who you mean) especially considering how much you disliked him. But I suppose it's the job of a writer to imagine things that hurt his oh-so-sensitive psyche.

I suspect there will be other things about my sex life that you will bravely reveal. You know I'm not a prude (remember I was all right with your handling of our sex scene) and yet I am disturbed, in this case, by being laid on the page like that, if you'll pardon the expression.

Carol

Dear Carol,

Yes, but it might have been more painful for me to make your lover someone other than Gabe. Maybe I chose him because I thought of him as a lesser man than I.

Writing is often painful for writers, but most of us try not to be cruel to others, and it certainly wasn't my intention to hurt you. I understood why, at that time, you felt in need of someone.

I don't believe Faulkner would have sold his grandmother for a good story, as he's supposed to have said, but he might have sacrificed bits of her, a little at a time. Writers pin pieces of even their most beloved ones to the page (laid on the page!) in their efforts to reveal their own sins, guilt, and hopes for forgiveness. And their desire to create something worthwhile from the torn remains.

Osiris was hacked to pieces and put back together in order to father a god. All right, maybe a bit over the top as a metaphor, but you get my point. For "god," read "work of art." Or, more modestly, a novel.

All the best,

Richard

N I N E

"WHO WANTS TO go first and read the scene you wrote during the week?" Richard asked.

"We will," Aiden said. "Kevin and I wrote an opening scene that's a takeoff of the original. Kyla has the flu and Max was too busy to join us. So, anyway, it's Scene One, The storm. Two sailors. We'll each read a part."

"I've never seen such a wicked storm before."

"Yeah, tornadoes and hurricanes are getting worse all over the world. Yet you still deny that climate change is real. Maybe you should pray to the Gods of Denial so we won't end up as bloody corpses on the rocks."

"'The Gods of the Nile?' Those Egyptian dudes?"

*"No, douchebag. Denial, like it's not happening. You think peo-
ple can clear-cut as many virgin forests as they like and the world
will go on as usual."*

"Are we in the Virgin Islands? I thought this was BC."

*"God save me from ignorant fucking deckhands! You couldn't
find your way from Kits Beach to Jericho Beach. Oh, shit. Quick,
take in the topsail. Down with the topmast. Hurry, the rest of you
slackers. I don't want to die because of slow asshole drunks."*

*"No, my friend, the real drunks are below, guzzling martinis
with Mr. Tony Prosper. Oh, here they are now, heads popping up
like gophers from a flooded hole."*

"Gophers! Are you a prairie boy at sea? Would explain a lot."

*"Oh Christ, oh Gods of the Nile, or Denial, any goddamned
gods, help us! We're running aground — the ship is breaking up.
Save yourselves! Jump!"*

"That's it," Aiden said. "Comments, anyone?" Richard asked.

"It kind of gets some of the goofy humour in Shakespeare,
like the bad puns," Anna said. "And introduces the theme of pro-
tecting the environment."

"I think we need to feel more scared and excited by the storm,"
Jacintha said. "We need to feel that it's real."

"I thought in performance there'd be sounds of wind and
crashing waves, and sailors moaning and cursing," Aiden said.

"That's true, but there could be more reaction in the dialogue,"
Richard said. "Anyone else? No? Are you all underwhelmed? Not
a bad effort, though, Aiden and Kevin."

The next group's offering was even less impressive. "A bit
short," "kind of stilted," and "boring" were some of the comments.

Third was Jacintha's group.

"We didn't do a scene," she said. "Beth wrote a poem in which
our Ariel, a member of the community who is a visionary, channels

a shaman of a local First Nation. The shaman tells how much their land has already been degraded. She's a kind of sympathetic Sycorax, not Shakespeare's hag. Beth asked me to read it."

> *Listen to them laugh and babble, this Prospero and*
> *   his gang.*
> *This island was mine to roam undisturbed, a*
> *   grieving spirit.*
> *Is he any better than those who destroyed my first home?*
> *My people's fault was this: We showed the strangers*
> *The abalone beds, shining and plentiful.*
> *They laid them waste.*
> *And fields of camas, vast and*
> *Blue as lakes, now dull as dry grass.*
> *Once we listened with joy to what sounded like*
> *Heavy rainfall — millions of fish,*
> *Splashing, foaming through the narrows,*
> *Salmon, herring, oolichan.*
> *Frogs sang in their thousands.*
> *Some still sing, but I fear the day*
> *When silence reigns forever.*

A long silence mirroring the last lines was broken by a single "whew" from Jason.

"Whew, indeed," Richard said. "You've evoked the abundance of a virgin land very well."

"All that still existed about a hundred years ago," John said. "I did some of the research. Camas is an edible bulb, very nutritious."

Another long silence. Anna was the first to speak. "It all seems so hopeless sometimes. I get depressed."

"*Yet in this captious and intenible sieve / I still pour in the waters of my love,*" Richard quoted. "From *All's Well That Ends Well*. About faith and hope."

"Trying to catch water in a sieve isn't exactly hopeful," John said.

"No, probably not an entirely appropriate quote," Richard said. "Anyway, a beautiful poem, Beth. Well done. In the next class, let's begin to work out who our characters will be. What they want will show us what's at stake, what the conflicts will be, and can lead us toward a plot. We already have the visionary Ariel; that's a good start. See you all next time."

TEN

BY THE END of the third class, the students hadn't come up with any kind of consensus about characters, and Richard despaired of them being any better at agreeing on a plot.

Afterward, Jacintha asked if she could speak to Richard privately after lunch. Now he sat waiting for her in his office. He was nervous. What did she want? Maybe she was just going to tell him she was quitting. But that shouldn't make much difference to him; the number of students would still be adequate. He had barely finished that thought when another one tumbled over it: *I want her to stay.*

Jacintha rushed in — he had left his door open — and sat down across the desk from him before he could speak.

"Thanks for seeing me," she said.

"You're welcome," he said. "I'm curious about why you want to see me."

"It's about the play, of course," she said. "I don't think the way we are doing it is going to work out. I thought maybe just some of us could write the new version. All these groups are cumbersome, and today was just chaotic. I've discussed this with Beth and Anna and John — they're all keen, and they're willing, as I am, to do it on our own time."

Richard, relieved, breathed more deeply. She wasn't leaving. A moment later he berated himself for caring — or at least for caring what seemed an inappropriate amount.

Jacintha stared at him, waiting for him to speak, and finally he said, "Well, that's a lot to take in."

"I know, but it's going to be impossible to do this whole class thing when we can't even agree on what form it will take. And I don't think the groups are ever going to work, either."

"It's not working at the moment, I grant you," Richard said.

"I think once we have a simple but powerful theme, the play will come together," Jacintha said. "I'd like to try to make it work."

She leaned forward eagerly. Richard was transfixed for a moment. He remembered how different she had been in the first class. Her first comment had been delivered in a dry, cynical tone of voice: all that "satisfying revenge" on the way to reconciliation.

"Professor Wilson?" she said, when he was slow to speak.

"Ah, theme, yes."

"Environmentalism is too obviously political. It really doesn't work as the central theme, don't you think? I'm an activist for the cause — I've started a protest group called the Gaia Collective — but writing a play about the subject without proselytizing could be very difficult, could easily become preachy and boring. I think a better theme would be the marriage of male and female, which includes gender equality and power versus powerlessness. These things are crucial to saving the earth.

"But the way we were headed this morning, emphasizing saving an island from developers who want to clear-cut it, was too on the nose. If we're going to even approach the sensibility of *The Tempest*, magic has to be central. And the kind of poetry that magic inspires."

"I'll have to think about this. What to do with the rest of the class while you are doing the writing is one of the questions."

"I'm sure you can figure that part out," Jacintha said with a smile.

Richard thought again of what Jenny had told him about her vision for the play. Prospero's care of Miranda was certainly central, but Miranda and Ferdinand's love story might just be the real key.

As though reading his mind, Jacintha said, "So, I thought the climax could be Miranda and Ferdinand's wedding. And then the denouement —"

"Hold on! You've come up with some good ideas. I'll think about them and talk to the class about your group wanting to take the writing on, and we'll see where we might go from there. Thanks for caring and thinking so deeply about it."

"Right. More another time."

As she was getting up, she held his gaze and smiled so warmly that Richard's heart beat faster. After she left, he sat for several minutes, lost, not so much in thought as in the lack of it.

E L E V E N

THE GROUNDS AROUND City Hall were buzzing with activity. The turnout was good, about seventy-five, a lot of the usual suspects — earnest seekers of justice and inveterate agitators. Greg and Brian had put up posters at UBC and on Commercial Drive asking people to bring sheets and blankets and anti-Olympics, pro–affordable housing placards. Tanya had posted the same information on Facebook. It was a Sunday, so city hall was closed.

Brian had managed to bring two dozen shopping carts in a borrowed van and people were draping them with sheets and blankets to represent where the homeless kept their pitiful belongings.

"Where the hell did he get them? Must have stolen them," Skitch said to Jacintha. "Greg said he'd be a good gofer. And torches. There's about twelve freakin' giant torches, tarred rags on poles. He's fuckin' good."

"And what did you do, my little layabout?"

"Nothing so far, but I'm here to raise hell."

Brian was directing some of the protesters to parade along Twelfth Avenue with signs reading Houses, Not Circuses, and Olympic Excess Means Human Suffering, and similar things. One proclaimed, not mincing words, Fuck the Olympics. Skitch grabbed that one and proceeded to march and yell the same words to the traffic passing by.

The elegant art deco city hall, with its broad lawns and formal flower beds, made a nice contrast to the scruffy blanket-and-cart campground. More signs came out: Home Sweet Home, and My Stinking Low-Cost Housing. A few people spread blankets on the ground, opened picnic baskets, and offered around sandwiches, buns, fruit. The posters advertising the rally had stipulated no alcohol or drugs, but now and then pot smoke enhanced the air.

All six members of the group were there: Tanya, Brian, Greg, Beth, Skitch, and Jacintha. The Gaia Warriors — "Collective" was too tame a word, they'd decided — were ready to fight the power.

Beth stood with a group of protesters near one of the carts, and Tanya and Greg had joined Skitch on the sidewalk parade. Brian scurried around, keeping an eye on everything, and Jacintha watched for a while from a place off to one side, holding a large carrier bag.

The light was dimming as Jacintha walked over to look at the torches piled together on the lawn. They were impressive, as Skitch had said. Five-foot-long poles with generous wrappings of tarred cloth.

When darkness fell, Brian shouted, "I need twelve torchbearers!" and out of the twenty who rushed forward, he chose the lucky ones. When he lit the torches, a cheer went up, and everyone started chanting, "Housing! Housing! Housing!"

The bearers, under Brian's direction, marched up and down the sidewalk, also chanting.

People gathered to watch on the porches of the large, expensive houses across Twelfth Avenue, and a security guard, who had perhaps been dozing in the bowels of city hall, suddenly appeared. He said nothing, just took out his phone. Within five minutes several police cars had arrived, and close behind them a fire truck, all with sirens blaring.

"Overkill," Jacintha said to Skitch.

"Move off the grounds quietly and there'll be no trouble," a policeman shouted over a bullhorn.

A few people started moving down the hill to Broadway. Most stood their ground.

"Lay the torches down. Now!"

A fireman advanced with a hose. Some of the bearers put the torches down and stepped away. The ones who held on were hosed and fell to the ground.

Tanya took pictures with her cellphone, until Greg shouted, "There's no way we're getting hosed — come on," and they both ran to the back of the building and down to Broadway.

Brian grabbed Beth's arm and said, "Come on, the hoses are bad enough, but it'll be tasers next."

"Are they tasering people now?"

"Not yet, but some of those guys are bound to resist arrest, and things could get ugly."

It was then that they both saw Jacintha picking up one of the torches from a man the fireman hadn't got to; she dashed over to a cart covered with a blanket.

"Get back," she yelled at the two women standing near it, and after they'd run away, she lifted the blankets and threw in the torch. With a great whoosh, flames shot six feet high.

A man started to throw cardboard signs onto the cart. Within moments, a fireman was blasting water at the cart and managed to keep the fire contained.

As Skitch and Jacintha raced down to Broadway, a TV news crew pulled up on Twelfth, too late to get pictures of the hose-downs.

"I'm going to phone the station and give our group credit for organizing this," Jacintha said.

"Yeah, okay. But shit! Jacintha. What was in that cart?"

"An open container of gasoline," Jacintha said. "Just a small one," she added with a smile.

"Wow. You're amazing. Someone could have got hurt, though. Did you see that woman? Maybe she was burned."

"No, she was okay. Almost drowned, but not burned. And now she knows who we are — now everyone knows who we are: the Gaia Warriors!" She pulled off her black, knitted cap and her hair cascaded down and shone under the street light.

"Yeah, you're a goddamned warrior. An Amazon. The others might be a bit pissed, though. Especially Brian. He likes to think he's in on all the final decisions."

"He'll have to get used to being wrong about that."

Jacintha called the local TV stations: "The Gaia Warriors will strike again, like we did at city hall tonight, unless action is taken to provide housing for the homeless. We'll go much further."

"What do you plan to do?" asked the reporter at each station.

"Tell the mayor to act now or he'll find out," Jacintha said. "End of message."

"What's 'much further'?" Skitch asked.

"I don't know," Jacintha said. "We'll play it by ear."

"Fuck, that was exciting," Skitch said. "You're exciting."

He pulled her close, kissed her, and groaned, and Jacintha felt him hardening against her.

"Why won't you sleep with me?" he asked. "I know you want to." He put a hand on her breast.

"You know nothing," she said, slapping his hand. She wiped her mouth and started walking again.

"I know I make you hot. I'm not stupid. So why won't you? You're driving me nuts."

"Look, those roses are gorgeous," Jacintha said, as they passed a front-yard garden.

"Jacintha!"

"You wouldn't be able to handle me."

"That's crazy. Of course I can *handle* you. I can satisfy you big time."

"Big time?" she said, and laughed.

"Yes. You'll cry for more."

"I repeat: you can't handle me. You don't know what I need. I'm complicated."

"Tell me, then. Tell me what you need."

"Maybe later. I need to get to know you better. Know that I can trust you."

"Ah, Jassie. You can trust me. Don't torture me."

"Don't whine like a big baby. Come on now. Let's get a bus. I need to get home and get my beauty sleep."

"All right," he said. "But I don't know if I can put up with waiting much longer."

"You'll wait, my little friend. You'll wait," Jacintha said, looking at the sharp outline of his upper lip and the deep groove above. *Like lips sculpted by Michelangelo*, she thought, as she had before, then quickly pulled her mind away from the danger, for her purposes, of such an indulgence.

She took his hand and ran, pulling him after her and feeling smugly pleased when he started laughing.

TWELVE

CAROL WAS IN the living room of Janet Warren, psychologist, whose card said Traditional and Alternative Counselling. Janet sat opposite her in a matching armchair upholstered in dark-blue cotton. A small oriental rug in blues and reds lay on the oak floor between them. A forest of plants covered a table beneath the window, and on the walls were oil paintings, mostly of landscapes and flowers.

"Did you paint these?" Carol asked.

"Some of them. The flowers."

"They're good. I like the way you've liberated the flowers from vases. And the colours are excellent. There's some of the dissonance that Matisse used to such masterly effect."

Carol was reassured by Janet's good taste, then realized what a snob she was being. She remembered having chastised a friend who'd stopped seeing a counsellor because he was inclined to use malapropisms. "Well," the friend had said, "if he doesn't understand words, should I rely on him to understand me?"

There was something motherly about Janet, even though she was younger than Carol, maybe forty to Carol's forty-eight. Janet had short, straight, brown hair and wore black-framed glasses, a green shirt-dress, and sandals. Her hands had been soft and warm when she touched Carol's arm lightly as she greeted her at the door.

"Thank you," Janet said. "Do you paint?"

"No. My father was quite a well-known painter — Aubrey Leland. I teach art history."

"A professional eye, then. I'm flattered. And I've heard of your father. I'll look for his work. Can I see it locally?"

"They have a few of his paintings at the Carlton Gallery on South Granville Street."

"Good. Well. We should probably get down to business. Why don't you tell me what you'd like to deal with in this session, and then we can discuss which approach you'd like me to take. We can use meditation, hypnosis, or past-life regression, for example. Or," she laughed, "all of the above. Then there's dream work and journalling, among other things."

God, Carol thought. *Maybe she's flaky. At least she doesn't have unicorns and fairies on the walls.* "Oh, I don't know. Could we just talk for a while?"

"Of course. Would you like to talk about your father?"

"No."

"Perhaps later, then."

A sudden vision of her father's eyes came to Carol, eyes that could be fierce when he was disappointed in her. She heard his voice saying, "How's my girl today?" and she felt a moment of grief. Grief didn't surface too often now, ten years after his death. Anyway, it was something she knew how to deal with.

She didn't know exactly where to start today, but it was costing her one hundred dollars an hour, so she thought she'd better say something. "I'm having an affair," she blurted, without knowing she was going to say it. "And I don't really want to."

She started to cry, and Janet moved a box of tissues to the arm of Carol's chair.

"Why don't you want to?"

"Because I love my husband."

"I see. Go on."

Her nose was running and the tears wouldn't stop and wet tissues were piling up in her lap. Janet moved a wastebasket nearer to Carol's chair.

"He won't make love to me anymore. Richard, my husband. We had an accident. I mean, our house came down in a landslide and our boarder, Jenny, was killed." Carol took a deep, gasping breath and waited a moment. Then she went on. "Richard was badly injured, but he's healed well. I wasn't hurt physically as much as he was, but I think we both thought, during the slide, that we were going to die. Now Richard wants to change his life completely, do good works or something. He thinks sex is selfish and trivial, I guess. Anyway, he seems to have given it up and I've become kind of … well, obsessed with it. Maybe not obsessed. I don't know. In the first weeks after the landslide, I was just horny a lot — oh, I hate that word, but it's appropriate — but lately I've been getting these *surges*, almost electrical, and then I have an ache that lasts for hours. When that began to happen, I started the affair. It's been helping a little."

"I see."

"It feels good to cry. I haven't really cried like this. Not full out. I didn't realize how much I'd bottled up."

Janet was silent as Carol's tears and sobs gradually subsided, then said, "I've heard about this kind of situation before — not with a married couple, but with two male friends who barely escaped death in an accident. One who'd previously liked his beer and his casual affairs became celibate and highly spiritual; the other went from being quite a mild, average Joe, to being wild and promiscuous. Near-death experiences often bring about big changes, a hunger for reassessing one's life, everyone in his or her own way. And the death of a friend has intensified this for you and your husband. We might say you have developed a lust for life. Pun intended!"

Janet laughed, but Carol didn't.

"I suppose it's interesting to know it might be a kind of syndrome," Carol said, "but it's not really comforting. Did the two men ever go back to normal — you know, to their previous selves?"

"I don't know. They weren't my clients. Anyway, whatever happened to them wouldn't predict your outcome. We need to focus on you."

"You make it sound like it's a psychological thing. But my experience is very physical," Carol said.

"It can be hard to separate the psychological from the physical," Janet said. "Each can have a strong effect on the other in many kinds of situations. But listen, you have choices — you're not a victim of these feelings, whatever their origin. Would you like to try an exercise? A simple meditation?"

"Yes, all right."

Carol felt better after meditating. She'd gone to her "peaceful place," and had invited Richard to visit her there. She'd assured him of her love.

Her homework was to start writing letters to Richard, not for him to see, but as a way of refreshing her memory about all the good things they'd shared. Janet said it was important not to show them to Richard, because he might interpret them as pressure.

"Give him more time to sort things out," Janet said.

"What about my affair?" Carol asked.

"Quit if you can. But be patient with yourself. Here's a suggestion. When strong sexual feelings arise, talk to them. Personify them. Have your sexually needy self talk to your peaceful self."

"Okay," Carol said, but doubted that she would. *Flaky* raised its embarrassing head. On the whole, though, she had found the session helpful. It was good to talk to someone so openly. She missed her dearest friend, Sandra, who had moved to New Zealand with her husband, who happened to be Richard's best friend. They kept in touch, but Carol had so far been embarrassed to reveal her worries about Richard or her struggle with her hypersexual state. Face to face, she might have told her, but it was difficult over the phone or in a letter or email. Adding to the difficulty was that they had been "happy couples" together, and a bit smug about their good fortune.

THIRTEEN

RICHARD HAD WALKED a block when he saw a woman on her knees on the grass, digging up buttercups, happily unaware of the futility of lawns. A couple walking their dog smiled at him, content, it seemed, to regularly pick up excrement from the boulevards. A man, one of the many in the neighbourhood who mowed his lawn what seemed like every other day, was cutting the already-short grass, the noise and gas of his mower polluting the street. *Do they have any inner lives at all*, Richard wondered, and he thought of his mother, constantly vacuuming. Perhaps their inner lives consisted of enumerating with satisfaction each chore completed. Perhaps the noise drove all other thoughts from their heads, and they enjoyed a type of meditation. Was there a happiness in that kind of life that he would never achieve? Of course, the avid clippers and dust-suckers might be slowly going mad, the only evidence of it the increased frequency of their obsessive activities.

Richard was thinking grimly of all the silent madness in the world, when his heart lurched at a sudden, terrible cry coming from an elderly woman sitting on her porch, her back straight, her hands folded neatly on her lap, her mouth wide open. Her cry seemed to be coming from so deep inside her that he could hardly bear to listen, and when he moved toward her to see if she needed help, he was stunned to see her start to smile, apparently not agitated at all.

"Are you all right?" he asked.

She didn't answer, kept smiling, so he slowly turned and walked away. He'd gone no more than half a block when the awful sound rose again from her chest, her throat, her mouth, like an alien being trying to escape. He kept walking, but he was shaking, and an echo of that wail seemed to be building up in his own chest. He walked six more blocks before he felt reasonably calm.

When he returned home, Carol called him into the kitchen, where she was working on her lecture for the next day.

"Sit beside me here," she said when he joined her. "I want you to look at this painting and tell me what you think. What's the story?"

She pushed a book toward him. Richard sat down and felt Carol leaning into him without moving physically, as though her aura was nudging his. He moved his chair back a few inches, and she looked at him sharply but didn't comment. On the table was a reproduction of a painting by Bonnard called *The Dessert*. In it, a young man and woman sat at a table holding coffee cups and plates that were empty except for one with a few cherries on it. The wall behind the pair was red-orange, as was the woman's blouse. The young man wore cool colours, blue and green, and he had a stub of cigarette hanging from his mouth.

"The story?"

"Yes, I'm going to have my class study it, but I wondered what you would make of it. Why, for example, are their postures so different? She's looking downcast, it seems to me, and he's, what? Matter-of-fact? Cocky?"

"The meal wasn't very good, maybe. Or she has indigestion."

"Richard! You've always had insights in the past that have helped me. Be serious, please."

"All right, let's see." He picked up the reproduction and studied it for a moment or two. "I'm guessing they're brother and sister, and she's pining for a boyfriend, and the brother is not sympathetic."

"I don't know how you can say that! Look at the predominant colour. It's hot, passionate. And look at the flowers on the sideboard. They're leaning way over, sort of drooping, not like a normal bouquet at all. It suggests the couple have just had sex, that sex was the 'meal' and coffee and fruit the dessert. And that she was disappointed in their lovemaking. And probably just generally disappointed in him. Look at him! A punk."

"That theory seems like a stretch."

"No, it isn't at all. I'll bet if I surveyed people, nine out of ten would agree with me. I think you're being wilfully obtuse."

"If you were already so sure of the 'story,' why did you ask me about it? The minute I sat down, I felt like it was some sort of test."

"Yes, well, I didn't intend it to be, but it seems to me now that you can't even *recognize* a sexual situation. Never mind be part of one."

Richard stood up. "Good night," he said. "I'm going to bed."

"I'm sorry," Carol called. "I just blurted that out. It wasn't fair."

"Yes, well, we're a sorry pair," Richard called back.

February 2012

Richard,

I remember that evening. I think I was baiting you, but I was so frustrated and angry.

I don't know if it was the same night — it was a night of one of your long walks — when I watched a documentary on Bob Dylan's concerts in the 1960s. Joan Baez took the stage, and when she had sung, started calling for Dylan to come back on. "Come to the stage, Bobby. Is Bobby there?" *Poor deluded girl*, I thought. The "Bobby" was so telling. She thought he was hers, tame, a lovely, tame poet — an oxymoron if there ever was one.

I believed you were tame, that you would never be beyond my wants, never out of reach. But no one owns anyone and no one stays the same forever, and you had your reasons for going into the wilderness.

Carol

Dear Carol,

I was tame, and now I'm tame again, whipped and in a cage.

Richard

Richard,

I think the very fact that you've written this book disproves your last statement.

Carol

FOURTEEN

"CAROL, THERE'S SOMETHING I have to tell you. Come and sit down."

It was 10:00 p.m. and Carol had just come home from a faculty meeting, having gone for drinks afterward. "You're scaring me. You look so grim."

"No, no. It's nothing serious. Well, it's serious, but not really for us."

"Who, then? Stop pacing. I need a glass of wine. Sit down." Carol opened a bottle of chilled white wine, poured herself a glass. "Want one?" she asked, and Richard shook his head.

They sat at the table. "Okay. Who's dead or dying?"

"No one. There's this girl, Emily. She works on the street."

"Selling flowers? Jewellery?"

"No."

"She's a hooker? You know a hooker?"

"Yes, well, but she's in trouble. I saw her one day a while ago and spoke to her and I didn't have a class today and I was going to the drugstore and she was at the edge of the park on Nanaimo Street and she recognized me. She has a black eye and bruises and said her boyfriend was threatening to hurt her more and could I help her?"

"Jesus, Richard."

"Anyway, she's here."

"Here? In the house?" Carol's voice rose with incredulity.

"She's resting in the spare room. She was in worse shape than I first thought."

"Shit, Richard. What were you thinking?"

"I didn't know what else to do."

"You could have called the police."

"It didn't seem right. She was stoned — might have ended up at the police station instead of being looked after. I couldn't just leave her there. The boyfriend might have come back."

Richard stood up and paced from sink to fridge and back again. He glanced into the sink at the empty glass Emily had drunk milk from, gulping it like a parched child. That was all she'd wanted before she went to lie down on a cot in the spare room. He'd wanted to take her to the hospital, but she'd refused. She'd been wearing the same red tank top and white plastic boots as the first time he'd seen her, with only a thin white shirt, unbuttoned, over it. He hadn't noticed, that first time, how extremely thin she was. Her breasts were small beneath the tight top, and her thighs were no bigger than his upper arm. He'd wanted to pick her up and carry her to safety — she would have been no heavier than a twelve-year-old — but she'd managed to get into the taxi and then into the house without help. He'd looked in on her as she slept. She'd taken off her boots and he'd almost cried when he saw her white ankle socks, decorated with Japanese cartoon kittens. He'd adjusted the blanket to cover her shoulders and her feet, then left quietly.

"She can't stay here," Carol said.

"Just overnight. She's in bad shape. Tomorrow I'll see if I can get her to a safe house of some kind."

"You're not a goddamned social worker."

"No, and you're not hard-hearted. Try to be sympathetic."

"I'm only trying to be practical. We can't look after such a ... such a troubled girl. We might get into trouble with the authorities. How old is she?"

"She said she was eighteen."

"I guess child welfare won't be after us, then, if she gets sicker in our care. If she's telling the truth. I'll go and talk to her."

"She's asleep. Wait until the morning."

"How bad is she?"

"Black eye. Cut lip. I gave her Polysporin to put on it. Bruises on her arms and legs. And weary. God, Carol. So weary. As though she's lived eighty years, not eighteen, and seen everything. Everything horrible."

"All right, Richard. All right. I know you're being kind, but we don't really know anything about her. These damaged girls are complicated, and sometimes dangerous. At the very least, she means heartache for you; at worst, trouble. Honestly, I can't take the stress of this right now. And I just thought of something else. Could her boyfriend look for her here?"

"How would he know where to look?"

"Does she have a cellphone?"

"I don't know. But she was so desperate to get away from him. Why would she call him?"

"I guess you're right. Desperate and weary, as you say. I'll just look in on her, though. Make sure she's not in any distress, breathing normally and everything." She stopped in the doorway, looked back. "I'm really pissed off with you, you know."

Richard followed her into the spare room. The girl was curled up in the fetal position, the blanket kicked off. Carol went closer. She put her hand on the girl's forehead. It was cool and her breathing seemed normal.

"I think she's all right," Carol said. "I'll see if she'll let me take her to a clinic tomorrow morning. I hope to god she doesn't lapse into a coma or something in the meantime."

Richard and Carol both slept fitfully. At 2:00 a.m., Carol shook Richard awake. "I hear noises," she said.

She got up and ran out of the bedroom, Richard close behind. They found the front door ajar. Emily was gone.

"I think I heard voices, too," Carol said.

Richard went out the front door to the sidewalk. He saw Emily with a man. They were about a block away, running. He shouted, "Come back!" He started to run, too, but they were faster, and he stopped and went back to the house.

Why was he chasing them, anyway? Emily had always been free to go. But why was she running?

When he got into the house, he got his answer. Carol shouted, "They've taken my soapstone carving. And my grandmother's emerald-and-gold brooch. The only keepsake I have of her. I fool- ishly left it by the sink in the bathroom last night. How could you, Richard? How could you? Call the police."

"No."

"No? Richard, she stole my things. Call the police."

"It could have been her boyfriend who stole them. I don't want to get her into trouble. He might have coerced her. Probably did."

"I don't care." Carol picked up the phone and started to punch in 911, but Richard grabbed it from her and slammed it onto the table.

Carol stood stunned in the middle of the kitchen, the harsh ceiling light shining on her dishevelled hair and making the circles under her eyes darker. She seemed to have had a lot to drink that evening. One strap of her short, blue-satin nightie slipped off her shoulder. Her lower lip trembled.

"You look like a mess," Richard said and immediately regretted it.

Carol's reaction made him step back, wobble, hold the table for support. She screamed, a high-pitched shriek, ran to him, and pounded his bare chest with her fists. "Bastard, bastard," she kept repeating.

Richard grabbed her wrists and held them, and after struggling for a moment, she let out a long sigh and cried, her body drooping. He tried to embrace her, but she pushed him away, sat down at the table.

"You take away my husband — no, you know what I mean. You withhold yourself from me. Not a proper husband, and now, now, you rob me of my belongings and make my home unsafe."

"It's not unsafe."

Carol stood up and ran to the hallway. She came back to the kitchen with the spare key that was kept under the blue pottery bowl. "She could have taken this and nothing else, hoping we hadn't noticed the key was missing, and come back and cleaned us out."

"But she didn't. We're safe, Carol. She won't be back."

"First my house falls on me, almost kills me, and now this. My new home feels dangerous. It has been violated. Oh, shit, Richard. You make me do things I never dreamed I would ever do."

"What? What things?"

"Yelling at you like that. Hitting you. I'm so angry and hurt that you put that pathetic girl ahead of me. Ahead of my security. And now you won't call the police."

"It's just that it wouldn't do any good. They'll pawn or sell the things before the police could ever track her down. We have no evidence. And I don't know where she lives — not even her last name."

Carol stared at him, and Richard saw something in her eyes, some pain deeper than that caused by the night's events.

"What other things, Carol? That you never dreamed you would do? There's something else, isn't there?"

He could see she was struggling with whether to speak or not. He waited, hardly breathing.

"I had an affair," she said.

Richard felt his blood turn to ice. He heard a moth battering itself to death in the light fixture, heard the fridge motor, heard a car engine starting, heard his heartbeat thundering in his ears.

"Richard, I'm sorry, I can't go on like this."

"Who is it?" he asked coldly.

"It doesn't matter."

"Tell me who it is."

"No one you know. It's over now, anyway."

"How long?"

"Not long. It doesn't matter."

"It matters — it all matters." He left the kitchen and came back, wearing a shirt. "I was cold," he said. It was about twenty degrees Celsius in the room. "Tell me, Carol."

"Richard, please. I've started therapy. To help me deal with everything. It won't happen again — the affair, I mean."

Richard stared at her until she looked away. Finally, he said, "I can't go on like this, either. I'm causing you pain, craziness. I'll move out."

"Richard, no!"

"I'll find another place this week. I can't give you what you need, and I can't bear thinking of you with another man. We don't even have honesty between us. You're not being completely open with me even now."

Now it was Carol's turn to stare, open-mouthed. "What fucking condescending, egotistical nerve!" she said. "You giving me an ultimatum, after bringing thieves into the house. After becoming a goddamned monk. And that girl. Did you have a thing for her? Is it just me you can't get it up for? Bloody well go, then. I won't stop you."

"That's unfair, Carol, and you know it."

Carol opened the fridge and pulled out a bottle of white wine. "I'm tired of talking. I'm going to sit here and get drunk."

"You've been doing that a lot lately."

Carol glared at him.

"I'll sleep on the couch," he said.

"Why bother?"

"I'll be gone by the end of the week." He left the room.

"Fine," Carol said. She stood, lost her balance, and bumped her thigh sharply on the edge of the table. She swore.

Richard, in the bedroom, stood staring into the closet, the way people stare absent-mindedly into a refrigerator.

Carol found him like that. "What are you doing?" she asked.

"Looking for a blanket," he said.

She went to him, put her arms around him. He stood with his arms rigidly by his sides and continued to look over Carol's shoulder into the closet.

"Richard, let's not do this. Please don't go."

"I have to," he said.

Carol let him out of her embrace and crouched down to get a blanket from a basket on the closet floor.

"Here," she said. She gave him the blanket and a pillow from the bed. Richard looked back as he was leaving the room and saw her tears. He recalled her emphatic "fine" when he said he would leave. But he was afraid that nothing would ever be fine again.

FIFTEEN

CAROL HAD BEEN sleeping poorly since Richard had moved out a week earlier. Tired and sad, she'd been finding it hard to concentrate on her work. Luckily, she had taught today's class many times and knew the material thoroughly. It was "The Importance of Women Artists," part of her Art History 101 course, to which she devoted two classes.

She began, as always, by reading part of a letter written by Gustav Mahler to his wife, Alma, before she had consented to marry him. Carol had developed a fascination for her through studying the painter Kokoschka, who had been madly in love with Alma, a muse to several prominent artists of her time. One biographer said she had seemed to need around her "the mystique of the artist" — the male artist — even though she was a composer herself. *Why wasn't* being *the artist enough?* Carol thought, and felt the accelerated pulse in her throat. Each time she read the letter aloud, she felt as angry as she had the first time.

"The roles in this play must be correctly assigned," Mahler began. "The role of 'composer,' the 'worker's world,' falls to me — yours is that of the loving companion and understanding partner! Are you satisfied with it? You must renounce all *superficiality*, all *convention*, all vanity and delusion. You must give yourself to me *unconditionally*, shape your future life, in every detail, entirely in accordance with my needs and desire nothing in return save my *love*."

"And he wanted her answer 'before Saturday,'" Carol said, anger evident in her voice. "He said having two composers in the marriage was ridiculous, degrading, and competitive. This even though Alma was considered a promising composer." Carol leaned against her desk to steady herself. "Any comments?"

She always felt nervous at this point, afraid some dismissive remark might make her temper flare. There were fifteen women and three men in this class, but it took only one man, as had happened last year, to push her over the edge. He'd said, the chauvinistic asshole, "Well, there haven't been a lot of great women artists, so maybe he was trying to save her from disappointment."

She'd railed then about how so many women had been relegated to artistic oblivion; most of her students leaned back rigidly in their seats, as though pinned there by a strong wind.

Now a young man put up his hand.

"Connor?"

"Mahler was a great composer," Connor said. "Probably a lot greater than Alma would ever have been."

There it is.

The class remained in tense silence. Carol took a deep breath.

"How can we know that?" she said, quietly, reasonably. "If Alma had no opportunity to develop her talent?" A vein in her neck was throbbing and her cheeks felt hot. "The same thing applies to women painters — which, of course, is what this section of the course is about. If they aren't given time and space, and if galleries don't show them and critics don't discuss them, how can they reach their full potential? And who are the arbiters of aesthetics; who are the gallery owners? And who defines greatness?"

"Men!" a woman called out, without a second of hesitation.

"White men!" another called.

"Half-dead white men!" another woman shouted, and almost everyone laughed.

"Yes, well, too bad it isn't funny," Carol said. "This was all well argued and documented in the nineteen-seventies, so you'd think some progress would have been made, but very little has changed. Google it. Find out what percentage of artists shown in galleries today are women. And how many are given one-person shows."

She walked over to the slide projector. "I'm starting with a painting by a man, the seventeenth-century Dutch artist Jan Steen. You'll soon see why. Could someone please turn out the light? … This is *Woman at Her Toilet*, meaning grooming, of course. Painted between 1665 and 1660. Not exactly pornographic, is it? I chose it precisely for its subtlety. A subtle male gaze, at least to the modern eye."

She said nothing as everyone looked at the woman sitting on a bed, one leg crossed high over the other as she took off a red stocking. She wore a blue jacket trimmed with white fur. A dog slept on the pillow on the bed, where the woman had probably recently lain. On the floor were slippers and a chamber pot.

"Notice how the fur, the dog, the warm tones of her skin, and the sweetness of her face make this a sensual picture. And there's nothing wrong with that. But where does your gaze go first? Or where does it settle? Connor, where does your gaze go?"

"Straight to the crotch."

Again, almost everyone laughed.

Carol thought suddenly of Nick Wallinsky, whom she'd seen at his recent art show, and felt a hot pulse between her legs. She had stopped seeing Gabe after her second session with Janet Warren, so he could no longer offer any relief. Meditation, as recommended by the therapist, hadn't helped much, but masturbation had, a little.

She pulled her attention back to the class. "Karen, what do you think?"

"The dark gap is a bit obscure," Karen said, "like you can't be sure her leg is raised high enough for you to see anything, but it triggers your imagination. Kind of titillating."

"You long for a flashlight," a student named Owen said.

The heat between Carol's legs turned to an ache. *Pull yourself together*, she thought.

"In fact," Carol said, "this is a portrait of a woman of 'easy virtue.' The stocking she's taking off is a *kous* in Dutch, which is also slang for female genitals. The objects on the floor — the slippers and the chamber pot — are symbols of lust. The Dutch word for 'chamber pot' is also the word for 'slut.'

"To be fair to Steen, he was a great painter and painted many pictures of respectable families and chaste women, although all his women do tend to have their legs immodestly apart. And it's worth pointing out that there's no male equivalent in English, and probably most languages, for the designation 'of easy virtue.'"

"What about 'horndog'?" Owen again.

"Notice the admiration in Owen's voice. Enough said. By the way, Owen, you are older than sixteen, aren't you? Try to act it.

"The next slide is a painting by Artemisia Gentileschi, *Susanna and the Elders*, 1610." She left the slide on for a full minute, saying nothing, letting the students observe the two elders, fully clothed, leaning over a railing and looking toward the naked Susanna. One elder whispered conspiratorially in the ear of the other, who looked intently at the woman. She leaned her head away at an extreme angle, eyes downcast, both arms raised to protect herself.

Carol clicked to the next slide, a painting of the same subject by Carracci, a man. In it, Susanna looked directly at the men, appearing relaxed, with the hint of a smile, as though she might be half-willing to accede to the men's wishes.

"Did you see the difference? Ellen, what did you see?"

"In the one by the woman, Susanna is scared. In the other one, she isn't."

"Right. And which one do you think is more in keeping with the Bible story of a woman of great virtue suffering a seduction attempt by two men?"

Carol showed more slides: paintings by Suzanne Valadon, Mary Cassatt, Frida Kahlo, and Emily Carr, most of them portraits of women, or self-portraits. And she showed some of Georgia O'Keeffe's flower paintings and Judy Chicago's *Dinner Party* flower sculptures, the former said to be suggestive of female genitalia, and the latter definitely so. Then she showed some of the angrier and more rebellious work of feminist artists of the 1970s. One was a performance piece from 1975 in New York: Carolee Schneemann reading naked from a scroll she was slowly pulling out of her vagina.

"The scroll is more than two feet long and is titled *Interior Scroll*," Carol said. Schneemann also wrote a book, *Cézanne, She Was a Great Painter*, an account of the ways in which women artists were erased from history."

"I don't see what calling Cézanne a woman accomplishes," Connor said.

"It shows," Karen said icily, "that if Cézanne had had a vagina, his work would have been buried in it."

"That's gross," Owen said.

"The artist is commenting on exactly that opinion," Carol said. "The vagina isn't gross to women, but it evokes disdain in a lot of men if it isn't directly connected, so to speak, to their own sexual needs and fantasies.

"All right. Your assignment for next class is this: choose a woman artist and analyze one of her paintings or sculptures in terms of a 'female gaze.'"

"That'll be easier for the women," Owen grumbled.

"But think how lucky you men are," Carol said. "You'll learn the most from the exercise."

February 2012

Richard,

Thanks for showing me in my professional life, someone who is more than a disappointed wife and apparently sexually voracious. Although you did mention that I was suffering from the horrors of the landslide, you didn't show that I was screwed up by it! Pun intended.

Carol

Dear Carol,

You're welcome.

Richard

SIXTEEN

"PEOPLE ALL OVER the world will one day live in floating houses. The water is coming." The speaker on the radio was quoting a resident of an experimental housing estate on the River Meuse in Holland. The houses, he said, were tall and narrow, resembling a row of toasters, and were moored to poles and set on hollow concrete pontoons so they could rise and fall with the river.

The water is coming.

Richard turned off the radio. Rise and fall, indeed. He lived now in a dungeon of a basement suite on Sixteenth Avenue, near the university, as lonely as he would have been in a house on stilts far out in some dark lagoon, with the waters rising all around him, the house bobbing and swaying, about to topple at any moment. The memory of the landslide came crashing back and it took him a few moments to banish it.

He missed Carol, but he couldn't bear to be around her now, even if she wanted to be with him. Her unfaithfulness sat like a hard lump of dough in his chest. Sometimes, alone in the evenings, a groan escaped him, a cry of *angst*. The German word captured it onomatopoeically. *Anguish* worked, too, as did the good old English word *pain*, short and stark. He looked the latter up in the dictionary. From the Latin *poena*, penalty. Pain was a penalty.

He wanted a word like *weltschmerz*. "World pain," literally, although the dictionary defined it as "a vaguely yearning outlook on life." Vaguely? Not bloody likely.

He turned on his computer, intending to do some work for his class, checked his email, and found one from Carol:

Dear Richard,

I'm so glad you deigned to talk to me on the phone the other day. I've tried to reach you again since, but it seems you won't answer my messages. I went to your office a couple of times, but you weren't there.

You said you must start to devote yourself to serious matters. I'm not sure what you mean. It seems to me that teaching young people puts you in a position to do important things. You can be socially relevant. And not just during class hours. You said you're worried about climate change. You could organize marches against the use of fossil fuels, for example. You could encourage some of your students to become architects and engineers who would build energy-efficient buildings and solar-powered vehicles, and things we've not even imagined so far. You could stay in the thick of things, if you wanted to.

I still love you, Richard, you know that, and I believe, fervently, that we can get back together again after you've had time to recover. After both of us have. I didn't real- ize at first just how shaken I was by Jenny's death, and I blamed you alone for the rift in our marriage. So I have things to work through, too.

I don't even have your apartment address. Please email it to me and I'll forward your mail to you. There's a postcard for you from Imogen with a view in Tuscany.

Much love,

Carol

Richard emailed his address at once, a small flicker of hope dancing across the screen. And then guilt: he really must write to Imogen. She'd sent him an email several days ago. He opened it and read it again:

Dear Daddy,

Italy is super fabulous, great food, sweet, exuberant people, and all that art and history. Next, back to Spain. Pete and I fell in love with it and will spend some time there in a small apartment near the sea where we stayed earlier. Very cheap.

We lift a glass of Valpolicella to you.

Love, Imogen. Love to Carol, too.

He hadn't seen Imogen in more than a year. When she was younger, she visited for a month every summer, and he and Carol went to England on four different occasions, twice at Easter, twice at Christmas. But once she started university, she travelled abroad on most vacations, lately with her boyfriend, Pete.

Richard had had, before the disaster, a boxful of photos of her that he'd found painful to look at. One of the few that were bearable was one of her at six, smiling impishly. In most of the other photos, he saw sadness in her face and his throat would ache with what seemed years of his unshed tears. She had a touching seriousness at the best of times, as though she'd seen into the heart of the world and found it wanting. How much of that was his fault?

He thought, not for the first time, that maybe he should have fought for his marriage to Grace. They'd had eight good years. At least he'd thought they were good.

A year or so after he and Grace started seeing each other, she'd asked him, "Don't you think we should get married?" He'd said he wasn't sure, he'd have to think about it. And Grace had immediately begun to cry copiously, sobbing like a child. She thought he loved her, she'd said, didn't know how she could go on, and he relented, said he hadn't meant never, just not right away, but, no, no, he was ready, don't worry, we'll set a date.

Had his reluctance been a premonition, his vision of her as a child accurate? She had had trouble with adult responsibilities like housekeeping and bill paying and making practical decisions once they were married. She'd phoned him at work a little too often to help her sort out some simple problem. And she'd been overwhelmed with caring for Imogen as an infant, barely able to cope sometimes. He suggested she get a part-time job, that they could afford a babysitter a couple of days a week. But the only job she'd ever had was clerking in a clothing store, and she said she'd rather be a full-time mother. *I should have helped her with Imogen more.*

Maybe the end had been in the beginning. Maybe his hesitation about marrying her had been lastingly hurtful to her. Had he done and said other things over the years that had made her doubt his love?

In the months before she left, she said he had put his work and his ambition first and her and Imogen second. She was lonely, she said.

Her affair with James, the man she later married, had been going on only a short time when he found out. His pain had been terrible, his imaginings of her in James's sexual embrace almost unbearable. And now Carol. Two wives unfaithful. *One might be considered a misfortune, two seems like carelessness*, he thought, riffing on Oscar Wilde's great line. *Christ, this isn't funny.*

Later, though, after the divorce, he thought sex might not have had much to do with it, since he and Grace had never stopped making love. Had he overreacted? He could have pleaded for a reconciliation when she said she was going to live with James, but he'd acted as if divorce were inevitable, withdrew, and left her little choice but to go. If James had fought to keep her, Richard could have threatened to sue for alienation of affection. A colleague had done that and won; his wife's lover had sloped away and his wife had been impressed with such steadfast love and had stayed.

How empty the house had been. He'd longed for the old clutter, longed to have Grace phone him at work over some small thing. And Imogen. How many times had he said no to reading her a bedtime story because he was writing a short story or marking papers or preparing a lesson? Oh, Imogen, how could he not have known that time would pass quickly and he'd rarely have the chance again to please her, indulge her, hold her tiny body in his arms?

At least he and Carol had no children.

But he'd *volunteered* to leave Carol. Defeatist again.

S E V E N T E E N

September 2005

Richard

My therapist suggested I write letters to you — a kind of diary, to help me sort out my feelings about you and our marriage. I won't send subsequent ones, but I felt the need to send this first one. Here it is as an attached file.

Diary Entry

I hardly know what to do with myself these evenings since you left, Richard. I have a hard time concentrating on anything and can't read anything that doesn't pertain to my classes, and even that is difficult. Sometimes I channel surf, but after a few minutes, I give up.

Last night, though, I tuned in late to a movie called *The Virgin and the Gypsy*, and the climactic scene caught my interest. Near the village where the young heroine lives, a dam bursts and floods the village and the heroine's house. Water rushes in, fast and terrible, and the gypsy and the virgin try to rescue her elderly grandmother, but are too late and she drowns. Then the pair go upstairs. (When I think about this now, I wonder if the whole scene is a fantasy of the girl's, because they leave the body of the grandmother without a backward glance.)

Then the gypsy — dark and handsome, of course — removes the virgin's chaste, white petticoat and makes love to her. The scene is quite lovely, although the camera cuts away before too much happens. Even without seeing the whole movie, you know this was a long time coming, if you'll pardon the expression.

The reason I've told you all this is that it brought back memories of our time in Venice, when we stayed in a hotel overlooking the Grand Canal. (Whenever I utter or write that sentence, it feels like I'm making it up, it's so impossibly romantic, and yet we were there.) I suppose it's the wateriness of it that triggered the memory. But of water rising, not roaring down a hillside, freighted with mud. I don't think I could watch a minute of that.

It was in April, remember, before the smells of Venice ripened, and the gauzy white curtains billowed in the window, and noises came in, too — people talking below on the promenade, vaporettos on the canal — but the sounds were exciting rather than intrusive. They seemed like a soundtrack we'd chosen for our own movie. It was hot and we'd thrown the covers off the bed and the sheets were cool and pure white and we made love while almost a foot of water covered St. Mark's Square.

But there was nothing to fear. We walked barefoot later, remember? And laughed and splashed our way to a restaurant where we ate the most delicious meal, one of my most memorable ever, of fritto misto — scallops and sole and clams and shrimp. They were so succulent, weren't they — gently infused with lemon and rosemary and olive oil.

The delicate juiciness of the scallops as I bit into them reminded me of your mouth on me such a short time before. And I looked at you and smiled and I believe you were thinking of the same thing, the way you smiled, too, your fork poised in front of your lips.

Can we have it that good again, do you think?

Richard, I'm still not going to tell you who I slept with. I have my reasons — mainly that it would do no good, and also I want you to forgive me without demanding that, because your withholding yourself from me for so long was partly why it happened. I know that was because of the trauma of the landslide and Jenny's death, so you weren't really to blame. But I wasn't myself, either.

What I do blame myself for is not being more understanding of your pain, and more patient. If I had been, I never would have told you about my affair. So forgive me for that, please. You need never have known.

Have you looked for Emily, and if so, did you find her? I feel bad about how I acted. I know you had a sincere desire to help her. My interest in this has nothing to do with my jewellery. I've let it go. Anyway, she probably traded it for drugs, and some dealer's girlfriend or mother is wearing it now.

Love, Carol

I don't think I'll send you any other entries, but I will keep
in touch. Is your place all right — livable and not depressing? I'll come and see you there soon, bring your mail and
a couple of other things you left behind.

xo

Carol

Richard still felt the pain of her affair, the fact of it, but he
could, he *would* forgive her. He started to write a reply saying
so, but ended up deleting it. Nothing he said rang true to him.
In most of what he did these days, he was just going through
the motions.

He wrote a short email back, avoiding questions of forgiveness.

Dear Carol,

Thanks for the memories of Venice. It was certainly a
wonderful time.

I like the idea of a momma's boy drug dealer — the stuff of
TV crime drama!

No, I haven't looked for Emily. Partly it's because the
thought of scouring the Downtown Eastside with so few
clues is depressing and a bit daunting. The other thing
is that I don't think she wants to be found. Damn, that
does sound cowardly. Maybe I will look for her in the near
future, when my energy level rises. I'm still kind of drag-
ging myself around.

xxoo

Richard

He read it over. Was it enough? Should he reword it? Add something? No. Let it stand. It was all he could manage.

Richard thought too much about death these days. Not *every third
thought*, like Prospero, but episodes, chunks of time carved with
hallucinatory sharpness out of otherwise ordinary days. Everyone
around him would look hollowed out, soulless, but apparently
unaware of their state.

Today, as he walked along Tenth Avenue to the grocery store,
he looked at each person for a spark of life and saw only a blank.
*You don't know you've died and are now only going through the
motions*, he said in his mind to a woman as she walked toward him.
He laughed out loud, startling her, and she was for a moment alive
again. A baby in a stroller looked into his eyes and seemed to be saying, *Yes, I see it, too, but we have to go on pretending*. It reminded
him of the children in the film *Wings of Desire*, the only ones who
could see the angels — so much better than seeing the dead.

His first experience of this — mirage or revelation? — had happened after seeing his father in his coffin. He'd died suddenly of a
heart attack, aged sixty. The shock and horror of the waxy, empty
face had caused Richard to move into this walking-dead world for
days afterward. When his mother died of cancer a few years later,
he made a point of not seeing her body.

His father had made his mother miserable for most of their
marriage, with his emotional distance and his constant criti-
cisms. Not a great role model, Richard realized after Grace left.
He hadn't been as bad as his father, but before that he'd believed
with the hubris of youth that he could be *entirely* different.

He was glad he hadn't seen Jenny dead. After the first weeks,
his dreams of Jenny changed. She was still as alive as ever, taking

his hand and leading him to the baptismal waters of the sea. But
now in the dream, he was pale and waxy, struggling to find enough
strength to wade in the water.

Sometimes, awake, he thought he caught a glimpse of her walking ahead of him, turning a corner. Once he ran a block to catch
up, before he realized the madness of it. Sometimes he felt her
presence: once in a crowded café and once in a dark theatre, the
one time he'd tried to sit through a film. He'd walked out in half
an hour, unable to bear looking for her in each row any longer,
knowing he wouldn't be able to see her.

Walking was a form of relief but that, too, failed him when he
entered one of the dead zones. The only thing he could read was
The Tempest, because of his commitment to Jenny. And teaching
kept him going for the same reason. What would he find to save
himself — if he still wanted to be saved — when that was over?
He knew what he *should* do: find a way to make a difference in the
world, as functioning altruists would have it. He had brochures
from various organizations, like the Red Cross and the Stephen
Lewis Foundation. He didn't necessarily need to go abroad (or he
could prove Carol wrong, be more courageous), but whether he
could find a spark in himself with enough heat to enable him to be
of use, he didn't know.

February 2012

Richard,

How I poured my heart out to you all those years ago. How I wanted you back. I feel sorry for my past self — not a healthy emotion. As for people walking around hollowed out, I was one of them for a while, and so were you. It seems to me now that as painful as that state is (and it comes more than once in most lives), it's a mistake to rush headlong into something new to fill the void, as we each did in our own way, your way, of course, causing more dire consequences. What wiser people say about boredom can apply to the more serious state of hollowness: sit with it, breathe it in, wait for the right action to come slowly.

Carol

Dear Carol,

You are one of the wisest people I know.

Richard

EIGHTEEN

"SORRY I'M LATE," Beth said, out of breath from hurrying her heaviness up the stairs to Jacintha's apartment above a bakery on Commercial Drive, as the intoxicating aromas of butter, yeast, caramelized sugar, and cinnamon seeped into the room. Beth's breasts, white as bread, swelled out of her pink tank top, and her surprisingly small feet and puffy calves protruded below a bright-green peasant skirt.

"Be on time, next time," Jacintha said. It was the first meeting of her newly invented women-only Gaia Circle, a branch of the Gaia Warriors. There were three members, Tanya being the third.

Beth had told Jacintha, the day after the city hall protest, how alarmed she'd been when Jacintha lit the fire.

"You have to push the limits when you're fighting the establishment," Jacintha had told her.

Beth had escaped, as had the other members of their group, but several protesters, the most vocal and belligerent ones, had been taken into custody for a few hours, then released for lack of evidence of who had started the fire. The TV coverage was minimal and Jacintha suspected International Olympic Committee censorship — or at least that they had some sort of "understanding" with the media.

"It's unseemly to come late to a Circle," Tanya said to Beth.

"This isn't a Wiccan Circle," Jacintha said.

"It could be. Maybe it should be," Tanya said. "Let's at least read *Charge of the Goddess*, so we can ask for her help. I brought a copy with me."

"Without a proper casting of the Circle? Are you all right with that?" Jacintha asked.

"Yes, I think we'll be forgiven," Tanya said. "This once, anyway."

Tanya read, and when she got to "Naked in our rites," Jacintha saw Beth's startled look and smiled coolly at her, making Beth squirm.

The *Charge* was over and Tanya was looking at Jacintha expectantly. Tanya was also a "mature" student at UBC. She'd completed her BA in English and had taken a couple of years off. She was now in the Theatre Program to get her MFA. The two girls had been in high school together, not close friends, but they'd been in the same Wiccan Circle. Neither was in a Circle now, and Jacintha had abandoned the practice, not sure how much of it she believed in. She'd originally turned to Wicca out of a need to set herself above other girls. She'd wanted no repetition of the ignominy she'd suffered in elementary school.

In grade one, lonely, she'd told her classmates her mother's claim that she was a Russian princess, and that her grandmother, also called Catherine, was related to and named after a queen called Catherine the Great, Empress of All the Russias. "We have one of her crowns in a safe place," she said. "But I can't tell you where because it's a secret." After that she had friends to play with at recess, and girls to eat lunch with.

But her second-hand clothing, scuffed shoes, and sometimes-tangled hair were too much of a contradiction to her claimed status, and one of the older girls started calling her a liar and made up hurtful chants to plague her in the playground: Jass the Ass, Jacintha the Stinka, Princess Poo, Stinky Pants. The torment went on for weeks, until an actual Stinky Pants, a boy who shat himself in class one day, took the gleeful attention away from her.

During the worst of it, Jacintha begged her mother to let her stay home from school, and Catherine, seeing her distress, acquiesced. During the second week, a social worker came to the door. Luckily, or perhaps unluckily considering what happened later, Catherine was dressed modestly in sweater and skirt and had that morning washed the encrusted dishes and swept the floor. If she'd been out, as she was most days, leaving Jacintha alone, Jacintha might have been removed from her mother's care then. *Before the terrible thing happened.*

In high school, living with her adoptive family, Jacintha was tall and beautiful and wore fashionable clothes, but nevertheless she still felt the need for something to set her apart, something to give her power. She began by reading tarot, and then, with the help of library books, started casting spells for her friends. Her first successful spell was for a girl who wanted a particular boy as her boyfriend. The spell involved a pink altar cloth, a magnet, a pair of pink candles, and rose petals. "I am the magnet, he's the pin" was the incantation.

She cemented her success, and thus her reputation as a witch, by taking the boy in question aside and asking him if he was interested in the girl. When he said no, she told him that if he pretended, took the girl out a few times, then she, Jacintha, would give him ten dollars plus whatever he spent on dates. She had a generous allowance from her parents. He agreed happily.

"If you tell," she said, "I'll make your life hell." The look in her eyes was all he needed to be convinced.

"Can we do a spell now?" Tanya asked.

"Just a short one," Jacintha said.

"Okay. Let's do one to call our heart's desire to us."

Jacintha found paper and pens.

"I'll need a metal bowl, too, or a saucepan if you don't have a bowl. And matches." Equipment assembled, Tanya said, "Write down one thing you desire in your life now, then fold the paper and place it in the pan."

Tanya finished quickly. Beth took longer, writing earnestly, frowning. *Wishing for a lover*, Jacintha thought. *It's probably ages since she's been laid, if ever.*

She herself had been celibate for several weeks, believing sex would distract her from her plan. There was a tradition — she didn't know which one, maybe several — that said sex squandered energy, depleted personal power. It didn't seem to be in the Wiccan tradition, with its rite of god and goddess having sex, usually sym-bolically but sometimes in actuality. A holy copulation. When she'd told Skitch about it, he'd said — how could he resist? — "Holy fuck!" She smiled, remembering.

Jacintha had written one word only: *Richard*. She placed the paper in the metal bowl, set it on fire, and watched it burn.

"All right, down to business," Jacintha said. "Let's come up with an idea for a new action."

"Greg says we should find out where that developer lives, the one who's planning to cut down a bunch of trees on the North

Shore to build houses for fat cats, and throw paint and garbage at his house and maybe graffiti it, although it could be tricky if he's got fences and alarms, and maybe we should do his offices instead."

"Tanya, Tanya," Jacintha said. "I'm asking for women-originated actions."

"Can't I even consult Greg?"

"'Can't I consult Greg?'" Jacintha mimicked in a little-girl voice. "You need to stop consulting Greg about everything, asking him for permission."

"We've always talked about everything. No secrets, even."

"What? In the great tested maturity of your one-year relationship?"

"Sarcasm doesn't make for a great group dynamic, you know," Tanya said.

"I thought of something," Beth said, and waited for permission to go on.

"Let's have it."

"Well, I was reading the story of Spider Woman, and how she spun the world out of herself, and that inspired me. You know how some housing developments don't allow clotheslines because they say they're unsightly? I think it reminds them of poor people. Anyway, not using dryers saves energy. So I thought we could tie lots and lots of clothes together into huge webs and string them down a whole city block between trees and telephone poles, and put up signs saying things like Clean Up Your World Without Wasting Energy, and Clothes Dryers Suck."

Everyone was silent for a long moment. Then Jacintha smiled one of her rare, wide-open smiles, and said, "Great, Beth. And signs saying The IOC Sucks, and Hang the Politicians Out to Dry. But the largest signs will say The Olympics — Greatest Energy Suck of All. Everything we do now needs to be about the Olympics."

"How do we do it without anyone stopping us?" Tanya asked.

"That's Beth's problem," Jacintha said. "You'll be the commander, Beth. You can enlist the services of Skitch and Greg and

Brian. One of the real benefits of this idea is that you'll get a lesson in having men *do your bidding*. Don't you love that phrase?"

"I'll help Beth organize it," Tanya said. "What will you do?"

"I'll alert the press, when the time comes."

"I don't know if I can do it," Beth said. "Be in charge, I mean."

"Think of Spider Woman and have courage."

Skitch arrived minutes after the meeting was over, carrying a bottle of red wine and some cinnamon buns. "I saw Tanya and Beth leaving," he said. "What were you doing?"

"You'll find out soon enough."

"Yeah, yeah, okay." He set the buns on the table, opened the bottle, gripped its neck, drank long from it, and gave a loud sigh of satisfaction. He offered the bottle to Jacintha and when she shook her head, he put it down, held out his arms, and gave her a hooded-eye look. "Come here."

"Come here? Do you think you're in a romantic movie? That supposedly sexy face is just silly."

"Harsh! Listen, Jacintha, we have to fuck — we just have to. I don't care what you said about me *handling* you. It's just a simple fuck." He grabbed her, held her tight, pressed his erection against her.

"You can be such an asshole."

"Lie down with me, Jass. Please. Give me something."

"No. You need to learn patience. I'm going out now, but you'd better stay here for a while. You've got a big wet spot on your fly."

"Jass, please."

But she was out the door and gone.

NINETEEN

CAROL STOOD GAPING at the street where Richard lived. It was barricaded by police cars, and pieces of cloth of every colour were tied together, the ends fastened to tree trunks down the length of the street, blocking traffic — of which there was little, the street being a quiet, residential one. When she looked more closely, she saw that the cloth was clothing: jeans, shirts, printed dresses and skirts, bedsheets and towels. At intervals were what looked like very large dream catchers — clothes woven across huge hoops hanging in the middle of the street. More sheets and garments had been flung over tree branches and dripped nightmarishly as far as the eye could see. It was like a bad Christo and Jeanne-Claude installation — their most recent had been the hangings of beautiful orange banners all through Central Park in New York. This installation on West Sixteenth was chaotic, except for the carefully made webs, as though every person on the block had gone mad on washday.

It took Carol a moment to notice the sign in black pen on cardboard tied to a telephone pole: Up with Clotheslines, Down with Sucking Dryers, and further down the street, The Sucking Olympics. Police cars were parked at various angles to prevent vehicle access, although who would try to drive into the mess of sheets that would drag across their windshield, or into the hoops that would snare them, she couldn't imagine. Leaning against one of the cars was a striking young woman, talking to two policemen. They had notepads out and seemed to be taking a particular interest in her.

Carol started down the sidewalk, but was stopped by another policeman, outside the yellow tape.

"No access, ma'am."

"I just want to visit someone."

"Who might that be?"

"It might be my husband."

"What's his name and address?" His pen was poised over a clipboard. He was good-looking, about thirty-five, tall and lean. Attractive.

Carol had one of her sexual surges and became thoroughly disoriented.

"Ma'am?" the officer said. "His name and address?"

And she realized she'd been staring at him stupidly, probably for several seconds.

"Oh!" She told him Richard's name and address. She could feel her face flushing.

"And you don't live with your husband?"

"No." She gave her name and address, as requested.

"Did your husband have anything to do with this?" He gestured to the carnival of cloth behind him.

"No, of course not."

TWENTY

IT WAS SUNDAY afternoon, the day after the Spider Web protest. The knock on Richard's door startled him. He wasn't expecting anyone — only Carol knew he lived here, and she hadn't emailed him to say she was coming. When he opened the door, he saw Jacintha standing before him.

"Jacintha! What are you doing here? How did you know where I live?"

"Beth told me you'd moved nearby and told me which house she thought it was. I was in the area yesterday and saw it, so I thought I'd try my luck. I hope you don't mind."

"No, it's all right," he said, setting aside his embarrassment at having been caught in such a dishevelled state. "Please come in." He asked, "Were you involved in that demonstration here yesterday?

The beautiful blond woman shouted, "It's all my doing, officer. Leave her alone."

A car drove up and a man with a video camera and a woman with a microphone got out. A local news team.

"Over here," the woman claiming responsibility called. "I'll make a statement."

"No, you won't," an officer near her said, and stood in front of her. "You can take pictures of the street," he said to the reporters, "but that's all."

"I represent the Gaia Circle, the women's branch of the Gaia Warriors," the woman said, shoving past the officer.

The officer opened the police car door and said, "Get in." He held her arm and she jerked it free, but she obeyed and got in.

She rolled down the window and shouted, "We're tired of most people's passivity. We want thousands to join us."

The cameraman swung her way and tried to photograph her just as the officer blocked the window.

"It's quite funny, isn't it?" the woman reporter said, pushing her microphone toward the officer.

"No comment."

"What are you going to do now?"

"We're waiting for a city crew to come and take this mess down. I can't tell you more, pending an investigation."

"Get a shot of that sign, Doug," the reporter said. "Our MLAs Have Lint Traps for Brains. That's funny, Officer, you have to admit."

The officer was admitting nothing.

Carol tried again. "Please, my husband's place is just a few houses down."

"Sorry," he said. "You'll have to come back later."

She had a class and then a faculty meeting to get to. "Later" would probably be tomorrow.

But she said, "Later, then," and smiled the slightest bit suggestively. *Oh, please let this stop.*

I remember you said you were with a protest group. Presumably Beth is in the group, which is why it was on this street."

"Yes, Beth was in charge. I was actually arrested, but they let me go with a warning. We got insultingly little attention from the media. They didn't mention the Gaia Circle or Warriors, the names I gave them. They went from thirty seconds of footage of our signs to some Olympics official saying how wonderfully safe the Games were going to be. Typical bias."

"I'm sorry you weren't as successful as you wanted to be."

"I guess we'll have to go bigger next time."

"I hope that won't involve violence."

"No, it will just be a lot showier."

"I see."

"Wow, it's gloomy in here," Jacintha said, after she had sat down at the kitchen table. She said she had just come from Beth's house, where she, Beth, Anna, and John had been working on the play. Richard had given them permission to not attend classes and to work on their own. She had brought some manuscript pages with her for Richard to read.

Richard had told the rest of the class that they wouldn't be working on the rewrite anymore, that they would be studying Shakespeare's *Tempest* and would be assigned essays on it. Most seemed very relieved by the news. He was probably more relieved than they were. It had been a brave experiment, but it was failing. Maybe it was more foolhardy than brave.

Jacintha looked around the apartment. "Is that a mousetrap by the fridge?" she asked. "You should have a cat, but on the other hand, I'd fear for the cat, given the state of this place. What's that smell?" She peered into the sink at the caked, piled-up dishes.

"I wasn't expecting a guest." Richard was in sweatpants and a T-shirt, both in need of washing, and he hadn't shaved or combed his hair.

"Oh, sorry, that was rude of me," Jacintha said. "How long have you lived here?"

"Two weeks."

Richard's embarrassment was growing. He could smell his sweat, feel his hair signalling his haplessness in a spiky semaphore.

"Do you have any coffee?" Jacintha asked. "Shall I put the kettle on? Unless you want me to leave."

"No, sit down. I'm fine. I'll make some coffee."

As he fumbled around with the kettle and the coffee tin, Jacintha startled him by saying, "You suffered a great shock, didn't you, with that landslide? Has it made you depressed?"

At first, he was tempted to say, "I'd rather not talk about it." But her eyes held such a look of concern that he said, "It's been hard, but I'm coping. How do you know about it?"

"It's general knowledge on campus. Everyone feels sorry for you. I don't mean in a pitying way. I mean everyone, including me, empathizes."

"Thanks."

"Do you believe in karma? You know, that things happen to us because of past sins? Oh, I don't mean you. I was thinking about Prospero's exile. What was his sin? Being too bookish is what Shakespeare suggested. Maybe out of touch with the needs of the people. You're bookish, but being interested in saving the planet keeps you in touch."

"Saving the planet?"

"The environmental theme you were originally keen on."

"Ah, yes, but you and I agreed that love and magic and poetry were to be more central."

"We're having fun giving the villains their punishment. But about karma: What do you think of the concept, generally?"

"Well," he said, "millions of people in the world suffer through no fault of their own. When an individual crime is punished, that's cause and effect, not karma. Maybe some people call it 'karma' without really knowing what it means. I'm unclear on it myself, but from what I do know, I don't think I believe in it."

He thought suddenly of Emily. "For example, what have those poor young women in the Downtown Eastside ever done to deserve being abused or murdered?"

"I wouldn't have thought you knew much about the Downtown Eastside."

"You can't live in Vancouver all your life without knowing about the Downtown Eastside," Richard said. "And I've had occasion recently to pass through the area."

"Pass through. Yes." She gave the phrase a significance that puzzled Richard.

"I knew a young woman who lived down there," she said. "A desperate young woman."

"Knew?"

"She's not there now."

"I knew a young woman there, too."

"What happened to her?"

"I don't know."

"That's where we differ."

He could feel she had a lot more to say about it, but her sombre expression made him think he'd upset her by asking questions.

"Well, maybe punishments aren't karmic," Jacintha said, "but there can be a nice symmetry. Like when a rapist gets cancer, or a murderer dies in a car accident while leaving the scene of his crime. Although probably that happens in fiction more than in real life. Too bad, really."

Richard's head was beginning to ache. He was still picturing Emily — thin, bruised, and permanently wounded.

"The kettle's boiling," Jacintha said.

"I'm sorry, but I'm not feeling well. I can't offer you that coffee, after all."

"Oh, no, I'm sorry. I'll be going, then."

Richard held the door open as Jacintha put on her coat. She hesitated for a moment on the threshold, turned around swiftly, and darted at Richard.

Carol arrived just in time to see her kissing Richard on the lips. Jacintha pivoted slowly, looked Carol up and down, smiled, and glided away, disappearing around the side of the house.

Carol stared open-mouthed at Richard.

"It's not what it looked like," Richard said. "She came here uninvited, a student, to bring me some of the play rewrite. I have no idea why she did what she just did."

"Oh, really?" Carol said. "Here's the cashmere sweater I bought for you." She threw the bag with the sweater in it, striking Richard in the face. "Bastard! Liar! That was the woman who was on your street yesterday!" She turned and ran from the door.

"Come back — I didn't do anything. Carol, please."

He chased her, grabbed her arm. She struggled, punched his shoulder, ran again. He stood defeated, watched until she was out of sight, and went back into the gloom of the apartment.

He tried to think what to do. Should he phone Carol, write to her? Surely he could convince her of his innocence. And then, unbidden, it was Jacintha's beautiful, glowing face he saw, Jacintha who filled his mind. Her mischievous look after she had kissed him was, god help him, charming. He could still feel her mouth on his, ran his tongue along his lower lip. A taste of berries. He realized with horror that he felt aroused for the first time in a long time.

No. Not her. It should be Carol. If anyone were to reawaken him, he wanted it to be Carol.

He stumbled to the sink, scooped cold water from the tap, battered his mouth with it until his lips were numb and the front of his shirt soaked. He leaned there for a long time, elbows on the rim. He tried to pray. *Please, God.* But a buzzing in his head that seemed to spill out into the room mocked him like a spirit unconvinced.

TWENTY-ONE

JACINTHA THOUGHT HER visit to Richard had gone well, although the kiss might have been too soon. She had vowed to move slowly, but there was something about his bedraggled appearance that had touched her in spite of herself. And then when she saw his wife near the door, she couldn't resist the opportunity to stir things up.

On the whole, she felt satisfied with what she'd done and had expected to sleep well that night. But she'd been awakened by her own scream at 4:00 a.m. She'd dreamed about her childhood rape again, for the first time in a long time. She hadn't had one of those since she had recovered from a kind of breakdown while she was at Simon Fraser University. She had been working on a short film with some fellow students. The premise of it was hers and she had written most of it. (She was an English major but was taking one film course.)

The short was called *The Portal* and was about a gate that the dead could step through from a parallel world, neither heaven nor hell, to visit the living. She had taken a lighthearted approach to it. Period-costumed actors played the parts of Keats, Jane Austen, Alexander the Great, Julius Caesar, and Cleopatra, all of whom, individually, had brief, enigmatic conversations with present-day students as they strolled together around the campus. The film was well received and had earned those involved an A.

Not long after the film was shown, she'd told a friend that she had seen The Dirty Man, a man who had raped her, come through the Portal, and that was good because it meant he was dead, but she was still frightened. She'd said evil people shouldn't be allowed to come through, not just Jack the Ripper and Hitler and people like that, but all murderers and rapists. Maybe they could still do terrible harm.

"Anyway," she'd said, "evil people must not be allowed to come back to revel in how they're still thought about and talked about, and gloat over how abuse and carnage are still rampant in the world."

One day, after she had been feverishly ranting along those lines for several days, and cowering in corners to avoid being seen by her rapist, a friend took her to the nurse's office and from there she was escorted home. The family doctor prescribed a tranquilizer and recommended that she return to her therapist, but she ran away instead, to a boyfriend who always had a good supply of pot.

One night, stoned and unable to stop crying, she'd shot up heroin with him. The next day, she'd realized with horror that she had broken the most important promise she had ever made to herself: that she wouldn't follow her mother's path into addiction and self-destruction; would never use heroin or any other hard drug.

She'd moved back in with her parents, who convinced her to see the therapist who had helped her as an adolescent, and with the additional help of medication she got better. But she wouldn't go back to school. She asked her adoptive parents to give her money for travel instead of for tuition, and they, always kind, agreed. She went to England, France, Italy, Germany, India, and Indonesia, spending several months in both France and Indonesia, taking lovers from time to time. Finally, feeling rootless, she'd returned to Vancouver.

For a while she was idle, not knowing what she wanted to do. And then one day she had seen a protest against the Olympics on TV and thought it might be exciting to join in the drama. She had energy and skills to offer. And then, almost simultaneously, she'd found the Richard she thought she was looking for, and had a more important reason to stay.

But why the nightmare now? Was it some kind of warning? About what? If it was about her plan, too bad. She wouldn't give it up.

She found some pot at the back of a drawer, put on a Miles Davis CD. Jazz and pot had always helped when she had sleepless nights. (She rarely smoked at other times.) She let the abstract patterns created by the smoke and the music carry her away to a place where fear couldn't touch her.

She would tell Richard what had happened to her as a child. But not yet.

TWENTY-TWO

THREE DAYS AFTER Carol had arrived at Richard's doorstep and seen Jacintha kissing him, Richard received an email from Carol:

October 2005

Richard,

I'm disappointed in you. And hurt. Even as I was writing my tender memories of you and me in Venice, you were probably asking your "student" to tell you about her sexual experiences. She's probably had more than her share, by the look of her. She's a criminal, by the way. I saw her being arrested on your street the day of that ridiculous display.

You always liked my stories. Do you know I made most of
them up, in the spirit of fantasy? It was what you wanted.
Examples: I never left a restaurant table to fuck a waiter in
the washroom, or fucked a fellow passenger in an airplane
washroom. And I never had an English teacher who quoted
poetry while he finger-fucked me, or had sex with my professor on his desk. Those last two make me shudder now.

I know you'd like to know who I was recently mainly
unfaithful with, but I won't tell you, mostly to protect him
and partly just out of stubbornness. Yes, *mainly*. I took
another lover while my interest in the first was waning.

His name was Ari. I picked him up in a bar. He was gorgeous, tall, and muscular with a smile that made me weak
in the knees, and sex with him was juicy as hell. We met
in a hotel five times in a two-week period. He wanted me
more often, but with work and home, I couldn't manage it.

He spoke English, but it wasn't his first language. He would
lie naked next to me and whisper words I couldn't understand between kisses. I suspected he might just as easily be
whispering crude words to me as loving ones, but he was
such a skillful lover that I didn't care. His voice was honeyed,
and his thigh bones — oh, his thigh bones — were so long
that they alone could have seduced me. After we made love
I would curl up inside the tent of his chest and arms and
long legs and wait, knowing that soon, without preamble,
not even whispers this time, he'd fuck me again, quickly and
hard. After he left, I wouldn't wash. If we'd been together
in the morning, I'd walk around wet all day. My pelvis and
thighs felt loose and so receptive that I fancied if he'd suddenly appeared around a corner on a street, I'd have taken
him right there, behind a bush or a parked car.

He had been in Vancouver on vacation and went back to his own country. I missed him a lot for a while. I hadn't intended to tell you about him, but I've been so unhappy and I want to hurt you as you hurt me with *her*.

Carol

Richard read Carol's email with horror. He would have shouted, sworn, but he could hear the footsteps of the upstairs tenants. His pain was familiar, the kind he'd felt when he found out about Grace and James. He went to the fridge and pulled out an open bottle of white wine and took long gulps straight from the bottle.

His laptop screen, shining with its awful artificial light, sat on the table next to a patch of sunlight that had managed to sneak in through the small, low window. *What's the point of sunlight, its innocent cheerfulness?* he thought, or almost thought — it was more of an awareness at the edge of his mind of the contrast between himself and the oblivious, carefree world, in which everyone else was happy.

A mouse suddenly appeared on the breakfast table in front of him, smugly eating a morsel of toast. Richard picked up a dirty coffee mug and aimed it at the mouse's head. He missed. Immediately he felt ashamed — a trap was one thing, but blood and guts via his own hand was another. But he'd wanted the goddamned, contented little bastard dead.

He jerked the curtains shut, dousing the sunlight, and took another swig of wine.

It was the *visuals* that killed, the goddamned sticking images, the stick-it-to-the-sucker knife, the technicolour movie clips, moving him to tears and nausea. "I had an affair," was one thing; revelling in the fucking greatest thighs and wettest cunt was another.

Once, after he and Grace had separated, he'd gone back to the house to pick up more of his things and he'd walked in on Grace dressing for an evening out with James. She'd put on her sexiest bra and panties, black lace, ones she used to wear for him before they made love. That had hurt a lot. He'd pictured James slowly undressing her and had felt sick. But he'd never had a blow-by-blow description of them together. No visuals.

How dare Carol do this to him?

He moved to delete her letter, then stopped. He certainly had no desire to read it again, and yet he was unable to delete it. He turned off the computer, guzzled the last of the wine, then went to the fridge and got a bottle of beer. After a while, when he was somewhat numb from the alcohol, he thought that at least he hadn't actually seen them in bed together. But he kept imagining Carol curled up against the guy's stupid fucking thigh bones, waiting to be fucked again, and then Carol lifting her skirt and lying down behind a parked car on Hastings Street, legs in the air, and *him* — Richard couldn't bear to think of him by name, even a false name — falling on her gleefully.

He drank some more. He was definitely drunk. He should make some coffee. No, too much trouble. He got himself a glass of water. Sat down. Tried not to think of Carol and Mr. Thighs. Impossible. He thought of the example he had heard about suggestibility, "don't think of a pink elephant," and laughed a crazy-sounding laugh.

After he'd been sitting numbly for a while, he got up and managed to make coffee. After he drank it, his head cleared a little and he remembered a story Carol had told him about one of her favourite painters, Oskar Kokoschka, who had been madly in love with Alma Mahler for three blissful and painful years. One day he'd arrived unannounced at the house they were redecorating and found that Alma had a man called Kammerer staying there, probably another lover, although she wouldn't admit it. Kammerer was a scientist who'd been conducting experiments with toads, and the living room was full of them. They'd escaped from their tanks and were wetly, sloppily copulating by the dozens, jumping and sliding all over the floors and furniture. They must have seemed to

Kokoschka like ghastly amphibian surrogates for the lewd coup-
lings of Alma and Kammerer. Talk about a killing visual.

No fucking toads here, anyway, he thought, and went and lay
down for a much-needed nap. When the number of toads copulating on cars, under cars, and in the middle of Hastings Street got
completely unmanageable, making him frightened to take a step
— other people were squashing them as they walked and green
slime and yellow ooze were spurting everywhere — Richard woke
up, relieved, until he remembered what had inspired the nightmare. *He* was Kokoschka, and the slimy fucking toads were here.

February 2012

Richard,

Beautiful Ari! I still think of him sometimes. Am I sorry I made you suffer? No, not entirely, which is an anomaly for me because I don't believe in revenge.

Carol

Dear Carol,

I believe you have just hit on a truth. I think that acts of revenge are rarely completely regretted, even by the noblest of us, and that a small thrill remains to trigger, now and then, a contented smile.

All the best,

Richard

TWENTY-THREE

RICHARD HAD LEFT a phone message telling Jacintha to report to his office on Monday at 11:00 a.m., and now she sat across from him. The office was overheated and sunlight blazed in, making him squint. He got up and pulled the blind down. A philodendron wilted on the windowsill. He would have taken off his jacket, but didn't want to show any hint of casualness in his appearance or demeanour.

For three days and nights he had struggled with his devastating visions of Carol with her lover. But on the fourth night, the previous night, he had slept undisturbed by graphic dreams for a solid eight hours — no thighs, no toads — and felt relatively sane again. *Let it go, it's in the past,* he kept telling himself, and it seemed to be working. The images had recurred only twice this morning, and only for a few seconds.

He looked at Jacintha. She was wearing a grey tweed jacket over a pale-blue turtleneck and grey slacks. She'd tied her hair back into a low ponytail.

His jacket was tweed as well. Was she mocking his seriousness, the formality she'd expected?

"I'm sure you know why I called you here."

"Yes."

"You committed a serious breach of student-teacher ..." He was going to say "relationship," but decided against it. "Student-teacher ethics," he said. "Why did you do it? Come to my house? Do what you did in front of my wife?"

My wife. The vision of Carol with horrible Ari flooded in, and for a moment he forgot everything else.

"Are you all right?" Jacintha asked. "You look a bit stunned."

"Yes, I'm all right. Why did you do it?"

"I didn't know she was your wife. Sorry. It was on the spur of the moment. The kiss, I mean. I came to your house because I wanted to give you pages of the play. In the end, I forgot to."

Was she lying? Most English literature students knew Carol was his wife and knew her by sight.

"You did more than that," he said.

"I can be a bit too impulsive. Will you make a complaint against me?"

"No, I don't want to waste my energy on the complications a complaint would entail. I'm prepared to let it go if you promise to curb what you call your impulsiveness."

She smiled happily, as though he'd called her in specifically to compliment her.

"But you must promise not to come to my house again, or to ..."

"Kiss you?"

"Yes. That should go without saying." Now the memory of the kiss was uppermost. His lips felt acutely sensitive and his cock throbbed. *Carol had every right to rail against that kiss.*

"I'll put it in writing, and then you'll have evidence against me if I break my word," Jacintha said.

"That isn't necessary." He was having trouble concentrating now. *Must remain stern.* "Look, I want you to know you've hurt my wife and our relationship. Made her doubt me." Shit, what had happened to his resolve not to get personal?

"She loses faith easily."

"You've no right to say anything like that," he said.

"No, sorry again," she said, but she didn't sound sorry.

Her brashness was back. Richard had seen another side of her in the two meetings he'd had with her as a representative of the rewriting foursome. When he had confirmed that her group could take over the work, he and Jacintha had spoken again in his office.

She had elaborated excitedly on an idea she'd mentioned earlier. They would build on the original scene where a great feast is offered to the villains and then snatched away before they can take a bite. They would "take it over the top," with luscious-looking props and exciting music and seductive women dancing, until the men were convinced they were guests of honour, and then the music would clang horribly and the dancers would jeer at them, mock them, call them vile names.

"Maybe they could bite them and pull their hair, too," she had said, laughing. "In a few other scenes, I want to have some of the enchantment of the opening scenes in the film of *A Midsummer Night's Dream.* You know, the one from the nineteen-thirties, with fairies flying like sparks in the darkness? So beautiful. Have you seen it?"

"Yes," Richard had said, and had had an almost irresistible urge to touch her cheek.

His attention was jolted back to the present when Jacintha stood up, went to the bookshelf, and picked up a clay figure Imogen had made, a black dog with short legs and pointy ears and small blobs pressed on to simulate fur. "Did a child make this?" she asked.

"Yes, my daughter, when she was six years old."

"Little children have a knack for getting to the essence of things, don't they? This is the very essence of Dog." She ran her fingers over its rough back, then looked up at Richard. Her gaze lasted only a moment, but the sadness in her eyes, and something more than sadness, a deep hurt, stunned him and time stood still.

He was tempted to take her in his arms, say soothing words.

Instead, he said, "You'd better go now." *Oh, hell. What just happened?*

She placed the dog carefully back on the shelf and when she turned to him, her invulnerable face was back again, her smile bright and hard. But he had seen her, had seen behind the facade. His heart was pounding.

A moment after she left, Gabe came shambling in. "I just saw a beautiful girl leaving here. So lovely and innocent, some of these students, aren't they? But these beauties can be too seductive. We have to watch out for what amounts to transference in the Freudian sense. They admire us, Richard, not just for our intelligence or even our virility, but because they want their daddy."

"What?" Richard had never heard Gabe expound this theory. "Not fucking Freud!"

"He wasn't wrong about everything," Gabe said. "Didn't someone else say that? Someone recently, someone famous? Anyway, most of the little dears never got enough encouragement from their fathers, and they see us as the father figures who can give it to them, if you'll pardon the expression, with the added charm of possibly helping them further their academic careers."

"Oh, I don't think that's the case. Rare, anyway."

"They want to fuck us, Richard, to get approval. But if we let them, there's a good chance they'll ruin our academic careers." Gabe burped loudly, and a strong smell of pepperoni filled the air.

A vision of Gabe lewdly embracing one of the "beauties" made Richard feel a bit sick.

"Are you all right?" Gabe asked.

"Yes. What brought on this cautionary little lecture?"

"Well, you're more or less single now — so sorry about that — and more at risk than you used to be. As head of the department, it's my duty to remind you of the danger. Besides, that young woman who was in your office got my juices flowing." Gabe grunted his way out of his chair. "Must be going — busy man. I have a budget meeting, where, by the way, I might be able to get you a raise in salary for next semester."

"I won't be here next semester."

"So you say. We'll see."

As Richard's annoyance subsided, a terrible thought arose. *Did Gabe know what had happened with Jacintha? The kiss. How could he know? And anyway, nothing further of that kind was going to happen. Ever.*

But Carol could have told him. She and Gabe were friends, something he'd never understood. Presumably he didn't speak so coarsely, or burp so enthusiastically, when he was with her. She said he was a kind person underneath the bluster.

He'd wanted to ask Gabe if he'd seen Carol lately, if she'd confided in him at all, but decided it was too demeaning.

No, he didn't think Carol would have told. She was hurt, but surely not that vindictive, and she wanted him to keep his job. If she'd told Gabe, he would almost certainly have mentioned it. "Carol tells me you're having some trouble with a female student," he would have said, frowning with false sympathy. No, Gabe didn't know.

And then, as he thought of what had just happened with Jacintha, his whole body became suffused with tenderness. His arms and legs felt weak, and he slumped in his chair.

TWENTY-FOUR

ON THE FRIDAY before the Thanksgiving long weekend, Doug Price, a fellow English literature professor and friend, knocked on Richard's office door and asked him if he'd like to go for drinks on Saturday afternoon.

Richard had always enjoyed Doug's company — he had an enthusiastic nature, was cheerfully witty — and before the landslide, they'd lunched together at the faculty club every couple of weeks and had often chatted in one or the other's office. But after it, Richard had socialized with no one, had made excuses. What could he say? Even if it were possible to explain his limping psyche, he had no wish to reveal it.

Maybe he could have confided in Dan, his best friend, but he was in New Zealand. And he wasn't even sure about how honest he could be with Dan. Everything was so complicated.

An ache stabbed Richard's chest and he realized he was lonely. He hadn't been in touch with Carol since *the* email. He'd tried to compose an email telling her how hurt he was and that he was willing to forgive her, and also to renew his plea of innocence regarding Jacintha. But he couldn't get the tone right, and anyway, how strong could his claim to innocence be now, in light of his recent feelings?

"Yes," he said to Saturday drinks. "Yes, that would be great."

Doug named a pub on Pender Street, downtown, where they could meet. "It's a place I go for an hour or two sometimes when I need to be by myself. It's good because I'm unlikely to run into any of my students there. My wife's unlikely to find me there, either, and tomorrow she'll be hell on wheels, getting ready for Thanksgiving dinner."

"At least you know where she is," Richard said.

"Oh, damn, sorry, Richard. You and Carol. So sorry."

"It's all right." But of course it wasn't.

On Saturday morning, Richard left his apartment much too early for his appointment, unable to bear the smothering gloom. He walked around for a while, looking for a café that served something other than pizza or sushi, and, failing, sat on a bench on Pender Street, resting his aching legs. Someone was crouching a few feet away and pointing a camera in his direction, and before Richard could react, the young man jumped up, grinning broadly, and said, "Do you want to see it?" He thrust the screen of his digital camera a few inches from Richard's nose.

What Richard saw made him laugh for the first time in a long time. It seemed that a seagull was sitting on his head. It had actually been perched on a sandwich board advertising a sushi menu, and the photographer, by shooting from a low angle, had created the illusion of Richard behatted by a bird.

"You like it?" the young man said. He was hardly more than a boy, dressed in baggy jeans, an oversized sweater, and a knitted hat of orange, green, and yellow stripes.

"Yes," Richard said. "It's quite funny. I look the fool, which is good for me at the moment."

"Are you a teacher or something? You talk very proper."

"Yes, I am."

"Don't get me wrong, man. Like, I'm okay with properness, only not everybody has to talk proper, and if they don't, they don't need to be looked down somebody's nose at, you know what I mean?"

"Yes, I do."

"I'm Tom," he said and held his hand out to shake.

Richard took his hand. "Richard," he said.

"I'm kind of a Zen guy, like, you know, take it like it comes. Do what feels right, you know? Like, I don't frame my pictures, and if that means some potty little gallery won't show them, I don't, like, give a shit. You gotta be true to yourself, you know, like everybody has a seed or something that's just theirs. A youness. Is that a word?"

"Well, I think you mean 'essence.'"

"It's a word now, anyway, because I said it. You've got your youness and I've got mine. Shit! Just thought of something. If I had a kid, I'd call it Youness. Holy fuck, that'd be great. Would you like a copy of this photo? I could send it to you if you give me your address."

Richard thought of Emily's "visit" and the debacle that had followed. He couldn't risk another orphan on his doorstep.

"Sure, I'd like a copy," he said, "although I think the image will be firmly planted in my brain for quite a while. Can you email it to me? It'll cheer me up whenever I look at it. Keep up the good work." He wrote his email address on the back of someone else's business card he found in his wallet. His own card had his phone number on it and he didn't want Tom to have it. "This isn't my card," he said. "Don't even know where I got it."

"Thanks, Prof. Thanks for digging the pic. I'll send you some other stuff, too."

As Richard watched him walk away, Tom waved the card in the air and smiled so joyfully that it made Richard's heart ache.

The boy had the kind of gait that makes a person look like they're bouncing on springs, a happy gait. Richard hoped life wouldn't take too much of Tom's bounce away.

Richard walked back toward Granville Street, found the bar Doug had suggested, and settled in a corner dark enough to suit him. He downed a beer quickly, ordered another, and thought about "youness." Was it just delusional to think there was some part of oneself that was unique? It was a popular idea. As a young man, he'd been sure of who he was. He was consistently himself, a solid, unified entity. Now, at forty-eight, he knew he was different than he had been, but not better. He was a suffering, guilt-ridden ass, completely unlike his twenty-five-year-old self. If he had an essence, it was deteriorating. His youness was fucked.

After he'd guzzled a third beer, he thought, *Shouldn't that be Me-ness? Or I-ness? Or I Am the Ass That I Am?* He was tempted to say the last sentence aloud for the other lurkers in dark corners to hear, but luckily Doug arrived at that moment.

"I just talked to a kid who told me about 'youness.' Said it was a word because he'd made it a word. The arrogance of youth, eh?"

"U-ness?" Doug spelled it.

"No, y-o-u-ness. As in the essence of a person."

"Aah. Clever, in a naive way. How are your students these days? Any of them insufferably clever?"

"One or two." Jacintha immediately danced into his inner vision and moved toward his lips. He took a large swig of beer and wiped his mouth with the rough tweed of his sleeve.

"Have you noticed," Doug asked, "how most of the male students, regardless of their background, have Celtic first names? My classes are full of Kevins and Keirans and Seans and Liams. Any idea why?"

"Yes, I have them in my class, too. As to why — who knows? Influence of the movies, maybe?"

"Speaking of Celts — are the Scots Celts?" Doug went on. "Anyway, there's this young Scottish guy in one of my classes and he keeps using the word 'kanga' all the time, until finally one day I asked him if there were kangaroos in Scotland and he was highly puzzled until we both figured out that he was saying 'kinda' for 'kind of.'

"And then there's 'like-speak.' Drives me crazy, although it occurs mainly in the hallways, thank God. Do you want to have a contest with me? See how many 'likes' we can use in one sentence?"

"No, no, my head's too fuzzy," Richard said. "But you go ahead."

"I don't know like if I can like do it because like I'm not like young like anymore you know like not you know in that like demographic."

Richard began to laugh. He laughed until he hiccupped and went on laughing and hiccupping until he was gasping for breath.

A couple of beers later, Doug said, "I'll get us a taxi."

Richard hiccupped half the way home.

TWENTY-FIVE

RICHARD WAS GOING out for Thanksgiving dinner. He'd been unsure about whether he should go, and decided in favour of it at the last minute.

A week earlier, he had talked to Beth at a local grocery store. He'd run into her a few times before, once on the bus they were both taking to the campus and another time at the same store. They had chatted easily and he had learned a bit about her, that she was planning to be a teacher after she got her MA, and that she also wanted to continue writing poetry and maybe publish her work.

He found her intelligent and sensible.

She said she was shopping for some things for Thanksgiving dinner, and Richard asked if she'd be celebrating with her parents. She said, "No," they were away, travelling.

"What about you?" she asked. "Will you be with your family?"

"No, I don't have any family in town," he said, swallowing hard at the implication of the words he had uttered.

"But you won't be on your own?"

"Yes, I will be."

Beth's forehead creased with concern. "Oh, that's not right," she said. "On a holiday."

"I'll be all right," he said, smiling.

"No, look, why don't you come to my house for dinner on the Sunday. I'm having a few friends over and you live so nearby and ..." Her face had flushed pink.

"That's nice of you, but I'm not sure it's appropriate."

"Oh, well, my old history teacher will be there — a friend of my parents."

"You mean as a chaperone?"

"Sort of, I guess. Not that we need a chaperone."

"No, of course not." Richard was about to decline as kindly as he could, when he pictured himself on the day, sitting in his dingy apartment, eating scrambled eggs and crying into his Scotch.

"Yes," he said. "Thank you. I accept." What, after all, could go wrong? He would eat and, after a reasonable time, politely take his leave and let the kids and the old history teacher go on partying.

"Great, see you next Sunday, then." She was about to walk away when she turned and said, "Oh, I guess you'll need my address. We're neighbours, sort of, but just in case. And here's my number, if you want to call."

Does she look a bit too happy about it? Richard wondered. No, she was just a kind young woman, happy he wouldn't be alone on a holiday.

He could always change his mind, plead the flu. Or insanity. But here he was, on his way with a bottle of good red wine.

He hadn't liked parties in recent years. At the ones he'd attended, he'd stayed close to Carol, doing that "hold your wife by the elbow" thing his dad used to do, partly out of possessiveness, but more, Richard guessed now, in his dad's case and in his own, for security.

A young woman dressed all in black opened the door. "You must be Professor Wilson," she said. "I'm Tanya. Come on in."

The stained glass in the door, amber and blue, let in such a murky light that he felt like turning around and going home. The floorboards creaked. A stairway of darkly varnished wood rose to the right. Voices from the kitchen. The smell of roast turkey.

Beth was at the stove, stirring. "Oh, Professor Wilson, let me grab your coat." She put down the spoon, looking flustered, splashing gravy. "Oh, wine, great. Thank you."

A kid with a shaved head and a gold ring in his eyebrow sat at the table with his feet on another chair, wolfing down nachos as sour cream blobbed on one side of his mouth.

"Skitch," a familiar voice said. "Manners, please."

Richard turned to see Jacintha and his heart jumped. He hadn't admitted to himself that he'd hoped she would be here.

"Hello, Professor. Here, sit." She pushed Skitch's feet aside and they fell with a thud. "Good news, Professor. I'm your new neighbour now, Beth's new roommate. I moved in this week."

"Aah," Richard said. The sound was almost a groan.

"You don't look happy about it."

"Oh, no, I'm just surprised." But he was both alarmed and excited, the latter to his dismay. He sat down, feeling suddenly weak.

Jacintha poured him a glass of red wine from the open bottle on the table, and sat down beside him. She wore a short red dress, sheer stockings, and red high heels. Part of her hair was piled up like a golden crown; the rest hung loose. He glanced around the room. Besides Skitch and Tanya, there were two others.

"That's Greg," Jacintha said, "and the other is Brian — both in my gang. Everyone here is in my gang." She laughed. "Tanya let you in, and this bozo is Skitch. Jesus, Skitch, eat with your mouth closed. Behave yourself."

"You're hot when you're bossy," Skitch said, between chews.

"You can't get me off your back that easily."

"Hop on any time," Skitch said, and then suddenly let out an ear-piercing howl.

Richard reeled back, almost toppling his chair. Bozo, indeed. More like a wolf in heat.

Greg offered Richard some of the joint he was smoking. As he bent toward Richard, his bangles clanked and his long beads and loose, white shirt flopped forward.

"No, thanks — I should eat first." Richard felt simultaneously very old and in a time warp. Hadn't he been to parties like this twenty-five years ago?

"Gang?" Richard asked, the word only now registering. "What kind of a gang?"

"An environmental protest group," Tanya said. "We organized that anti-Olympics protest at city hall. The Gaia Warriors."

"Oh, yes, Jacintha told me. Are the Olympics an environmental issue?" He knew it was a stupid question as soon as he'd asked it.

"Of course," Brian said in a lecturing tone that matched his earnest appearance. In jeans and a corduroy jacket, with a wispy beard, he looked like a very young professor trying to look older. "The Olympics take money away from transit and green spaces and bike paths and things like that. Millions, probably billions of dollars. And affordable housing. People lying hungry and cold on the streets are part of the environment, too. You should know all that. Aren't you writing an environmental play or something?"

"Too fucking right," Skitch said, whether about the Olympics or Richard or both was unclear.

"Brian is studying political science and environmental studies," Greg said. "A double whammy."

"You should join us on one of our forays into the Vancouver corporate jungle," Brian said. "We'll be in touch." It sounded more like a threat than an invitation.

They all helped to carry the turkey, mashed potatoes, yams, green beans, gravy, salads, and cranberry sauce to the dining room, where places were set in a splendour of white linen and red candles and a centrepiece of maple leaves and twigs with red berries and white chrysanthemums.

"You did this?" he asked Beth.

She gave an embarrassed smile and nodded.

"Where's your history teacher? The friend of your parents?"

"She has the flu, couldn't come."

They didn't talk much. Skitch, true to form, gnawed noisily on a drumstick and inhaled potatoes and gravy. At least three bottles of wine were sipped, slurped, and guzzled. Richard tried to drink slowly, with moderate success. Sadness overcame him as he remembered Imogen at five years old, her dinner consisting of a tiny piece of turkey breast, two carrot sticks, and French fries made especially for her, so she wouldn't have to eat yucky mashed potatoes or gravy, the latter garnering a double-yuck. And Grace in her party dress; he couldn't remember the colour now, but he remembered how the silky material had clung sweetly to her beautiful ass, and how she'd kicked off her high heels and padded back and forth from kitchen to dining room, serving just the three of them. God, his heart ached.

"Cheer up, Professor. There's a lot to be thankful for," Jacintha said. She smiled, licked gravy from her lips.

He looked away, turned to Tanya on his left, and made some remark about the mild weather and how Thanksgiving was early this year, wasn't it? It was only October 12 and why did the Americans celebrate it so close to Christmas?

Tanya looked bored and said, "I don't know."

"I'm surprised you young people aren't with your families today," Richard said. Christ, did he have to sound so old?

"My parents live in Ontario," Brian said.

"Mine, too," Greg said.

"My mother was going out to dinner at the Four Seasons with her boyfriend," Tanya said.

Skitch offered no explanation. Neither did Jacintha.

"Is this turkey free-range and organically fed?" Greg asked Beth.

"No, I mean ... no ... I ... they cost about seventy dollars and I couldn't afford one."

"Hey, we should all have chipped in. You know the chemicals they put in the feed and the way they cage the poor dumb birds."

"Well, I'm sorry, I ..."

"This turkey is delicious," Richard said. "I'm sure we'll all live. Thanks, Beth. The whole meal is wonderful. Did you make the cranberry sauce?"

"Yes, they're organic berries. You can use less sugar if you make your own sauce."

"Yes, nicely tart."

"Too fuckin' right," Skitch contributed.

Tanya gave Greg a black look, probably over the free-range remark. Richard assumed they were a couple. Probably Jacintha and Skitch were, too, although she treated him more like her spoiled child than her lover. A picture of them in bed rose out of the darkness of his mind, and lumps of turkey and yam and mashed potatoes twisted together evilly in his stomach. He took another large gulp of wine, making it worse.

When they'd eaten their fill, everyone helped carry empty plates and leftovers to the kitchen. Dessert and coffee were to follow.

Greg carried the empty wine bottles to the blue box on the back porch.

As he was closing the kitchen door, Skitch pushed past him and turned the box upside down. "Goddamned piss-poor guilt trip for the masses," he said. "Get the little guys to recycle and turn off all the fuckin' lights and wash in cold water and ride bikes till our asses fall off, while the big guys spew chemicals from their factories and fly around in their fuckin' jets. And these goddamned twisty bulbs." He unscrewed the porch bulb and threw it down and stomped on it until it broke. "Put everything on the backs of the little guys. Make us think we're saving the fuckin' planet."

Cold air streamed around him and into the room like an evil genie as he stood looking past the stunned faces, probably thinking about what to smash next.

Jacintha walked over and put her arms around him, holding his arms against his sides. "You're right, my little warrior, you're right. But let it ride for now. Just let it ride." She kept her voice soothing, getting ever softer, until it seemed she was only breathing in his ear. Wolf-whisperer.

Richard felt a stab of jealousy.

"Yeah," Skitch said. "Yeah." He came in, sat down, then stood up again. "Where's the broom. I'll clean that glass up."

"No, don't touch it. There's mercury in those bulbs," Brian said. He put on rubber gloves and grabbed a plastic bag and went onto the porch, closing the door behind him.

"Well," Beth said, looking nervously from Skitch to Richard, "would anyone like some pumpkin pie and whipped cream?"

After the pie, they all sat in the living room, and Richard accepted a cup of coffee from Beth. He'd had enough wine.

Tanya and Greg slumped on the couch, and Skitch sprawled, legs outstretched and apart, sliding halfway out of an armchair. The only movements the three made were to reach for the endlessly circulating joint.

Richard declined; his head was already a bit fuzzy. He watched Jacintha dance by herself to loud, pounding music, flinging her now completely loosened hair around, stomping, spinning. His heart pounded along with the music.

"Enough!" Tanya said, and jumped up with surprising agility from her semi-comatose position. "I want Billie Holiday."

The heartaching voice flowed richly, honey and whisky, into the air. Richard could almost taste it. Jacintha swayed now, hips, shoulders. Sinuous. She reached out her hands to him. *Come dance with me. No, no, I can't.* And then he was on his feet, swaying with her, her body pressed against him. *Come outside*, and he followed her into the hallway. *Here, put on your coat.*

"I should go home," he said.

"All right, but let's take a little fresh air together."

She wrapped herself in a shawl, hooked her arm in his, and they moved slowly down the stairs and along a sidewalk to the dark end of the garden. Not totally dark. He looked up at the silver stars in their indigo blanket. He remembered to breathe, and the cold air cleared his head a little. There was a smell of decaying leaves and something sweet. She took his hand and led him through a gate.

"They won't see us here," she said. "We're alley cats."

"You should go in. It's cold," Richard said. "I'll be going home now."

She held his face and kissed him lightly.

He stepped away from her, knew he should turn and leave, but found he was reluctant to move.

She took off her shawl, put it around his waist, then hers, and tied the ends behind her. "You can't escape now," she said.

He could feel his blood racing through his veins, heating and prickling his skin. He pulled away, pulled at the shawl, extricated himself.

"No!" he said. "We can't. You're my student."

"I'm twenty-five. And I won't tell anyone."

"No. We can't. I can't."

"We can. I'll put Skitch to bed on the couch and then I'll come to your place. You go now, and wait."

And he found himself walking down the shadowy alley the half block to his house. What was he doing? He wouldn't wait for her. He'd lock the door.

He sat hunched at his kitchen table, trying to resist the desire that kept creeping up, insistent.

After a while, he became aware of a sense of dread. *What if Carol finds out?* She believed the worst already, but he hadn't been unfaithful, and still believed he could convince her of that.

But it was more than Carol finding out. He didn't need an affair. He needed to find a way of being of service to others, being useful in some humanitarian enterprise, maybe in a war-torn country.

He laughed suddenly, a bark more than a laugh, at the way his mind had leaped from possible adultery to putting himself amid violence and bloodshed. He felt slightly mad, went to the sink and ran cold water over his head, the way he'd done when she'd kissed him here in his apartment that first time; ran the water until his head began to ache, dried himself with a tea towel, sat down. Beads of water slid down his forehead, into his ears. He rubbed his head again, roughly, angrily.

But no, it wasn't danger he craved. It was her.

Fifteen minutes. Longer? Maybe she wasn't coming. Please, God, don't let her come.

He waited. Another eon passed. He got wine from the fridge, but after a few sips, he felt sick. She wasn't coming. That was good. He was saved from making a terrible mistake. Yes, that was good.

He lay in bed aching, relief and desire alternating. His head pounded. He'd never be able to sleep. Masturbated. Got up. Took two Tylenols. Fell asleep. Dreamed he was at Jenny's funeral, which he'd been unable to attend, would not have been welcome at. Jenny, in her coffin, was in a long, red dress, her feet in thin-strapped sandals, red polish on her toes. He leaned over to make sure it was her and she smiled. "I thought you were dead," he said, and she said, "So did I."

He woke to grey light seeping in and wished to sleep again without dreams, but knew it was hopeless.

In the shower, the water was icy before he could adjust the taps; this was a baptism into a new and troubling world. How would he face the day? By hoping to see Jacintha. He said her name aloud, and it slid sweet and smooth across his tongue. Hyacinth in English. He remembered the heavy perfume of hyacinths, intoxicating, almost too much to bear. *No, she saved me by not coming to me. I must stop thinking like this. Stop feeling like this. How to stop feeling?*

What he was feeling was more than sexual desire. He wanted to comfort her, too, to hold her gently, to protect her the way he had wanted to when she held the clay dog. When she revealed herself. He felt a nervous happiness. Was he, god help him, in love with her?

On the Tuesday after Thanksgiving, Richard still hadn't seen Jacintha. He had no idea what was going to happen about her. That was the way he phrased it in his mind, in the passive voice. *No*, he told himself, *I should be thinking about what I'll do* about her. *I'll have nothing to do with her. I've had a lucky escape.* And yet he felt his will draining away and a heavy helplessness descending upon him. He felt he was at her mercy.

When he was about ten years old, before he'd learned to swim well, a neighbour woman had taken him, along with several other children, to a riverside picnic. He was dog-paddling happily and, after a minute or two, he decided to stand up and found the bottom was farther down than he realized. The current grabbed him, and he was many yards downstream when the woman — he still remembered her muscular arms, the coconut smell of her suntan lotion, and her soft breasts against his head — scooped him up and hauled him back to shore. He didn't go in the water again that summer, and never again in that river. But he hugged a secret to himself. As he was swept away by the river, he'd been afraid, but exhilarated, too. He hadn't known that word. He'd known only that every time his head surfaced and he gulped air, he felt a sense of wonder at the speed he was travelling and how the rest of the world had stood still and there was only the water, its strong arms carrying him to something unimaginable.

Now he was going under again, and again he felt both fear and exhilaration. But he had no rescuer this time.

February 2012

Richard,

I was surprised by the pangs I felt reading about your longing for Jacintha. It still hurts — not just reading about it, but also, from time to time, when I remember how I saw that ache in you, the true depth of which you tried to hide. (After I found out what had been going on.)

But thanks for finally admitting to me, all those years ago in England, that you loved her. Knowing that for sure was less painful than your denial of what I'd felt in my heart and my gut, and what I'd seen with my own eyes. The truth didn't set me free, but I had you back with me then, and I no longer had to doubt my perceptions. Of course, I told you all that at the time.

I say "surprised by the pangs," but I guess I shouldn't be. After all, we loved each other for many years, and I think love is never really lost. It lives not just in memories but has a half-life in the very cells of our bodies.

Carol

Dear Carol,

You did tell me "all that," but it's good to hear it again.

The half-life, yes, and sometimes more. I still have dreams
occasionally of you and me, happy, and much younger.
Once or twice, we've been making love. People in love do
imprint on each other. But still, I'm sorry. Thank you — if I
haven't said it enough — for being so gracious in reading
this book, in spite of the pain it might bring back.

With affection,

Richard

TWENTY-SIX

"WILL YOU POSE for me?" Nick Wallinsky said, smiling at Carol as she sat on the couch in his studio.

"Right now?"

"You look so beautiful in your red sweater and black jeans. And your hair is good like that. The auburn against the red is beautiful."

Carol liked his smile, his pronounced eye teeth. A David Bowie smile. "Pose?" she said. She'd been looking at a large, abstract painting that was almost entirely blue, four feet by five, with white shapes near the bottom of the canvas, some vaguely like bones or misshapen shells. "I thought you were doing only abstracts now. Like this one."

"I still do portraits, too."

"Well, if you'll take me as I am, I guess I could sit for a while." Carol had gone back to the gallery where she'd attended Nick's opening to have another look at his paintings, and he'd happened to be there, doing some business with the curator, and he'd invited her to dinner. Afterward, they'd gone back to Nick's place.

She liked his work. His more colourful paintings were reminiscent of Jack Shadbolt, but without any of his suggestions of landscapes or butterflies. Shadbolt was better — he was one of the greats, after all — but Nick was good.

They'd eaten at a Japanese restaurant where the prawns had been succulent, the sushi fresh as the sea, the hot burst of the wasabi as exhilarating as ever. Now she was sipping a chilled Sauvignon Blanc.

Nick sat down a few feet away, took up a drawing pad and some pastels. "Just relax," he said.

His jeans hugged his slender legs and hips, his T-shirt clung to his lean chest, revealed his muscular upper arms. His hair, blond with a trace of grey, flopped over his forehead and he pushed it back with long fingers. There was something of the street about him, as though he'd been undernourished as a child, had needed to be a scrapper, a smartass, in order to survive.

She was feeling a constant hum of desire for Nick, which she knew somehow could be sated in a way that had been eluding her for a long time.

Strangely, her disturbing sexual surges had diminished after the shock of seeing Richard and the one she thought of as *the girl*. She mostly regretted sending that brutal email, but she had moments when she was glad about it. And she didn't intend to regret any involvement with Nick. *Two can play at that game*, she thought, and then, *Have I really sunk to that level?*

"Have you always lived in Vancouver?" Carol asked. She would play it cool for as long as possible.

"Yeah, born and bred."

"Me, too. Where'd you grow up?"

"Kerrisdale."

"Ah." Not a poor neighbourhood; maybe not a scrapper, then. "You?"

"Point Grey."

"'Ah' yourself."

He reminded her of her first husband, Johnny, who had in fact come from a poor family. They both had thin, high-cheekboned faces and wiry bodies.

"You look great," he said. "Good. No necklace. The better to show off the long line of your neck. Take off your shoes and tuck your legs under. That's good. Lean against the arm of the couch. Get comfortable. You'll need to hold the pose for ten or fifteen minutes. Okay?"

"I have posed before, you know. Not since I was a student at Emily Carr, but I still know how to do it."

"Of course. Lovely, stay like that." He worked steadily, his expression serious. His very concentration was sexy.

Johnny had been a carpenter, not an artist like her father. She'd married him largely because of the dissimilarity, she'd realized later. To friends she'd said things like, "He's not pompous like my father," and "He's sweet, a regular guy, not elitist like my father."

She and Johnny were compatible in some ways — certainly sexually. And he had an eye for beauty, understood her passion for art, but had no words to express his appreciation. Like a cat who lays a gift mouse at his mistress's feet, he would bring her a pair of chairs with elegant bentwood backs, or a set of beautifully fluted wineglasses, and say no more than, "I found them at a flea market. Thought you'd like them."

He had had a scar on his face that toughened his almost-feminine features, but he'd got it from playing hockey at eight years old, not from street fighting. He had a way of looking at you, assessing you with a sly grin, which he directed at other women, too, but she was pretty sure he'd never been unfaithful. It was just that he was sexy and knew it and seemed to need others to know he knew it. Maybe he would have strayed eventually. The honeymoon period was a long one, most of the four years they were together, and even now she still sometimes felt desire when she thought of him. Sweet as he was, she'd realized in the end that his lack of education and conversation bothered her too much. She hated that her father had been substantially right when he'd told her Johnny was not suitable for her.

She was the one, in the end, who was unfaithful. She'd met an older man at a university party — a pedantic old fart, he'd turned out to be — but with their affair, the damage was done. They'd discussed books and movies, had gone to plays, and she'd felt as though she were drinking spring water after a long drought. She'd known then she needed an intellectual equal in order to be happily married.

She'd told the old guy, Sidney was his name, about her dissatisfaction with Johnny, her dear Johnny — a worse betrayal than the sexual infidelity. Sidney, in response, had quoted part of an Auden poem too gleefully, a line about a "dense companion." Later, she'd looked up the poem and written down three of its other lines: "The bond between us / Is chimerical surely: / Yet I cannot break it."

But she had broken it.

"Dense companion." Unkind, but true, by certain measures. Johnny was rough, not well educated, but he wasn't stupid. And it suddenly struck her that Nick was a blend of Johnny's physicality and her father's artistic talent, with no denseness on one hand and no grandiosity on the other.

"You seem to have gone quite far away," Nick said, holding up his pastel drawing for her to see.

"Oh, yes, just daydreaming."

Nick's drawing had caught her pensive look and the composition was beautiful, the negative spaces as shapely and interesting as the configuration of her body. "It's lovely," she said.

"It's yours."

They sat together on the couch and drank more wine.

"I'm sorry about you and Richard," Nick said. "Do you want to talk about it some more?"

"No, thanks." Carol had told Nick over dinner that they had parted. "He was difficult to be with," she had said. "He was so gloomy. He's probably depressed but he won't take it seriously because he can still dress himself and drag himself to work. And he's still teaching. He seems determined to change his life in some way that doesn't seem to include me."

Now she said, "No, I think I said enough about it already."

Nick took her hand in his. "I am so sorry."

"That was at first," Carol said, Nick's sympathy breaking down her resolve to say no more. "Now I think the bastard is having an affair." Her eyes filled with tears.

"You're hurt."

"Yes, I'm bloody well hurt."

He leaned in and kissed her on the cheek, then very softly on the mouth. He sat back and looked at her solemnly. "Was it all right to do that?"

In answer she kissed him back, a long, tonguing kiss.

"The artist and his model. God, what a cliché," she said. "Was there ever a male artist who didn't fuck his model?"

"I'm flattered by the Picasso reference, but posing for me once for fifteen minutes doesn't exactly make you my model."

Carol laughed. "No, you're right, but I've been teaching a feminist section in my art history classes, emphasizing how the 'male gaze' is detrimental to women in general and to women artists in particular. It's a view I hold strongly."

"Well, then, I'll never paint or draw you again, and I'll avert my eyes when we fuck."

"You're getting ahead of yourself, aren't you? That kiss might be a one-off, for all you know."

"And is it?"

"I don't know, either."

Nick poured more wine and said, "Tell me more about your art classes."

Carol regarded him for a moment, unsure if he really wanted to hear her feminist views. He had an ironic edge that she feared could sharpen into mockery or dismissal. For all she knew, he could be indifferent or even hostile to women artists and their plight.

Sensing her hesitation, he said, "No, really, go on, I'm interested."

Carol told him some of the main points in her classes on female artists, and how angry she still became over the attitudes of some of the young men.

"Quite shocking in the twenty-first century," Nick said. "When I was young, not surprisingly, I liked, and still like, the macho guys: Pollock and de Kooning and Jasper Johns. But when I studied the Impressionists, I was smitten with the mother and child paintings of Berthe Morisot. They're sensuous and she has a delicate way with light and colour and —"

"Stop," Carol said. "You had me at Berthe Morisot."

They talked for a while longer, until Nick said, "Let's stop now. I want to work on your mouth."

"Another drawing?"

"No, not a drawing."

Febraury 2012

Carol,

When you took up with Nick, I became very jealous. Then
I read a trick for letting go of a lover — or in my case, my
jealousy. One strategy I liked was to picture Nick in undigni-
fied positions, such as on the toilet, straining red-faced, pants
around his ankles.

One of my favourite images was of him naked, hopping
in circles on one leg, over and over, round and round, his
cock — very small, of course — bobbing up and down.

It helped.

After a while, I stopped. A sad acceptance took over.

And now you've gone and married him.

Richard

TWENTY-SEVEN

JACINTHA REMEMBERED THE exact moment when her perception of Richard began to change. She was in his office and had picked up the clay dog made by his daughter, when something strange and complicated happened. The hand holding the dog became warm at the same time as she felt a small stab of pain in her chest, and a throbbing in her head, and she looked at Richard and saw something equally complex in his eyes. He sat with his mouth slightly open and stared at her. Then he closed his eyes for a moment, and when he looked at her again, the tenderness she saw overwhelmed her. The very air of the room vibrated.

I think he loves me, she'd thought. And then, *Good — it will make things easier for me*. But she didn't feel as triumphant as she'd thought she would. Instead, she found herself pushing down doubts about her plan.

She had only ever loved one person. She was fond of her adoptive parents, but she couldn't say more than that. The one person, of course, was her birth mother. But that had been primal. Yes, primal. And now there was him.

She could hardly sleep that night, but in the morning wondered if she'd been wrong about what she had seen. Maybe Richard had simply been thinking of his daughter, whom he was missing, remembering her as a six-year-old. Still, what she had experienced had been intense, had not seemed to be triggered by a memory, but by the electricity of the moment that was generated between the two of them.

She was confused and hated the feeling. She had learned to survive by being sure of herself. It was never a matter of right or wrong, but what she *chose* to do. She had told herself the practical way to look at it was that he had shown her a moment of weakness; that if he had loved her in that moment, it needn't be important. It would just make him more malleable, more susceptible to what she had in mind for him. But the thought passed. She knew it wasn't what she wanted now.

At the Thanksgiving party, she had caught him looking at her with tenderness, too. And then, oh then, the kiss in the garden. His body felt so familiar pressed against her; so comforting. She couldn't remember ever feeling quite that way before. Of course, she reasoned, people feel most at home, most comforted by members of their family. The genetic bond. Even their smell is comforting.

She knew for sure now that he was her father. She had been almost certain when she'd learned his exact age. She had told him she was reading about the sixties and asked him if he'd ever been a hippie.

He'd laughed and said, "No, I was only ten years old in 1967, the so-called 'Summer of Love.' And I never wanted to have long hair or wear beads."

The DNA test result, which she received a few days before the party, had confirmed his paternity.

As she had been walking to his apartment that night, she suddenly knew she couldn't go through with it. She had meant to take him just to the edge and then take a photo of them half-undressed and tell him who she really was. He would be shocked and humiliated. She had planned to send the photos and the damning information to his wife and to the head of his department, to hurt him in retribution for how he had hurt her and her mother. She had been left fatherless and unprotected. But her plan had depended on her hating him, and she didn't hate him then. She wanted to forgive him, and more than that: she wanted him. *And he doesn't need to ever know who I really am.* The thought shocked her, but she wasn't about to let it go.

Almost at his door, she turned and ran, stumbling and almost falling. She couldn't seduce him, not now.

She arrived back at her house and awakened Skitch. She made love to him with a frenzy that was both ecstatic and unreal. She was there but not there, oddly detached.

The next morning, she left before Skitch woke up, not wanting to face his giddy gratitude. She walked to Jericho Beach, and as the sun came up and dazzled the water, she sat on a log to think. She took off her shoes and dug her toes into the sand. She liked the way the cold air made her shiver. Everything around her, all the sights and sounds and smells, made her feel more alive than ever. She had had a dream in which she and Richard sat quietly together, happy and peaceful.

A new plan was necessary. Maybe their love wouldn't be a sin. They were strangers except in their blood. There would be no need to reveal their history. Some people might disapprove of the age difference between them, but that would be easy to ignore.

She didn't even know why sin had come to mind, since she didn't believe in it. Crimes, yes, but not sin, and what she wanted, as far as she knew, wasn't a crime, either.

February 2012

Richard,

I know I recently told you, and also all those years ago, that I found it hard to excuse what Jacintha did, however hard her life had been. But the insight you've just given me has changed my mind. (Again, I presume she told you all that.) How desperate and confused she was. How wrong-headed. But, to her, not wrong-hearted. All I can say now is how greatly I pity her. I don't know what else to say.

Carol

Dear Carol,

Pity is right, and enough. Thank you.

Richard

T W E N T Y - E I G H T

CAROL WAS AT Nick's again.

"Enough of the husbandly sex," he said. "Let's get creative."

Afterward, as they sat eating pizza, Nick asked her if she'd like to go out with him to take some photographs in the neighbourhood, something he said he'd been doing regularly. It was a sunny Saturday afternoon.

They went to the alley behind Hastings, just off Main Street, with its poles that looked like scaffolding constructed to hang giants, and its Dumpsters and hookers and addicts.

Nick walked over to a young woman leaning against a brick wall and said, "Jackie, can I take your picture?"

"Hey, Nick, sure, how do you want me?" With a wicked smile, she lifted her skirt, showing sheer black panties.

"No, sweetheart, nothing special. Just be yourself."

She kept smiling, striking silly poses. Nick laughed and kept clicking.

"Thanks, Jackie," he said and gave her a couple of dollars.

"Can I take a picture of you?" he asked Carol.

"Here?"

"Yeah, that's good, stop there."

When he finished, Carol turned and saw a man shooting up a few feet behind her.

"What the hell, Nick. Why'd you snap me in front of him?"

"It's good — come and look." He showed her the digital shot, and she had to admit the composition was good: the juxtaposition of her, tidy and middle class, against the scruffy addict gave it a certain shock value, even social commentary.

He talked to a few more people and took a few more shots before Carol said she had to go. A lot of his subjects knew him.

"Come back soon," he said, as they walked back to her car.

"I will," she said.

On her next visit, Nick offered her cocaine. She'd used it only twice, many years earlier, and was reluctant to do it again.

"Come on," Nick said. "Have you ever had sex on it?"

"Once, and we went on so long I began to be frightened that we'd never stop. It seemed unreal — mechanical, even."

"But it felt great, too, didn't it?"

"In a way."

"You know I'm good. With me it'll be far from mechanical. Come on, you'll love it."

When they'd done a couple of lines, Nick said they were going out.

"I thought you wanted to have sex?"

"Later."

They walked toward Main Street in the rain. "The rain feels good on my skin," Carol said. "The air smells good, the cars sound interesting, don't they? Swish, swish, I feel like I could do anything, we could travel, get a boat, go to the Gulf Islands, do you like the islands?"

"You are so stoned."

"Yeah, talking a lot, is it laced with speed? I hope not, that's not good for you, but I feel great, except my butt is cold." She was wearing a skirt, but no tights.

"Let me fix that." Nick held her close and rubbed her cheeks. "Better?"

"Yes, but they'll get cold again."

"Not for long."

They were suddenly at the Main and Hastings alley.

"We shouldn't go in there," Carol said.

"It's fine."

It seemed so menacing, unlike the last time. She looked up at the ghastly grid of poles and wires and remembered how she'd told her students that the terrible could become sublime with a shift of perception, an inward gaze, but found she couldn't make the shift.

"Terrible," she said, but Nick was walking ahead and didn't respond. She licked at the drops of rain that were soaking her hair and face.

She looked down. Oily puddles. Grey bricks. Smells of fish and rotting vegetables and shit. She almost stepped in a pile of steaming shit.

"Nick, wait, damn it."

He stopped. She saw his teeth. Smiling? Grimacing?

She froze when she heard her name called loudly from somewhere behind her. A wail. "Carol! Carol!"

Nick took a step toward her, said sharply, "Don't look back."

"Don't look back? Why did you say that?" *Lot's wife. Wives lost. Husbands lost.*

"Someone's calling me," she said.

"No, the guy calls for Karen all the time. His girlfriend who disappeared. He doesn't like to be stared at, gets aggressive, so don't turn around."

Carol ignored the warning, turned back to the wailing man. He lunged toward her, steadier than she would have thought possible, given his wrecked state.

"Easy, man." Nick had her by the arm, was pulling her away. "Easy now, dude, no harm meant."

The man grunted, muttered, "Fuck off," stepped back until he was leaning against a Dumpster.

Nick led her farther along, past two young women shooting up. He held both her arms and positioned her against a wet brick wall. She noticed that she wasn't worried about the cold and damp seeping through her jacket and blouse onto her skin. He lifted her skirt, pulled down her panties, unzipped himself, and pushed in, all this before Carol had fully registered what was happening. She said, "No, Nick, not here," but her words seemed to come from a distance, and it felt good, and she stopped resisting.

Over Nick's shoulder, she saw a woman watching them. A man was pissing on the wall a couple of yards away. In spite of the acrid smell that assailed her, Carol came at the same time as Nick and she cried out.

"Nice work," the pisser called.

Everything seemed unreal. The alley scaffolding like a dozen guillotines. *Lose your head, pack up your heart, and go with your cunt. Not what I want, no, not what I want.*

The walk back was long, the air crystal clear but her thoughts far from clear, tumbling over each other. She talked: "God, that was awful, it was wrong, it was too weird, I should go home."

At home on Sunday morning, she felt ashamed and angry. The experience had been neither terrible nor sublime, only squalid. Like one of her sexy stories for Richard gone horribly wrong. She'd been stoned, or she never would have agreed. Maybe it was an aberration for Nick, too, not the kind of kink he needed to get off. But what if it was? And why had she been attracted to someone who could pull her to the edge like that? Was it a darkness she'd been waiting for? Had she wanted to go to extremes to feel alive again?

She remembered the hooker asking Nick, "How do you want me?" Her question had seemed personal, implied a history between them. Carol was very disturbed by her suspicions.

She went back to Nick's apartment the next evening, thinking it might be the last time, and confronted him immediately. "Have you taken photos of the women on the street? Pornographic stuff?" she asked.

"No, no pornography. A few candid shots, but mostly portraits shot here in my studio."

"Can I see them?"

"Of course." He opened a computer file. "Sit," he said. "Take your time."

The photos were beautiful. In the portraits, Nick had especially caught the eyes: many sad, some defiant, some with a glint of mischief. All of the pictures seemed to her to be loving and respectful, sensitive portraits of broken and nearly broken women.

"Sorry," Carol said. "I was freaked out by having sex in that stinking alley and thought the worst."

"It's all right. There are guys who shoot pornographic stuff in this neighbourhood, but I'm not one of them. I couldn't exploit the women like that."

Carol continued to scroll, and breathed in sharply as she saw a portrait of Emily. She was thinner than Carol remembered her, her eyes large and staring. "Jesus," Carol said, "I know this girl. Do you know where I can find her?"

"No, I haven't seen her for quite a while."

"Can I have a copy of this photo? Richard knows her and wants to find her, too."

February 2012

Richard,

I wish very much that I hadn't told you about that alley
scene when I was weak and decided to tell you everything.

Carol

Carol,

But it was such a gift to me as a writer! Not so much as a
jealous husband.

Richard

TWENTY-NINE

WHEN RICHARD ARRIVED at Jericho Beach, he found Jacintha and Beth waiting for him near the bonfire. Laughter and flute music and the smell of marijuana filled the air. Two of his other students, Andrew and Aiden, were standing nearby. The former was wearing a black cape and sombrero and the latter looked like an extra from *Romeo and Juliet*, with his tights and puff-sleeved, green velvet jacket. Both of them wore small, black "burglar" masks.

"Welcome to our revels," Andrew said, "our Bacchanalia," and he took a large swig of the bottle of beer he was holding. The full moon picked out the voluminous shapes of the capes and skirts of others around the bonfire and ribboned the incoming tide with its light.

Jacintha, who was wearing a blue velvet cape, pulled a black cotton one from her bag and draped it over Richard's tweed jacket. "I brought this for you," she said.

Richard had been unaware that the gathering was to be in costume. He'd been told the class was having a "wienie roast with wine."

"It's a farewell to *The Tempest* as we've known it, and a hello to *The Tempest* as it evolves," Jacintha said, laughing. "It's also going to be, I hope, an inspiration for some production ideas my writing group has."

Beth was wearing a satin dress with a laced bodice and a beaded Juliet cap.

"Where did you get the Elizabethan costumes?" Richard asked.

"The theatre department," Jacintha said. "Tanya and Greg raided the costume storage room and brought things over, but they couldn't stay, a rehearsal or something. We have to get the costumes back later tonight before someone notices they're missing."

Beth walked on one side of Richard, Jacintha on the other. Jacintha took his hand and he felt a charge of energy rushing up his arm. He waited a moment before he gently pulled his hand away.

"Beth," he said, "were you involved in planning this event?"

"Yes, a little."

"Well, a nice surprise," he said, in his most professorial voice.

Wild laughter came down the beach. The night smelled of too much excitement, the kind that could spin out of control. He wondered what other surprises Jacintha might have in store for him. She was unpredictable at the best of times, and this atmosphere — moonlit, pungent, evocative — was ripe with possibilities. He felt almost too alive. Almost young.

He remembered beach parties as an undergraduate, lying in the sand, half-drunk, kissing some eager girl, her breast under his hand, and then walking with her to find a private place. He was both nervous and excited about being here in the dark with Jacintha. He hadn't seen her since the Thanksgiving dinner a week earlier, and in spite of not knowing what he would say to her or what he would do, he had longed to see her. She had dropped off some of the play manuscript at his office when she knew he'd be in class. He wondered if her avoidance of him signalled the end of her ... what? Her flirtation? But when she had taken his hand, he was pretty sure it hadn't ended.

Two or three people were drumming, the beat heavy and insistent. Masked figures sat in a circle around a bonfire. A flute joined the drums, and then a violin, sweet and soaring.

"Here, put this on," Jacintha said.

"Oh, not a mask."

"Come on. Get into the spirit of it."

The mask was small, like the ones Andrew and Aiden and several men and women were wearing. He put it on. Jacintha put on a full-face mask, painted garishly — bright red lips and cheeks, black-rimmed eyes, skin dead white. With her long, golden hair framing the mask, she looked otherworldly, frightening.

"Are you anybody in particular?" Richard asked.

"I'm Juno, goddess of marriage."

"Not typecast, then."

"Great. A bit of dry wit. We could use more of that."

"Could we?" Richard said, but she'd moved away toward the fire.

Richard moved nearer, too, and saw that several others wore decorated masks like Jacintha's. He had a hard time recognizing anyone. The women all wore long dresses and capes, the men capes or Elizabethan jackets and tights. There were about twenty people. His class consisted of eleven.

"Who are these others?" Richard asked.

"Friends who didn't want to miss the fun," Jacintha said.

The women rose en masse, as though by some silent signal, and began to dance vigorously to the music, the light from the flames dancing with them. When they moved out of range, they seemed to disappear. One of them noticed the effect and started whooping each time she moved closer to the fire, and the others followed suit. The movement in and out of the light and the whooping sent shivers up Richard's spine. Young people could be so Dionysian, could slide so easily into the nonrational, the sensual and joyful.

Beth remained close to Richard. "It's a beautiful night, isn't it?" she said.

Richard didn't respond. She touched his arm. He turned and smiled vaguely at her.

"Beautiful night," she repeated.

"Yes, yes, beautiful." He looked away again quickly and Beth, after a moment, moved away from him toward the fire.

Jacintha appeared suddenly out of the darkness. "Smoke or wine?" she asked, a bottle in one hand, a joint in the other.

"Just a little wine, please." He took a sip.

She took his hand and led him down the beach. When they were well away from the others, she removed her mask and pulled him to her. As she kissed him, she reached down and undid his fly. In her hand he immediately became hard. She pulled up her skirt and his cock was against her naked belly. He moaned and she laughed. He didn't know what he would have done next, because two partiers came squealing past, very close, and he quickly pulled back and zipped up his fly.

"They didn't even notice us," Jacintha said.

His heart pounded and he felt out of breath, as though he'd been running, and he feared his erection was going to take its sweet time going down.

And then Jacintha whispered in his ear, "I love you," and his heart seemed to stop.

"I have to go and conduct a wedding now," she said. "Don't forget where we left off." She picked up her mask. "Listen, I want you to play Prospero in the ceremony. It's a handfasting; a Wiccan marriage ceremony."

"Marriage?" Richard was finding it hard to listen.

"Yes, I'm doing it for real for Anna and John. Haven't you noticed they're together?"

"No, I hadn't noticed."

"Do you know 'Sonnet 116' — the 'marriage of true minds' one?"

"I know it by heart."

"Wonderful. I thought it would be great if Prospero spoke the sonnet as his blessing. Let's go."

Back at the bonfire, Jacintha clapped her hands and shouted, "Attention, everyone. The handfasting will begin now."

A young woman shrieked and came running from the dark into the light of the fire, a young man close behind her, growling like a bear. It took a couple of minutes for everyone to quiet down.

Then another woman shouted, "We have to do our song first. Come on, everyone."

Almost everyone stood in a line, arms linked, and after a "one, two, three" began to sing "Stormy Weather" at the tops of their lungs, kicking high — a chorus line. Richard recognized where they'd stolen the idea. Derek Jarman had used the song, sung by a blues singer, near the end of his marvellous film of *The Tempest*, while sailors in white uniforms danced. Or had they danced afterward, to another tune? Anyway, it had made Richard smile for a moment, before he started thinking about what Jacintha had whispered. Could it be true? He'd had only a few sips of wine, but he felt drunk.

When they were finished, someone yelled, "Okay, on with the wedding for the poor, deluded fools!"

Jacintha had to ask Richard twice to begin his recital. The voice emanating from him sounded to him like an automaton. He had a feeling like stage fright.

It was only when he got to the fifth line that he realized how appropriate the poem was for present purposes: "… [Love] is an ever-fixed mark / That looks on tempests and is never shaken; / It is the star to every wandering bark …"

When he'd finished, Jacintha called Anna and John to stand in front of her, and, with her surreal mask in place, began the ceremony.

Richard only half listened. There were a lot of "blessed be's" and the pair were to recognize in each other the forms of the goddess and the god, and to know that whatever they did to each other, they did to the divine beings, too.

A vision came to him, strong and swift: Jacintha naked, wearing a crown of flowers, her legs wrapped around his naked waist as he carried her to an altar to make love to her in front of acolytes. How wonderful. He was a king. He was a god, and she was his queen, his bride, pressed hot and wet against his skin.

He forgot where he was until he heard gasps of surprise and turned back to the ceremony just as Jacintha raised a small dagger above her head, the blade glinting in the moonlight.

"Swear you now, on this sacred blade, that there is no reason this union should not proceed," she said.

They both swore.

"An' it harm none, do as thou wilt."

The ceremony was over.

"Say 'I now pronounce you husband and wife'!" someone called out.

"Not part of handfasting," Jacintha said.

"Well, at least say 'kiss the bride.'"

Everyone laughed and John and Anna kissed.

The chorus line stood again and belted out a heartfelt rendition of "Blue Skies," presumably a counterpoint to, or an overcoming of, "Stormy Weather." They might be Dionysian, he thought, but he was in the grip of Eros. "The bittersweet, the limb-loosener," Sappho had called the god. Bittersweet, yes. His Eros was fierce, biting into his flesh, knocking the wind out of him.

Jacintha had moved nearer the fire and was mock-conducting the choir. Several of the students, probably the drunker ones, started singing "Stormy Weather" again, drowning out the voices of the others. It was getting wilder.

When he saw a man in a ski mask and black cape rushing at him, brandishing a knife, he assumed it was part of the play, that they were moving on to another scene. Maybe Caliban was supposed to be menacing Prospero. He thought it was an act right up until the man plunged the knife in below his shoulder. He screamed. But the chorus line drowned him out, shrieking, "When my man and I ain't together."

His attacker put his arm around Richard's waist in a grotesque parody of an embrace, one hand still on the knife in Richard's flesh, and hissed into his ear, "Jacintha's your daughter. You've been fucking your own daughter, you piece of shit."

He pulled the knife out and the pain was even worse and Richard cried out again.

Beth, who had been standing nearby and about to approach Richard, screamed, "Help, Richard's been stabbed!"

Someone laughed.

"No, help. It's real!"

The attacker raised the knife again and Beth threw herself against Richard, knocking him sideways to the ground. The knife struck her. She fell, wailing, as people ran over to them.

Grunting, scuffling. Someone was trying to subdue the attacker. Shouting. Swearing.

"He's getting away! Across the road. He's heading into the trees. Go after him, somebody."

"Hell, no. He's got a knife."

"Call 911!"

Someone was pressing a cloth against Richard's wound. Someone else was tending to Beth, who lay close beside him.

His mouth was near her ear. "How bad?" he asked.

"Don't know."

Richard whispered, "If you know who it was, don't tell."

"What? Why?"

"I'm begging you. Will explain later."

"All right."

Jacintha was with him now, had taken over the pad that was staunching the blood. "Jesus, Richard. Who would do such a thing? Don't worry, you're going to be all right. An ambulance will be here soon." She kissed him quickly on the cheek.

"Don't … shouldn't. Was it your knife?" It seemed unimaginable, but what the attacker said was unimaginable and his head was swimming and … and … no.

"God, no. Richard, no. How could you think … See, I have the ceremonial dagger here, tucked into my belt, see, see, no blood on it. Oh god, Richard, no."

Richard reached out and pawed at the dagger. "Yes, sorry," he said.

He heard crying. More swearing.

"Fucking Christ. What the hell was that about?"

"The shit got away."

"Anybody know who it was?"

No one answered.

"Leave it to the police."

"Oh, sure, the fucking police."

When the ambulance arrived, Jacintha said, "I'll come with you to the hospital."

"No."

"Of course I will."

"*No.* I don't want you to."

One of the attendants asked if she was a relative, and Jacintha said yes and Richard said no.

"Don't want her to come," Richard said.

"Sorry, lady," the attendant said.

If what Skitch said was true — Richard had recognized his voice, his build, his smell — then Jacintha had told the attendant the truth, but it was too terrible to contemplate. He couldn't stand her to be near him at this moment, cooing sympathy, touching his cheek.

It couldn't be true. But where would Skitch get such an idea? Why would he make such a thing up? Was he crazy? Anyway, better she didn't come with him, because someone would call Carol to the hospital.

Please, God, let it not be true.

March 2012

Richard,

Shit, Richard. I've always given you the benefit of the doubt when you said you hadn't had sex with Jacintha. (Well, maybe not in the beginning.) But can you really claim that your naked cock against her bare belly isn't sex?

I'm disappointed in you. It seems you have trouble differentiating between lying and telling the truth, so I can't be sure now if you fucked her or not. Regarding that, I'm past caring. It's more your dishonesty that hurts.

Carol

Dear Carol,

Yes, *there it is*, the big question. What we did could certainly qualify as sex, but we never did have intercourse.

I suppose I could be accused of using the "Bill Clinton Evasion," but the difference is we didn't repeat our particular act again and again, as Clinton and Lewinsky were said to have repeated theirs. Ours was one time only, lasting only a few moments. Still, it added greatly to the disgust I felt about myself later.

Regretfully,

Richard

Hot on the heels of the above email, just an hour later, in fact, I received the following email:

Richard,

PLEASE, PLEASE DON'T PUBLISH.

I've been reading your manuscript without thinking hard enough about the consequences of your publishing it. What if we *were* identified? I realize I've been putting too much trust in your assurances about changed names and locations. Nick agrees with me.

I don't believe you committed the *unthinkable* act, but Skitch certainly believed you did. What if Imogen should somehow find out you wrote this book and have her doubts, too? You'd break her heart. Knowing *any* of it would hurt her.

I remember a poem by Adrienne Rich in which she says she came for "the wreck and not the story of the wreck / the thing itself and not the myth." Well, I've had the wreck (but didn't come for it), and I don't need the story. If you want to create a myth, Richard, one as profound as you can make it, I understand. I understand any artist's desire for that. But I'm real, and so are the others. We bleed.

Nick is angry and wants me to find out what I can do, legally, to stop you. I've been telling him about some of things in the MS and also reading parts of it to him. (He was not pleased about the "sex in the alley" scene.) But I don't see suing you, for example, as an option. There's always the risk of unwanted publicity. Also, it's very hard for anyone, generally, to prevent something from being published. And you have self-publishing options.

No, I'm appealing to your better nature and your love for Imogen. Don't hurt us. I'm begging you.

Carol

THIRTY

NURSES KEPT GLIDING past his door with potions and murmurs, like members of some mystery sect. Richard hated this room, with its eerie mixture of homeliness and sterility; wished it had a portal closer to death than life, one he could crawl through into a pit that awaited the unworthy, the unholy. If it were true.

Oh, please, let it not be true. Any misgivings he'd had he'd attributed to her being too young, and to his guilt about the thought of being unfaithful. But her seductive behaviour, things like the ambushing kiss, should have been warnings: her siren call.

When he and Carol were in Venice, they'd been told that when a dangerously high tide loomed, seventeen sirens were sounded. They'd laughed about how many warnings human beings needed before they got any message. They'd pictured the Venetians sitting, counting to seventeen before they put down their coffee cups and strolled to a higher level. They knew their version was silly, but enjoyed the joke. *Oh, Carol. I can't think about you right now.*

Had lust put his intuition to sleep, blocked its warnings? But no, he'd felt love, too. And how could even an awake intuition have conveyed to him the unthinkable? It was probably not true. Skitch must have lied after he saw Richard's attraction to Jacintha, and hers to him. He must have gone mad with jealousy.

He was glad Skitch had got away and hoped no one besides himself and Beth, and maybe Jacintha, knew who his attacker was. If the accusation became known it would be widely believed, even though false.

Carol had come to the hospital just after he arrived. She'd kissed him, squeezed his hand, wept, kept saying, "Oh, Richard, my poor Richard."

After a while, somewhat calmer, she said, "We've been so foolish. I've missed you so much."

He was groggy from painkillers, and when she asked him about the attack, he said he couldn't talk about it yet. She fell asleep in a chair by his bed and he slept, too. When he woke later, she was gone.

The police interviewed him briefly and left, apparently satisfied that he had no idea who his attacker was or why he had been attacked. Couldn't describe him. Kind of a big guy. Masked. Didn't say anything.

This morning, Carol was back with grapes and a large bouquet of red chrysanthemums, paired with maidenhair fern. "The doctor says you can go home tomorrow. You'll come back with me, of course. I'll pick you up in the morning. Gabe is teaching your class, says not to worry, take as much time off as you need.

Christmas break is coming up, so the new year will be a good time for you to return."

Richard looked out the window.

"Richard?"

He smiled. "Thank you." He wouldn't go back to her place, but if he told her now, she'd argue.

"Is it okay if I ask you about this now?" she asked. He nodded. "Do you know who did this? Or why?"

"No."

"Was it awful?"

"It was very fast. I hardly knew what was happening, and then it was over. Chaos around me. Shouting and screaming and then the ambulance. With the painkillers they've given me, it's not so bad."

"Not so bad? The whole thing is terrible."

"I'll be all right."

"Yes, of course you will. I popped in with some flowers for Beth on my way here. Her mother and father were with her. I didn't want to upset her by asking her what happened, just thanked her for saving you. The police told me what a witness saw her do. How amazing, risking her life like that. Her parents seemed dazed." She hesitated before she spoke again. "Maybe I shouldn't ask this, Richard, but could it possibly have anything to do with that student I saw you kissing that day?"

Richard saw she was holding her breath. "No, you were wrong about that. She just jumped at me. Nothing happened between us. This attack was unprovoked, random, nothing to do with her." *Lie, you bastard, keep on lying.*

"Maybe he was crazy or on drugs," Carol said.

"Maybe. We'll probably never know."

"Well, I wonder if the police have interviewed everyone who was there," Carol said. "About twenty people?"

None of his students besides Beth had ever met Skitch, as far as Richard knew, and, thankfully, Tanya and Greg and Brian had been absent. Anyway, with the mask and cloak, he'd be hard to identify. *Jesus, how banal. All Skitch's costume needed was a large initial on his chest, an A for* Avenger.

"Do you realize it's not even a year since you and I were in hospital together?" Carol said. "About ten months. A little over a gestation period, but giving birth to what? More disasters. Twin monsters. No, I shouldn't say that. You're alive and we'll have another chance. That's the main thing."

"Twin monsters?" Ice travelled up Richard's spine.

"You and me. You know, acting abnormally because of our trauma. Parting. All that."

Richard sensed she meant more, that she had recently been doing something she regretted, too. But whatever it was, it couldn't come close to the terrible act he'd almost committed. *If it's true.*

Twin monsters, yes.

After Carol left, a nurse brought him an envelope that had been left for him at the desk. He opened it with trembling hands. It was a DNA test report, confirming what Skitch had told him. He read it twice, three times. The letters began to blur. He read it again. His name. Hers. The percentile. Within the boundaries of certainty. All his energy seemed to drain from his body. He felt so weak, he was frightened. Until then, he'd had room for doubt, to think some terrible mistake had been made. A terrible mistake had been made, but it had been he who'd made it. He lay limp and numb for several minutes, until he realized there was one pressing action he needed to perform.

Beth's room was down the hall. He had to make sure she would go on saying she knew nothing. If it were his shame alone, he would scream it right now from the hospital window, but he needed to protect Carol. She'd be deeply hurt, and if the lie about an affair was publicized, her career would be ruined just because she was his wife. *And she would hate me.*

You are just thinking of yourself again, selfish bastard. He *should* tell her the extent of his involvement, admit that he had wanted Jacintha. Then he could suck Carol's hatred into his blood and bones and organs, fill himself with it, treat it as a precious poison. Will it to kill him.

He got out of bed, put on the dressing gown and slippers Carol had brought him. He went to the nurses' desk and asked for Beth's room number.

She was alone and looked so concerned when she saw him that it pained him. "Oh, Richard — I mean Professor Wilson, are you all right?"

"Yes, I'm fine. What about you?"

Beth's hand was bandaged and a bulky dressing protruded above the neckline of her hospital gown.

"How bad …?" he asked.

"Not bad. My hand is cut. And my neck was grazed. He missed anything vital. I'll be going home tomorrow. You?"

"I'm stitched up, going home, too. Beth, I'm so sorry. How can I ever thank you enough? You saved my life."

"I had to … I mean, thank you, but I could see what he was going to do, and anybody would have …"

"Don't underestimate your courage. Use it. You're talented. Write, or choose something else, but don't be afraid to pursue it, to succeed."

Beth blushed. "Thank you."

"Beth, do you know who it was?"

"Yes. Skitch."

"I thought you might have recognized him, too. Did you tell the police?"

"No, you asked me not to. I even lied about his height. Said he was very tall. Maybe six foot five." She laughed nervously.

"Thank you. Do you know why he did it?"

She grimaced.

"Is something hurting? Shall I call a nurse?"

"No, I'm all right." He could see the hurt in her eyes. "I think he did it because he loves Jacintha."

The truth flared like a migraine, and he closed his eyes. *She's in love with Skitch.*

She caught her breath, swallowed hard, looked at him from under her lashes so tenderly that he realized with horror it was him she was in love with. *God help me. God help her. Poor girl.* "He was jealous of you and Jacintha."

Pity overwhelmed him and he held her uninjured hand, felt her shiver. "That's right. Do you think you can continue to lie? To protect the people involved? The police might try to pressure you. I'm not asking for myself, but for the others. What do you say?"

"You really don't want him arrested?"

"No, there's my wife to consider. And Jacintha, of course. I don't think he'll try again, or hurt anyone else."

"You can't be sure of that."

"No, but I feel it in my gut." What Richard felt was that Skitch wouldn't hurt Jacintha. He wasn't sure whether Skitch would come for him again, but he felt unafraid at the moment. The shock of it all was probably numbing him.

"Thanks again, Beth. I'd better let you rest now." He kissed her cheek.

Her smile was heartbreaking.

Jacintha arrived not long after he was back in his room, and stood at the foot of his bed.

"Skitch said you've seen the DNA test," she said. Her hair swung loose, skimmed the collar of her green coat, glinted as if the sun had caught it, even though the sky outside the window was grey. Her eyes were huge with dark eyeliner and mascara, her mouth bright red.

Surely a clean-scrubbed, repentant look would have been more fitting, Richard thought, and then, just as quickly, he moaned inwardly. He was as guilty as she was; guiltier. He had no right to judge her. His head was pounding; his vision began to blur: a pale aura surrounded Jacintha's head, and the green of her coat wavered, watery, its edges melting into the darker green of the wall.

"I'm so sorry. For everything. You don't even know why I ... Do you remember my mother?"

"What?"

"Do you remember my mother?"

"No, I mean ... I mean, I don't know if ..."

"Did you abandon more than one pregnant woman?" Her voice was harsh.

"No, I didn't ... I ..."

"She had this photo taken at a pub. Here, look at it. She wrote on the back that she was there with Richard. At the Driftwood Pub. One of those guys must be you.

"And this book. 'Richard Wilson' is written inside." She held up the thin volume that was Blake's *Songs of Innocence*, an edition that reproduced all of the original colour plates. A purple border. An engraving of the naked piper, looking up at the infant on a cloud above him. Richard remembered vividly now: the place in Kits where he'd probably left the book, the pretty blond girl with eager eyes, how he'd gone with her, how after a couple of times he had had to escape from her neediness.

"Her name was Catherine," Jacintha said. "Catherine Peters. You met her one night and took her home. You had sex a couple of times more. Then you said you'd call her but you never did. When she found you again two months later, at the same pub, to tell you she was pregnant, you asked how she knew it was yours. She said she wasn't a whore and she was sure. You gave her two hundred dollars and told her to have an abortion and not to contact you again. She never told me this. She told my adoptive parents, who told me only recently. Maybe they shouldn't have told me, should have left me with the fantasy of a mysterious stranger lost at sea, or a soldier who died a hero in a war."

Richard moaned. "I wasn't sure it was mine."

"*It*, as you put it, is me."

She moved to the side of the bed and sat down and he saw then the dark circles under her eyes, the puffiness of her eyelids. She'd been crying. She reached out to touch his face and he said, "No!" She stood up abruptly, as though he'd slapped her, and paced back and forth beside the bed.

"I didn't want you to find out the truth. At first I did, but then my feelings for you changed. You know that. But Skitch saw the DNA report and put two and two together and got five. He thought I'd been sleeping with you. He's a lot more sensitive than he looks and probably picked up on my feelings for you. And then sometimes I went out walking at night by myself and didn't tell him where I'd been, and he got suspicious.

"I didn't want it to be true, that you were my father. I wasn't going to tell you, ever. I don't believe incest is a crime. Or anyway, there are degrees of it, and we'd never met before."

What is she saying? "You can't mean that," he managed to choke out, hardly above a whisper. "Oh Christ, this can't be happening."

"Please don't say that," she said, and stood up, ramrod straight and still.

Richard found it hard to breathe; hard to think clearly. Finally, he asked, "How did you find me?"

"Through the photo and the book, of course. And a lot of luck. Did you give the book to my mother?"

"No, I lost it."

"Do you want it back?"

"No, it's all right." *Nothing was all right.* "*Little Lamb, who made thee?*"

"I loved it as a child. Used to sneak it out of the drawer where she kept it and look at all the pretty drawings. She didn't want to read it to me. The snapshot was tucked into it. I knew the book and the photo were important to her. I've kept them ever since she died."

Richard groaned.

"How did she die?"

"A heroin overdose. When you met her, she was only nineteen and her parents were dead. It turned out to be a hard life for her, with no family and me to drag around. She did become a whore then. She started to use drugs after I was taken from her."

"It must have been terrible."

"Yes," Jacintha said, "the last time I saw her, I was twelve. She was just skin and bones, and after she died, I had a recurring nightmare that always ended with worms crawling out of her eye sockets. But you know, to paraphrase I forget who, 'Women have died and worms have eaten them, but not for love.' Not for love, but the lack of it."

"What?" Richard said. All her words were clear as crystal beads, but for disturbing moments impenetrable, hard to string into meaning. "Oh, yes, I see, but why, I mean why these things you did, this ..."

"Seductiveness?" Jacintha said.

Richard heard a high-pitched sound in his head, followed by a ringing in his ears. He didn't hear her answer. "What? Why?" he said, when an awful stillness had replaced the din. The air was heavy, dense as water.

"Because," she said slowly, "it was the way I knew you would suffer the most. I wanted you to want me, and then I was going to tell you and make you ashamed for wanting me, for almost committing incest. I wanted to avenge my mother. She used to moan that you had hurt her. 'Richard hurt me,' she said over and over when she was stoned. She said you hadn't hit her or anything like that, so as a child I didn't understand what she meant. I didn't understand the hurt of abandonment, but I do now.

"I thought I would say you *had* committed incest. People get so freaked out about it. Even you, but really you don't have to. I almost made love to you that night even though I knew who you were, but something stopped me. I don't know what. Love, I guess.

"Anyway, if I'd gone through with my plan, you would have been humiliated and disgraced in the eyes of your wife and colleagues — everyone."

Richard sank into his pillow, drained, shaking.

Jacintha watched him as he began to cry quietly.

Then another figure appeared so suddenly at his bedside that Richard thought he might be hallucinating, that this tall, stern being was a guardian angel come to set things straight, to say, *None of this is true. You've been dreaming. Rest now.*

"Is everything all right?" the nurse asked. "Are you in pain?"

"Yes. No. Not physically."

"I've brought bad news, I'm afraid," Jacintha said. "Family news."

The nurse frowned at Jacintha. "Not a good time for bad news."

"There's never a good time for bad news," Jacintha said.

The nurse took a slightly menacing step toward her. "He should rest. You'd better leave."

"Just another minute, please?" Jacintha said in a small voice, managing to look apologetic and sad.

"All right. One minute." She left, glaring over her shoulder.

Jacintha said, "I'm going to get us some coffee. I don't think she's actually going to check up on us in one minute, or even twenty. And please, don't despair. I won't tell anyone about us. And I've convinced Skitch not to say anything, you know, anonymously, because any scandal that came out would hurt me. And it would hurt you, and I don't want you hurt any more than you already are. He loves me, and he'll respect my wishes. We'll talk more when I get back. Figure out what to do next."

She kissed him on his forehead, her lips cool against his hot skin, and left, smiling at him.

He couldn't be there when she got back. He struggled into his clothes, his shoulder making it too painful to get his left arm into his jacket; he pulled on his shoes without bothering about socks and without tying his laces; he looked into the corridor to see if the nurse angel was hovering, but saw no nurses at all. He hurried to the elevator, went to the downstairs lobby, and phoned for a taxi. He was standing outside the door, waiting, when Frances arrived.

"Good heavens, Richard, what are you doing?" she said. "You look a mess. Carol's not taking you home until tomorrow, you know. She'll be visiting again this evening."

"I have to leave now. I'm not going home with Carol."

"Oh, Richard. Why not? She wants to look after you."

He started to cry great blobs of tears. Frances put her arm around him and he leaned his head on her shoulder, his crying becoming louder and wetter. People stared.

"Come, you're coming home with me." She led him to her car, buckled him in like a child. "You can tell me all about it when we get to my house, if you want to. And you can stay with me as long as you like. What do you say?"

"Yes, thank you, so kind." Snot ran down his face and he wiped it with his sleeve.

When he was settled in an armchair, drinking tea, he said, "I don't want to see Carol. Could you please ask her not to come here — not for a while, anyway?"

"Why? I don't understand."

"I can't explain right now. I mean, I could, but … Look, will you just promise me, please?"

"Well, I'd really like to know why, but … yes, I promise. But will you tell me soon what's going on? I know you've had a traumatic experience — the stabbing — but I sense there's more."

"Yes. Maybe soon. I think I should be by myself now. Rest."

"Of course. I'll make up the spare bed for you."

"Thanks."

Frances started to leave the room.

"Frances."

"Yes?"

"I was ... I was ... attracted to one of my students."

Frances said nothing for a moment, as the sentence rang in his ears.

"That's not the end of the world. Is that why you don't want to talk to Carol? Is your stabbing related to that?"

"Yes." *Not the end of the world.*

"Do you know who the young man was?"

"Yes."

"But you have to tell the police!"

"No, he accused me of something terrible. Something that all the denials in the world wouldn't erase from people's minds. If he repeated it in court, it would be awful for all of us. The police think the attack was random. I've said I have no idea who he was or why he did it. It's better that way. It's the only way. Please believe me, Frances, and don't tell anyone what I've told you."

"Well, I think you're wrong. He should be held to account."

"No, please, there'd be terrible consequences. Please promise me you won't do anything."

"All right, but against my better judgment. Whatever he said, he most likely wouldn't be believed."

"Some people would believe. Promise me, Frances." He was whining now, begging.

"Please calm down. I promise. Truly."

Richard began to cry. Frances sat on the arm of his chair and held his head against her shoulder, swaying, humming tunelessly.

After a minute or so, Richard stopped crying, blew his nose and said, "Thank you, Frances. I appreciate your sympathy even though I don't deserve it."

She straightened up. "You're very wrong about that. But I think you should sleep now. You look exhausted. Do you have some pills that will help?"

"No."

"I'll phone the hospital, see if I can find your doctor. Let's get you to bed. I want you to know I'm here for you, promise and all, and that you'll get through this. We'll talk about it later. Process it."

Process it? Come to terms with it? What's that other useless, hypocritical phrase? Find closure? "I don't think talking about it will help."

"We'll see," Frances said.

Under smooth, white sheets and a white down comforter, Richard lay rigid as a corpse, unable to roll from side to side to find a more comfortable position because of his wound, although the frantic tossing of his mind was the more serious impediment to sleep. Frances came in an hour or so later with sleeping pills, having miraculously got hold of his doctor. She'd had him phone a nearby pharmacy with a prescription, which she'd picked up.

After Frances left, Richard took an additional pill and fell, finally, into a blessedly dreamless sleep.

THIRTY-ONE

HE HAD LET her in. She had appeared at the door and he had let her walk right in.

He'd been sitting by the fireplace in his pyjamas and robe, staring into the flames. Fresh from a bath, he felt more comfortable than he had in many days. Frances had cleaned the area around his stitches and changed the dressing, and then went to have a bath herself. His wound, just below his collarbone, ached a little, and he concentrated on the ache, finding that doing so stilled his mind, made it almost blank. The licking and snapping fire had a welcome hypnotic effect. The room was cozy, cavelike, with its thick oriental carpet, warm beige walls, and red velvet drapes closed against the chilly night. He noticed, as if for the first time, that the fireplace had art deco tiles, with a border of stylized white lilies on a background of apple green. It reminded him of his and Carol's destroyed fireplace.

It was then he'd heard the knock on the door.

She came in before he could speak. He closed the door, followed her into the living room, and stood looking at her. She wore a navy peacoat and a Russian-style fur hat, and her cheeks were flushed. She smelled of the wind that blows down from the mountains, promising snow, fresh and pure.

"You shouldn't be here," he said. "How did you get this address?"

"You got the bouquet of flowers, didn't you, and a card from all your students? I needed this address so they could be delivered. Your wife told Aiden; she wouldn't have told me."

Richard had been touched by the card, but felt deflated now, knowing it had been engineered by Jacintha.

"Anyway, I am here. I used to be the one who should never have been, period. Not anywhere. But things turned out differently. Everything is different now."

Richard sat down stiffly, feeling as though he were splitting into two beings: one who wanted to recoil, to run and hide, and the other who wanted to hear her say something that would change everything, some denial. But that denial wasn't going to happen — there was something electric about her, sparking from her as though her words were going to strike him, peel away from him like burned skin whatever thin shield he still possessed.

"Listen. This is important. You loved me when you didn't know who I was. You should love me more now that you know who I am. I won't let go, now that I've found you. I love you and I know you love me and I want us to be lovers. We won't tell anyone I'm your daughter. Don't you see? We belong to each other in every way."

Richard couldn't breathe. *Breathe, must breathe.*

"Tell me it's what you want, too, Richard. Please. Oh, please. I know you want me."

"*No!* You have to go. Go. Leave. I don't want you."

"Don't lie."

"Do you want me to go insane? You have to go. You're making it impossible for us even to know each other."

"We can't take back what's happened. We can't deny the truth."

"You've got to give up this idea."

"I can't."

Jacintha, who'd been standing a few feet from him, walked over and reached out to touch his cheek. He pulled away as though he'd been hit. He felt both frightened and ridiculous.

He walked to the front door and opened it. "Please leave," he said.

She didn't move. The cold air that blew into the room seemed to clear his head, and he emerged from a kind of fog of panic. He left the door ajar. He knew what he had to say, but when he spoke it was as though he were watching someone else take command.

"The only way you can be my daughter is if we don't see each other again. You have to make a clean break. Forget me. Think of me as a dream. Or a nightmare."

"Melt into thin air? 'Leave not a rack behind'? Wishful thinking."

His clarity, mercifully, continued. "I've done you a great wrong. Before you were born, I injured you. And now I've done this most unforgivable thing."

"'Most unforgivable'? Only from your point of view. Living without you was the most unforgivable thing. I haven't told you, have I, why I was taken from my mother? I was raped by one of her johns. Afterward, I ran to a neighbour, who told a social worker."

He tried to speak, but his throat had closed up.

"But that was long ago, and now I have you. I lost my need to seek revenge, to humiliate you. I think it happened when I first saw that you wanted *me*, the child you thought had never been born. We have to stay together. I'm flesh of your flesh."

"No!"

She stared at him for a moment, then suddenly dropped into the armchair across from him, shoulders slumped, head down.

Finally, she looked up and said, "I should have come to you that night on Thanksgiving. I should have come to you."

It took Richard a moment to realize what she meant.

"No," he said. "No. That would have made everything worse. Unbearable. No. Not coming was the best thing you've done in all this."

She jumped to her feet, her fierce posture regained. "We would have been together now," she said, slowly, drawing out every word. "None of the bad things would have happened. Nobody would have known our secret."

"Jesus Christ, why can't you see? *That* would have been the bad, the terrible thing."

"Finding a lost daughter is never a bad thing," she said, and this time her hand touched his face and he seemed robbed of the energy needed to move.

"And on the beach, you were eager to make love to me. We were pressed *naked* against each other. You can't take back *how much you wanted me.*"

He dropped to his knees, moaning. Cold air blasted in from the door, making him shiver.

Just then, Frances came down the stairs, wrapped in a huge bath towel. "What's going on? Who is this?"

"Her, it's her," Richard said, barely audible.

"Do you want her to leave?" Frances asked.

"Yes."

"You heard," Frances said. "You'd better go. He's very upset. He hasn't been well."

"All right. But I'll come back tomorrow."

"No. Don't come again unless you're invited," Frances said.

"Richard, please. You'll see I'm right," Jacintha said.

Still kneeling, head bowed, he knew he looked, in his thick, brown bathrobe, as though he were a penitent monk, waiting to be whipped. He looked up, saw that the three of them, all perfectly still, made an absurd *tableau vivant*: the guardian angel, wild haired and wingless; the beautiful supplicant; and the doomed monk unable to pray or receive a blessing of any kind.

Then, fracturing the picture, Frances took Jacintha's arm and walked her outside, where Jacintha pulled free angrily.

She looked back and shouted, "Remember, Richard. We belong to each other now."

When she was gone, Frances helped Richard up and into a chair. "God, the nerve," she said. "Can't she understand nothing's going to happen? I just assumed you weren't going to pursue ..."

"No, nothing's going to happen."

"Dear Richard. Don't worry. She'll give up on you before long. But it won't help, you know, you falling to your knees, looking helpless. You'll have to be firm with her if you see her again, heaven forbid. Unless she's crazy. Do you think she's crazy?"

"I don't know." Truly, he didn't. Madness seemed like a pit they'd both slid into, a pit with slippery walls and no footholds.

"Well, I'll protect you from her as best I can. She's very beautiful. I can see why you ... well, never mind. I'll go and get dressed, and then I'll make some tea."

"Rather have whisky."

"Whisky it is. I could use one, too."

THIRTY-TWO

FOUR DAYS HAD passed since Jacintha's visit. Every time Richard heard footsteps on the porch or heard the phone ring, his heart lurched. She had sent two emails on every one of the four days. He read the first four and after that pressed "delete" without reading them. They were brief, begging him to see her, and repeating, with variations, many of the things she'd said on her visit.

He was surprised she hadn't come back. Or maybe she had come to the house or phoned and Frances had refused to let her in or to speak to him. Or maybe Jacintha was planning some different tactic. Some fresh hell.

He heard Frances on the phone now, talking to Carol. He assumed it was Carol by Frances's tone of voice, stern and sympathetic by turns, and by the few phrases he made out: "better not," "he's not ready to," "can't explain," "patience."

Patience. Patient. A sick man waiting. For what? Deliverance? Oblivion? Not for a cure in my case. He simply waited for each minute, each hour, each day to pass. To that end, Frances had assigned him household tasks, simple things he could do without putting a strain on his wounded shoulder.

"We can live only a moment at a time," she said. "Why not concentrate on our daily necessities and let the past and future take care of themselves?" She was full of Buddhist-inspired sayings, and sometimes they annoyed him, but mostly they soothed. Just a little. It was good to keep busy with mindless activities.

He was holding a potato in his left hand, his left elbow on the table to minimize the pull on the arm, and feeling some satisfaction as he peeled thin strips from the white flesh and released the starchy wetness. He cut the naked potato into four equal pieces and dropped it into a pot of cold water; picked up another, brown, rough to the touch, and pulled the blade down the length of it. Once, twice, three times. The rhythm was pleasant.

"It doesn't matter what the work is," Frances had said. "What matters is how much attention we bring to it. No job is more significant than any other. That's not only Buddhist teaching; it's part of many religions. The constant prayers and menial tasks of Christian monks, for example, are as much for developing attention as for praising and serving God. Well, maybe not quite as much, but learning how to be conscious in the moment must be a part of it."

So he was a monk now, paying attention to vegetables. He'd have liked to wear a medieval robe of rough, brown wool that punished his skin. Failing that, he'd have preferred to stay in his bathrobe all day. He smiled at how unlike punishment his soft robe was — it was more a symbol of defeat. But Frances insisted he dress every day in freshly laundered clothes, his shirts crisp and fragrant, ironed by her. He was required to shower and shave every morning, too.

She was his mother superior. His warden. His protector. He didn't know what he would have done without her sanctuary. Something drastic, maybe, but for the moment he was passive, childlike, in Frances's care.

Every day was much the same. The outside world had faded. He found it impossible to read the newspaper, listen to the radio, watch TV. He hadn't turned on his computer since Carol had delivered it along with clothes and toiletries on his first day here. Frances hadn't let her in, obeying his instructions.

The world had faded, except for the part that held the one who tormented him.

"Don't resist your thoughts," Frances said.

He couldn't have, even if he'd tried. They entered with a force that flooded his mind and body, and he'd find himself standing with a broom or a face cloth or a knife in his hand and not knowing how much time had passed as some lustful vision of Jacintha thrilled and shamed him, caused an internal Bacchanalia as wild as the one that night on the beach. He lived then in the moment, all right — an eternal moment of imagined bliss. That, he presumed, was not the kind of "being present" that the Buddhists advocated. Maybe he got points for not resisting.

Dinner consisted of mashed potatoes, rich with butter and milk, roast beef, green beans, and salad. Richard had eaten almost nothing the first couple of days, so Frances prescribed comfort food. She'd asked him what he liked, and mashed potatoes was one of the first things he'd named. And pancakes with maple syrup for breakfast and grilled cheese sandwiches for lunch. Childhood food. He and Frances made them all.

"The ritual of cooking and sitting down to eat three times a day will be good for you," Frances said. "Calm and steady, a reliable routine."

"Good for invalids and lunatics," he said, and Frances laughed.

After dinner, they sat by the fire and drank the last of the red wine from dinner, and then Richard had some brandy. He was drinking a lot.

"Richard," Frances said, "as I said before, I get the feeling that there's more going on with you than an 'almost' affair and the attack. Well, I've never been stabbed, so maybe I'm wrong, but some of your reactions seem a bit overboard, like refusing to see Carol. I bring it up again because I don't think you're going to resolve whatever's troubling you without sharing it with somebody. That would be a start."

"Overboard, yes — good word."

"Will you tell me about it?"

"I can't see Carol because I don't want to tell her about being tempted, coming rather close, you know ... And with the attack, she might think there's more to it, might not believe me. I can't bear to face her. That makes sense, doesn't it?" He'd raised his voice, slammed his glass on the end table and poured another brandy.

"I thought it might help ..."

"Sorry, Frances, I didn't mean to be harsh. You're being very kind, but please don't push me."

After Frances went upstairs, Richard sat and drank more brandy. He was drunk when he staggered up to bed.

Dreaming, he swam in a sea still as glass. In the distance, Jacintha watched him, her head and shoulders strangely high above the water. Was she smiling? Stern? He couldn't tell. No matter how fast he swam, the distance between them never diminished. Then, suddenly, he was a few feet away, facing not Jacintha, but Jenny. He cried out and sank beneath the water. Something was pulling him down. He struggled wildly and woke up gasping.

As he lay limp and sweating, he remembered how he'd kissed Jenny in his dream shortly after she died, how they'd held each other in the warm, caressing water. It seemed an innocent fantasy now, in light of all that had happened. But how long would it have stayed innocent? What was he capable of? Less than a year ago, he had been sure that he would never have touched Jenny. Now he was full of doubt. He must have had the seed of moral failure in him all along. He wasn't religious, but *sinner* was a word that came to him. He'd read that to New Agers *sin* meant "stumbling block," but surely "sin," with its snake hiss, was more serious than that. He knew everyone was capable of sinning, but he couldn't keep a philosophical distance, couldn't consider everyone else's capacity for it, only the particular weight and taste and smell of his own.

He had what he thought of as an odour of guilt. Probably most people wouldn't notice it; maybe he imagined it. He'd first become aware of it as an adolescent, when he'd stood before his father and said he'd done his homework when he hadn't.

"You're lying," his father had said, and Richard had noticed a sour smell rising from his armpits. "I can smell it," his father had said, and Richard had thought he meant it literally, but later realized he was probably speaking metaphorically, hadn't been close enough to smell his sweat.

His father had wanted to be a doctor, but at twenty-two he'd married Richard's mother when she became pregnant, and he'd gone to work in an insurance agency. He was a bitter man who'd died of a heart attack at sixty. He'd had no symptoms of heart problems before that. (Richard often worried that it was hereditary, as his paternal grandfather had also died of heart failure at fifty-eight, but that worry was far from his mind now.)

Richard had worked hard at university, but his father always seemed more jealous of him than proud. "You don't know how lucky you are," he'd said, when Richard graduated cum laude. Richard's heart ached, remembering.

He was surprised to realize that for several minutes he hadn't thought about Jacintha. But the heaviness in his limbs and the acidic taste in his mouth soon returned.

THIRTY-THREE

THE NEXT MORNING, he heard footsteps at the front door, when he was alone in the house. His heart pounded. Then he saw a letter had dropped through the slot. It was addressed to him. Trembling, he opened it. It was from Jacintha.

> Dear Richard,
>
> I've written you some emails but have gotten no response, so I'm putting pen to paper, as the old expression goes. I think it will be harder to ignore an envelope in your hand, and also they say that the writing hand is more connected to the heart than the typing hands. And everything I say to you is connected to my heart.

Dear, dear Richard. Once you're over the shock, you'll see that we belong to each other in a way that few people ever get to know. We'll own each other, always. Our connection isn't really about sex; it's an expression of our deeper connection, a marriage of our souls. Think of our bodies in the future performing a kind of holy ritual.

You must let me see you again soon. Tell that large, bossy woman to stay out of our way. I've been to the house again twice and phoned several times, but she won't let me see you or speak to you. Didn't you hear me at the door? I guess you were resting upstairs. I know we can work this out. We can't lose each other now.

I'm sorry I deceived you. Please forgive me for that. As I said, as I will say to you again and again, I changed when you looked at me with love. That's when I began to love you.

Your daughter, your soul,
Jacintha

Richard was sitting rigidly, the letter on the kitchen table in front of him, when Frances came in.

"Richard, what's wrong?" Frances said. "Is that a letter from her? It has upset you terribly, hasn't it? We can get a restraining order against her, you know. I've already told her that. And if she sends any more letters, simply don't read them. Would you like me to screen the mail, burn anything she sends?"

"No. Please. I can do that myself."

"But will you? You have the air of a fly caught in flypaper. But not hopelessly — I don't mean that. I mean, you look as though you have no fight in you." She touched his arm, leaned in, but he wouldn't meet her eyes.

"I'm going to go and lie down now," Richard said.

"All right, but will you come shopping with me for groceries later? We'll cook a nice dinner and then maybe play Scrabble."

"Maybe." He took two Tylenols and, after a miserable half hour, he fell asleep.

When he awoke, Jacintha's words still pounded in his head. How long would she keep tormenting him? How could he go on? He wished for oblivion, to feel nothing, to think nothing, to remember nothing. He got up, went downstairs, and drank more Scotch.

He was very drunk when Frances came back from shopping. She took the bottle away with her when she went to cook dinner. Richard managed to eat a bit of fried chicken with rice.

"Good shicken and rysh," he said, and laughed giddily.

After he'd eaten, Frances took him upstairs, changed his dressing and waited while he alternated between giggling and moaning as he struggled into his pyjamas. She made him drink a large glass of water.

"You'll feel better in the morning," she said.

"Liar," he said. "But thanks, anyway. You're a peach."

The next morning, Frances said, "It's a beautiful day, cold but not too bad. Let's go and sit in the garden for a while."

Richard's hangover had been muted by pills, and he'd managed to eat an omelette and green salad for brunch.

"I don't have a coat here," Richard said. His blood-soaked jacket had been taken from him in the ambulance, and Carol hadn't thought to bring one of his winter coats to Frances's.

"I'll get you something warm," Frances said and went up to her bedroom.

Aubrey's overcoat was still in their closet. She took it downstairs. "Look," she said. "Aubrey bought it on Savile Row in London. Feel how thick the cashmere is."

Richard, feeling something of a usurper, slipped into the coat.

They settled into cushioned deck chairs with their coffee. It was a day of clouds. Huge, cottony piles mounded like snow on the solid mountaintops. Frances said she saw an old god reclining in them, beard and Roman nose upward, but Richard couldn't see it.

"As a little girl," she said, "I used to be upset when the pictures changed. I'd see a rabbit and cry when it became stringy wisps. I hadn't thought about that in decades, and then one day my meditation teacher suggested an 'amusing meditation.' He said, 'Watch the image fade, wish for it to fade, say *going, going, gone*, and clap your hands.'"

"Auctioning off your attachments?" Richard said.

"You've got it!" Frances said. "Except there'd be no takers, because everyone has too many attachments of their own."

Richard watched but saw no clouds that reminded him of anything except the mountains they mimicked. They were oppressively large and static. They inched, eked out small wisps, were stubbornly unevocative.

As a child he'd been interested in the different types of clouds; had learned the names of many of them. And before that there were dinosaurs and bugs and stars and carnivorous plants to study and admire. Then, gradually, as he became enamoured of the world of literature, he had lost his keen interest in the mystery and beauty of nature.

There was so much he didn't know about the world. He'd thought he knew enough, and what most to fear hadn't been a priority. A cliff crushing his house and killing someone had never entered any list of what to dread. As for injury by incest, that was as far from being a possibility as a cannibal attacking him, cutting a slice off his leg and chomping on it, eyes glittering, blood dripping down his chin.

His leg started to ache insistently. The strong connection between painful thoughts and bodily pain was another thing he hadn't known about. (Maybe it was just him.) And then there was the unreliability of received wisdom — the truth had not set him free. He was caged by it, scrabbling and biting and squealing like a trapped squirrel he'd once seen throwing itself against the steel bars of a trap.

Frances suddenly clapped her hands and laughed. "A whale changed into a snake," she said.

"I can hardly believe we're looking at the same sky," Richard said. "In a way, we're not. Never mind. Come, let's go in and warm up."

T H I R T Y - F O U R

THE NEXT DAY another letter from Jacintha arrived.

Dear Richard,

I've waited to hear from you, but I'm through waiting. If you won't see me and then agree to continue
to see me, I'll tell Carol who I am and that we've
slept together. She won't want you anymore, once
she believes that. Most people are so conservative, so
boxed in by convention, that they recoil at anything
unusual, no matter how profound and beautiful it is.
She'd be disgusted. I'd be sorry to do that, but I'm
desperate.

I can't believe you want to lose me. We can be together secretly and you can go on living in your sham marriage, if you want to — loving both me and her, but me so much more. (You know that's true.) That's one option. Or we can go away together — a much better idea.

You can't stay with her. That would be agony for me. We must go away together.

Phone me, Richard. Very soon. Please.

Your loving Jacintha

Richard sat at the kitchen table while Frances made Earl Grey tea. He wondered if he'd ever be able to drink it again, or if the aroma would conjure up this terrible time forever after. He'd been drinking gin and tonic when Grace packed to leave him, and the smell of gin still made him nauseous.

He heard something at the window and turned to see bamboo flailing in the wind, brushing against the glass, whispering some sad, indecipherable message, something primal, something without hope.

Then a painting near the window caught his eye.

"I see you've noticed Aubrey's painting of Carol. It's been in storage, but I decided I'd like to be able to look at it again."

Carol's hair, so curly in its natural state, had been straightened and fell long and smooth, framing her face. The style Jacintha wore. Carol would have been about twenty-four, Jacintha's age. He angled his chair so the painting was not in his line of sight.

"Please tell me what's troubling you so deeply," Frances said.

"It's hard."

"I know."

He felt it was cowardly to want to tell. He should bear this by himself. The secret should burn in him, sear his insides, sear his soul. He deserved to suffer, should not make anyone else suffer by sharing his burden. But Frances could probably handle it. He trusted Frances. Maybe he should tell Frances.

"She's my daughter," he blurted, shocked at how quickly the words escaped him. "Jacintha's my daughter."

It was out. He watched Frances's face. She looked puzzled.

"How do you know? How do you know it's true? I mean …"

"Wait here." He went to his room and got the DNA result and handed it to Frances. Watched her face again. What was that look? Censure? Shock?

"Oh, you poor thing," Frances said. Not censure, then; not even much shock. She got up, put her arms around him. He cried and Frances wiped away his tears with her sleeve, kissed him on the cheek.

Finally, he said, "I can't take any more comforting at the moment, Frances."

She sat down.

Richard told her how he had "paid off" Jacintha's mother twenty-five years ago, how he hadn't known about Jacintha's existence, didn't know who she was until the time of his stabbing, and that Jacintha had known who he was when their relationship began. "You see now why I'm so wretched. Christ, Frances. I almost had an affair with my own daughter."

"The stabbing. The boy. Was he the one who told you?"

"Yes."

"Did he believe you'd slept with her?"

"Yes."

"Did you sleep with her?"

"No, thank god, no."

"But you were tempted."

Richard didn't answer, only hung his head.

Frances was quiet for a while, then said, "She's your daughter by genes only, not by upbringing. She was a stranger to you."

"Christ, you sound like her."

"Listen. It's not the disaster you think it is. That's the main thing, Richard. *You didn't know.* You've no need to blame yourself so severely."

"And yet I do."

"She's the one to blame. She tricked you. She's obviously emotionally unbalanced."

"And whose fault is that?"

"Not yours."

"I wasn't there for her."

"You were young. You believed her mother had an abortion."

"But did I? Or did I just not want to know?" *Knowing and not knowing again.*

"Richard, you've got to stop whipping yourself like this."

"Do you know what the most terrible thing is?" Richard said.

"No, what is it?"

Richard glanced at the bamboo, which had turned malevolent, hissing, "Say it, say it." No, it didn't need to be said. It shouldn't be said. He didn't say it.

He said, instead, "I don't think she'll let me go."

"You'll have to help her — help her to see that she must."

"How, for Christ's sake?"

"You could urge her to get counselling."

"And if she won't?" Richard stood up. He handed her Jacintha's latest letter.

"She really is terribly troubled, isn't she?" Frances said when she'd read it. "Does she have adoptive parents?"

"Yes."

"Then they will have to get involved."

"And have the whole sordid thing come out? No."

"You might have no other choice."

"What about Carol?"

"You must tell her, Richard. When someone tries to blackmail you, you have to take away their ammunition."

"And Imogen? What if Jacintha decides to lie to Imogen?"

"How would she find her?"

"Oh, hell, I don't know."

"Anyway, Jacintha will probably give up once she knows you've told Carol everything. Besides, you shouldn't underestimate Carol's or Imogen's capacity to understand. They both love you very much." After a moment's thought, she said, "You do love Carol, don't you?"

Richard nodded by way of an answer. He wanted to say, *yes, of course I do*, clearly and firmly, but the words wouldn't come.

"You must forgive yourself, Richard, for everyone's sake."

"You want me to 'be wise hereafter, and seek for grace,' but I may not be capable of it."

"Who are you quoting?"

"Caliban."

THIRTY-FIVE

FOR HIS DREADED audience with Carol, Richard was dressed as though appearing before a court of law: in a white shirt, grey slacks, and a grey tweed jacket. Only the tie was lacking. He sat waiting in a wingback chair, his arms on the armrests; too much, he realized, as though he were the judge and not the prisoner in the dock. He moved to a softer chair, let his shoulders slump. Sweat soaked the underarms of his shirt.

Frances showed Carol in and left the room.

"God, you look like death, Richard," Carol said, and put her hand on his forehead.

"No, don't. Please sit down."

She sat opposite him, leaned forward. "What is it, dear? Whatever it is, I'm here for you. Don't be afraid to tell me what's troubling you so terribly."

Richard reached into his jacket pocket and pulled out the DNA test result and handed it to her.

Carol scanned the document. "What's this? I don't understand."

Richard said nothing. Waited.

"Your DNA? And Jacintha's ... Is she your student? The one I ... I'm so sorry. I thought you and her ... You're related to her?"

"Yes. My daughter."

"Oh my God, Richard. Your daughter? But why didn't you tell me? I mean, a daughter. Why shouldn't I know? From an affair before your first marriage?"

"Yes."

"That's nothing to me. It happens all the time. The pity is that you didn't know. All those wasted years. That's why she was with you. Why she kissed you."

Carol got up, stroked his hair, his cheek.

"Carol. Stop. Sit down."

He watched as fear slowly filled her eyes.

"Someone said ... She might say ..." Richard said.

"What, for God's sake?"

"That we were together."

"I don't understand."

"I mean ... physically."

"You mean, slept with? She'll say you slept with her?"

"Yes."

"Jesus, Richard. You can't have done that. Did you? Did you sleep with her?"

"No. No. I would never even have told you about her, but she said she'd tell you that lie. She's been pursuing me, harassing me since the stabbing."

"I'm dying here, Richard. You have to tell me the truth. I have to know the worst now or I don't know what I'll do."

"I didn't sleep with her. That's the truth."

"But what she's doing, that's crazy. Did she know she was your daughter?"

"She was pretty sure. Then she got the confirmation. Just a short while ago."

"God, it's too awful to contemplate, to do something so … so … unthinkable."

Carol paced across the room and back, bumped into a chair, walked again in what seemed like a trance, and when she looked at Richard once more, her eyes were bright with revelation, wide and accusatory. She spoke slowly, with menacing emphasis. "You kissed her, Richard. I saw you — don't forget."

"I could never forget that." He thought of the torment Carol's letter had caused him after that kiss.

"Something more must have happened," Carol said. "To make her want to lie like that. To make her want to 'pursue' you. You must have done something to encourage her. Yes, you must have."

"Carol, no, I didn't encourage her. I'm telling you the facts."

She moved closer, put her face an inch from his. "You're lying. I can tell when you're lying."

He smelled the sourness of her breath, the smell of her anguish. He grasped her shoulders and she pulled away sharply.

"You did sleep with her. Tell me, goddamn it. Tell me."

"I kissed her. Once. That was all. Before I knew who she was."

"Once. Once more, you mean? Besides the kiss I saw at your apartment? I don't think once was enough for you. You wanted her, didn't you?" She looked at Richard so fiercely that he turned away, and then she let out a wail that brought Frances running in. "You wanted her!" Carol screamed, dashed at Richard, and pounded her fists against his chest.

Frances pulled her away with some difficulty as Carol tried to hit Richard again, and took her to the kitchen. Richard went out into the garden.

When Frances found him he was leaning his head against the garage wall. It was raining and his shirt was soaked.

"You should really be on a blasted moor, roaring and tearing out your hair," Frances said. "More Shakespearean. Come now. Come with me."

He let Frances guide him back into the house and upstairs to his bed, let her help him out of his wet clothes, accepted a sleeping pill. He felt as limp and passive as a sick child, all the fight gone out of him.

When Frances returned to the kitchen, Carol said, through hiccups, "What am I going to do?"

"Nothing, for now."

"How can I live with this?"

"You will." Frances poured them each a cup of tea, sat down. Both women were quiet for a while. A drop of snot was about to run into Carol's mouth. Frances reached for a paper towel, leaned across and wiped Carol's face.

"Stop treating me like a child!" Carol said.

They were both quiet again. Carol took a gulp of tea.

"Are you still seeing that psychologist?" Frances asked.

"Yes."

"Go and talk to her."

Carol gaped, eyes wide. "Talk about this? To a stranger?"

"I'm sure she's heard worse."

"Shit, who do you think you are: Mother Teresa? I have to get out of here. I can't stand this, can't stand your fucking *reasonableness*. Couldn't you just cry with me or something? Fucking hell."

Carol charged to the front door, Frances following. "I'll call you a taxi; you're too upset to drive."

Carol slammed her car door, shouted from the window, "Fucking leave me alone!"

March 2012

Carol,

Michel Houellebecq, the French writer, had a character called Michel Houellebecq in one of his novels, whom he killed off. I decided to do the same, to kill off Richard Wilson for your delectation. Hence the following short story, set in Victorian England, which I've written just for you. Perhaps you'll know why I chose this setting. Do you remember telling me you'd heard about a Victorian feminist who'd talked of a particularly dire consequence that could befall a man if he were to regularly, and for many years, frequent the same prostitute?

Here, then, is my story:

My Dire Transgression

My name is Richard Wilson and the story that follows is true. I am what my friends and acquaintances would have deemed a respectable citizen, a merchant in the city of London. I thought myself such a man as well, until the very foundation of my pride was shattered and my moral self was darkened with the foul stains of sin and shame.

I've had the usual habits, the same ones as most of my peers, which none of us thought of as vices: the occasional overindulgence in wine; the card games in which reckless losses sometimes occurred. And most of us visited ladies of pleasure regularly, some more frequently than others. I've not been excessive in this, but I became a widower when I was thirty-five and never had the inclination to marry again, so I sought satisfaction elsewhere.

Many a pretty lady had attended to my needs, and I treated each one with kindness. O, dear reader, I meant no ill. "How atone, Great God, for this which man has done?" Thus Rossetti spoke in his poem to the fallen Jenny, and thus I speak to those I wronged.

I fear atonement is not possible for me, only a cowardly escape.

My great sin against two of the fair sex (for it's false to say these women of the night are any less fair than their luckier sisters) and my sin against all that's holy began with my visits, eighteen years ago, to a house in Notting Hill, to a room as warm and welcoming as its lovely occupant, Mary. Over the course of six months, I saw her several times, taking to her wine and sweetmeats, and once a lovely piece of jonquil silk for her to have fashioned into a gown — this silk from my own warehouse, for I'm an importer of fine fabrics.

Then one night when I went to her lodgings, her landlady greeted me, saying, "Oh, Mr. Wilson, sir, I'm afraid Mary has gone of a sudden to the country, having taken poorly." She had left no forwarding address.

I see now that I should have looked for her, but it wasn't something a gentleman would do. She was neither my mistress, nor my betrothed, and had left me no message of farewell.

I enjoyed the company of other women over the years, some almost as beautiful as Mary, but none as gentle or as sincere in word and gesture. But I soon ceased to think of her. One of my paramours, plump, with coarse hair and a ruddy complexion, was nevertheless inventive in her art. Step by step she drew me up, taking me ever higher to a perfection of release. Words, sometimes sweet, sometimes rough, were her scaffolding. A clever architect of love. Then, after I'd known her for a year, she too left the brothel, and I heard a few months later that she'd died delivering a stillborn child.

I learned what had happened to Mary these many years later from the sad, broken lady herself. I would wish that I had never learned it, but not knowing would have heaped sin upon sin, and so I must be, in a small way, grateful, for it makes possible this confession.

Mary found herself with child and wrote to her sister to beg for help. Her sister's husband, a farmer, agreed to take her in on the condition that she give her baby away as soon as it was born. "I'll not have your bastard child here," he said. Mary was to earn her keep by cooking and cleaning and tutoring her niece and nephew, for she was clever with reading and sums.

Delivered of her baby girl, whom she named Ida, she was most heartbroken at the prospect of giving her away. She pleaded with her brother-in-law, but he was adamant, saying he wouldn't have the evidence of her debauchery in his house. "Leave her at the church door or drown her," he said.

Mary had a small, secret stash of money she'd brought with her, and seeing an advertisement in the village apothecary's window that a "widow with children of her own would accept charge of an infant for fifteen shilling a month," Mary decided this was a lesser evil than those suggested by the farmer. She contacted the widow and tearfully handed over to her the baby and a month's fee. She told her sister and brother-in-law that she'd given the child away, out-right, to an eager couple who couldn't have their own.

"You charged them nothing?" was the farmer's indignant response.

Mary was sickly after the birth but hoped that within two or three months she could reclaim her child and return to London. What she would do when her money ran out, if she didn't regain her health, she dared not think about.

One night, a month later, "by the grace of God," Mary said, she dreamed her baby was dying. The next day she rushed to the widow's house and found Ida painfully thin, with bruises on her arms and legs. She snatched her up and ran, the child grey faced and weak in her arms, and the widow following her to the gate, shouting curses.

The widow, Mary found out later, was one of the "baby farmers" who were responsible for the mon-strous abuse and slaughter of countless infants. Some — like Ida, if Mary hadn't rescued her — were left to die slowly of starvation so that the monthly fee could be collected as long as possible, while thousands of others were killed outright, for a flat "adoption fee." (The government has finally acted to stop these monsters, shockingly late.)

Back at the farm with Ida, Mary took the last of her money and threw it on the table where her sister and brother-in-law sat, and said, "Here, this is for enduring my child, and feeding and caring for her until she's well enough to go to London with me." The farmer, shocked by the terrible condition of the child, and somewhat cowed by the fierce, powerful look in Mary's eyes, agreed.

In London, Mary turned a closet into a room where Ida could be shut safely away when Mary was with a "customer."

When Ida was five, Mary's sister, still ashamed of what had transpired, asked her to send Ida to live on the farm. "I'll suffer no more vile nonsense from my husband," she said. So Mary sent Ida there, and visited her from time to time.

When Ida was seventeen, she ran away. Mary, distraught, looked for her in London, not even knowing if that had been her destination. A year later, she still hadn't found her.

It was at that time that I met a lovely girl with eyes the blue of forget-me-nots and hair only a little less bright than the yellow of daffodils. It was springtime and it seemed to me she carried about her the scented air of that season. She worked in one of the finest brothels in London, a place furnished with oriental carpets, crystal chandeliers, and golden silk curtains that I recognized as made from silk I myself had imported.

When, one night, Mary entered the downstairs parlour on her ongoing quest to find her daughter,

I was just kissing my inamorata goodbye until my much-anticipated next visit.

Mary saw us, cried out, and fell to the floor. The girl in my arms ran to her, calling out, "Mother!"

When Mary had recovered enough to speak, she looked at me with eyes such as the Angel of Death might possess and said, "Richard, Ida is your daughter."

"How can you possibly know that?" I said, and immediately felt ashamed.

She paused for a moment, anger upon her still lovely face, and said, "Have you not seen the birthmark, that strange mouselike shape on her arm, exactly like the one on yours?"

"No," I said, still not believing, not wanting to believe.

Mary pulled Ida to her and pushed up her sleeve, revealing the mark. I should have cried out, should have fallen as if struck by hammer blows, but I was frozen to the spot, dumb with horror.

Some time later, I found myself sitting with the two of them, not remembering how I got there. Was I led to the settee, blind, my legs as heavy and clumsy as those of an automaton?

Ida cried quietly as Mary held her hand. And so the three of us, three pale souls withdrawn from the fleshly scene nearby, sat in a corner of that gaudy, falsely comforting, falsely embracing room, as Mary told the story I've just recounted.

And, gentle reader, you are no doubt gentle no longer. (If I am to have a reader at all.) Mary was indeed the proclaimer of my death, which I shall in a moment accomplish with the pistol on the table in front of me. My penultimate act is to put this account in an envelope addressed to the *Times*, in the hope that they will publish it as a warning to other men, and as an opportunity for condemnation of men's misuse of women.

I have used my own name, but changed those of the two innocents.

Goodbye, and shed no tear for me, but only for the girls and women who have suffered from the likes of me, that whole monstrous horde of men.

END

Carol,

This Richard Wilson could be a previous incarnation of me, or a surrogate pound of flesh. Except that *I didn't sleep with Jacintha*. That brief moment on the beach was far from a *consummation*, and I'm thankful I never went any further.

Love,

Richard

Carol,

I had hoped you would send me a response to this story, but you seem to be sticking to your resolution. Maybe you will relent.

Still hoping,

Richard

THIRTY-SIX

CAROL SAT WITH Frances over tea in the kitchen while Richard rested upstairs. Last night she'd dreamed Jacintha was a little girl and Richard was molesting her, and woke thinking, *No, it's not as bad as that.* But the reality was awful, unheard of. No, not unheard of; it must have happened before, a father and daughter thinking they were strangers. But had it happened like this, a daughter attempting to seduce a man she knew to be her father, and he ignorant of the fact? And what if it had gone further than kisses? Sometimes she couldn't help picturing them together and would groan with pain.

"I've been doing some research on incest," Frances said.

"Mother, please, no." Carol gulped her tea down the wrong way and coughed frantically.

Frances patted her back and waited for her to get her breath back.

Carol, lifting her hand to wipe her mouth, knocked over her cup. She watched the tea flow across the polished table, watched as it began to drip into her lap.

Frances grabbed a tea towel and wiped the table and dabbed at Carol's skirt. Carol pushed her hand away. "It's all right. I don't care about my skirt. I don't care about anything."

"Will you just listen for a couple of minutes? I found out some interesting facts. It gave me some perspective on Richard's situation, to learn about actual incest."

"'Richard's *situation*,'" Carol said, watching the stream of hot tea Frances was pouring into her righted cup. Frances pushed a plate of digestive biscuits toward her.

"Have you been eating at all?"

"No, just drinking." Carol had been eating very little and had been unable to sleep. She was lonely, too, and had thought once or twice that she might go to Nick for comfort. But she hadn't done so, and her body was numb now, with not a whisper of desire. She hadn't told Nick that Richard wouldn't come home to be with her, only that he was going through a bad time because of the stabbing and she needed to be there for him. That had been true; she had realized she still loved Richard as much as ever. What she felt for Nick, she wasn't sure about. After all, she had known him for such a short time.

Nick had been disappointed and told her if things didn't work out with Richard, he would be waiting for her.

"Carol," Frances said, "I'm talking to you. You need to eat. I'll bring you some bread and cheese. And I have some nice tomatoes, last of the harvest."

"Please, please, don't fuss. I can't stand it. I don't want anything."

"All right," Frances said and dropped down into a chair opposite Carol. "Listen, I've discovered in my reading that the taboo

against incest had some almost comically practical reasons in earlier times and in primitive societies."

"Oh, comical, I'll bet. I guess if I don't want to hear this, I'll have
to leave," Carol said. But she made no move to go; instead, avoiding Frances, she looked out the window at the intense green of the
rhododendron leaves, kept staring at them as though to memorize
the particular shade for all time while Frances continued.

"Really. Let me make it clear I'm not talking about the use and
abuse of children. That, of course, is universally repugnant. So.
Practical reasons. Plutarch said if a girl married her father, she'd
have no family to run to in case of a quarrel. Seems unbelievable,
doesn't it? And in New Guinea, when Margaret Mead asked a
man of the Arapesh tribe about the idea of marrying his sister,
he objected only on the grounds that if he did that, he wouldn't
have a brother-in-law to hunt with and to visit. But, of course, in
ancient Egypt, kings and queens married their sisters and broth-
ers, and at least one pope had relations with his daughter, Lucrezia
Borgia, and —"

"Stop. I don't want to hear any of this. What makes you think
history could help me deal with this pain? Just shut up."

"All right. Sorry."

Carol stared out at the cold rain that had begun to batter the
windowpane as unrelentingly as tears of rage or mourning. When
she turned, she caught a look of pity on Frances's face, and became
acutely aware of what Frances must be seeing: her tangled hair and
her baggy and crumpled clothes. Her body smelled, too.

She started to cry and Frances went to her, pulled her up and
held her tight. They stood swaying together for a full minute.

"He didn't know. Christ, Mother, he didn't know."

"I know, darling. He really did nothing wrong."

"You can't say that. Wanting her was wrong."

"You are being illogical. He thought she was a stranger."

"He *desired* her."

"He says he didn't."

"Oh, shit, I'm so confused."

"I know. But listen. It's rare but not unheard of for a father and daughter who've been separated since the daughter's early childhood to meet and be attracted to each other, and knowing they're related, to still go ahead. And Richard didn't know and didn't go ahead. No matter how he felt, that's a couple of degrees away from culpability."

"Culpability. Histories. Just words. What I can't bear ..." Carol's voice cracked. She fought off tears. "What I can't bear ..."

"What is it, dear? What can't you bear?"

Carol sobbed, trying to get the words out. "I can't bear that he was in love with her."

"No. There's no reason to think that. We don't know that."

"I know."

"You can't know."

"I saw him, Mother. I saw it in his face. That's what's so terrible. For him, too, don't you see?"

"No, you've imagined it. Any attraction was a passing thing, and now he feels nothing for her but anger. And he has a great fear of losing you, Carol. It's you he loves."

"No," Carol said, but she felt a faint tremor of hope.

THIRTY-SEVEN

RICHARD PHONED JACINTHA two days after he'd told Carol what Jacintha was threatening him with. His hand trembled as he pushed the buttons. Jacintha answered on the third ring.

"It's me," he said.

"Richard, I'm very glad you called." Her voice was eager.

"No. No. Listen. I told my wife."

"Aah."

"So you've nothing ... I mean, there's nothing you can do ..."

"I have no leverage?"

"Yes."

"I could tell her you're lying, that something did happen. Or I could tell the university that something happened."

"I'm quitting, so the university doesn't matter. But I beg you not to lie to Carol."

"I wouldn't, anyway. I wanted to hurt you in the beginning, but you know how much I've changed. I just thought if Carol was the only one standing in our way … How did she take it?"

Richard was shaking. He dragged the phone toward a chair, jerking the tangled cord, tripped, righted himself, sat down. How could Frances not have a cordless phone?

"How the hell do you think she took it?" he said. "She was devastated. Horrified."

"Of course."

"Anyway, it's none of your business. I want you to leave us alone now."

She was silent for several heartbeats. Then, "I love you, Richard. We can still go away together where nobody knows us, and start again. I know you love me."

"Haven't you been listening? No, goddamn it! No!"

They were both silent through several of Richard's pounding heartbeats.

"Don't hang up, Richard."

"Did you believe any of it?" Richard asked. His anger felt good. It stomped on other feelings he didn't want to allow to surface.

"Any of what?"

"Olympics protests. Saving the environment. All that."

"I believe in anything that upsets the stupid, greedy bastards of this world."

"But you're not really committed to any cause, are you?"

"I do care about the environment, but you're right. I'm more interested in general shit disturbing. But I can let that go, for your sake. For you."

"I'm going to hang up now. Don't contact me again. Don't make it any worse."

"Not worse. Truer, better. I know you love me."

"No, I pity you. I regret that I've hurt you."

"You haven't hurt me. You've given me —"

"Get help, Jacintha." It hurt to say her name.

He hung up and sat for a long time, trying to calm himself.

He prayed that she wouldn't try to see him or talk to him again, and, eyes closed, his prayer was like a dark, protective shroud around him. And then the shroud was filled with her presence, and he groaned aloud.

Two weeks went by without any calls or emails from Jacintha.

He phoned Beth: "How are you? Has your wound healed?"

"Yes. Yours?"

"Yes, well, some wounds never heal."

"I know."

"Uh, Beth, how's Jacintha? Is she … is she still living with you?"

"No, she left without saying anything, about two weeks ago. I phoned her parents. They don't know where she is, either. They said that in the past she sometimes went travelling without telling them. Maybe she did that."

Has she gone away with Skitch? Richard thought. *But surely she wouldn't take up with him again, after what he did?* But he didn't know what she might do, what she was capable of.

"Good news, though," Beth said. "The UBC theatre department has promised to help us stage our *Tempest* when John and Anna and I have finished writing it. Isn't that great?"

"Yes, great." He was ashamed of how little he cared.

THIRTY-EIGHT

RICHARD COULDN'T BE sure that Jacintha had given up on him, but it seemed she had, and because of that hope, he resumed his routine at Frances's more calmly than before. After his daily walk, he spent an hour on chores — vacuuming, doing laundry, cleaning the bathroom. He liked the mindlessness of the work, could stop thinking about himself as he scrubbed, sorted, folded, and pushed and pulled the vacuum cleaner. It was literally mind-numbing. *Poor stay-at-home housewives*, he thought, and felt a flicker of self-approval for having sympathy for someone outside his immediate concern.

He made lunch, which was engaging rather than numbing because he looked forward to it so much — the sizzle of a steak or a hamburger in the pan, the pungency of onions as they fried.

He'd taken to eating mostly meat, fanatically and slaveringly. He sometimes sliced a tomato or threw a few lettuce leaves on the plate, mostly to please Frances, who warned against constipation and high cholesterol. If Frances was there at lunch, she made herself a large salad and accepted a few thin slices of meat. She urged Richard to eat fruit. A full bowl of oranges, apples, pears, and kiwis always stood on the table. Sometimes he would eat half an apple or pear.

"Is it a childhood thing, I wonder," she said of his meat gorging, "or something atavistic?"

"I don't remember liking meat very much as a child — not beef, anyway — so it must be something else. A new taste for blood, perhaps," he said with a grim laugh.

After lunch he always walked again, going farther afield. Sometimes he walked to within a block of Jericho Beach, but he always turned back before he got there. As in a waking dream, he would see a madder version of that mad night, see himself lying bleeding as Jacintha and a crowd of wild-haired women danced around him, and men drummed and shouted, and the moon poured down too brightly, making sharp, frightening shadows.

On his way home, he picked up more meat and planned dinner as he walked. He'd never cooked much before, so he kept it simple. At first Frances objected, partly in self-defence, to his cooking all their lunches and dinners, but quickly realized that cooking was the one thing that gave him some small pleasure, and so she put up with the house smelling constantly of beef and bacon.

Frances had started teaching watercolour painting at the Carnegie Community Centre at Main and Hastings, two afternoons a week. Richard didn't know exactly what she did on other afternoons, and he didn't ask. Most evenings she was either in her bedroom or her studio. Sometimes she sat with him and they talked a little, or she read while he watched TV, but he preferred to be alone. (Being indoors felt relatively comfortable now; somewhat

safer than being outdoors. The claustrophobia he'd suffered after
the landslide had disappeared.)

He watched TV for hours at a time, but avoided anything
romantic. He couldn't bear to see people either happy or unhappy
in love. Comedy programs were banal and maddeningly cheer-
ful, and movies were almost always about love and sex when they
weren't about violence. And there was always too much plot. He
found he couldn't stand *stories*, he who had been an avid devourer
of plays and novels. He couldn't read anymore. There was poetry,
of course, but if a poem had even the slightest whiff of a narrative,
the emotion was usually too intense for him.

What he'd discovered were reality shows. *Hoarders* was the first
one he found: men and women drowning under piles of their useless possessions. They were all seeking security. No one could get to
them without wading through garbage. And since no one could heal
their broken hearts, there was no point in letting anyone reach them.

Richard thought of them as unwitting gurus who demonstrated
the futility of lusting after security in *things*. They took the quest
to its absurd end, mocking the rich who attempted to buy security
with cars and mansions and diamonds. All were things to wade
through. None impenetrable. You could triple-bolt doors, carry a
gun, build a seemingly solid house, but there were battering rams,
other gun-wielders, and cliffs that could fall and bury you; storms
that could drown you.

He watched *Hoarders* until any episode became too confronta-
tional, mother or father against son or daughter. Then he'd turn to
a sports channel and watch hockey, basketball, car racing, whatever
he could find, often with the sound off. Tonight he'd just turned to
TSN when Frances called down from upstairs.

"Richard. Will you make sure the front door is locked?"

"Sure," Richard shouted. (He checked the door frequently. The
irony didn't escape him — a modicum of security against one small
woman.) "And the back door and all the windows, too," he added.

"What?"

"Nothing. Good night, Frances."

Richard sat on Frances's front porch, watching a film crew working outside the house, across the street. Hardly anything was going on, but he found it fascinating, nevertheless. A high energy stirred the air and belied the casual postures of the men and women standing around the parked vans. The vans had wheezed and roared into position the day before, and soon the workers clanked lengths of metal and cables and other pieces of equipment onto the sidewalk and carried them, along with furniture and lights, into the house. The movie had two stars, neither of whom interested Richard. Anyway, they'd probably be whisked in and out of the house pretty quickly.

A lot of the time, the crew members were quite idle, waiting for something. He liked the mystery of it, and the unaccountably high energy that persisted in spite of the endless waiting. He waited, too, but after a while he didn't care whether anything happened or not.

The workers seemed to him like magician's helpers who knew how the illusion was being created but weren't jaded, still felt the magic the way a future audience would feel it. After a long while, he heard a voice from on high saying, "Quiet, please. We're rolling." The atmosphere shifted slightly — ears pricked, noses lifted, bodies shifted.

Richard thought of the actors in the house. One would maybe feel lucky to have got the role. He would move to his mark, speak the line until he got it right. It didn't matter what the line was. It had been written by someone else, and another someone had positioned the light and shone it on him. And maybe on the third reading he would start to believe he was the character he was playing, and a heat, a bliss of satisfaction, would fill him. He'd done what he came to do.

Cut! Good work. You nailed it!

Why, Richard asked himself, was he enjoying this whole thing so much? He'd seen hundreds of movies and he knew how they were made, but still, this was in the nature of a revelation. He couldn't dismiss the feeling that he'd been shown something important as he sat watching a world being created behind closed doors a few short steps away, a written and directed world with the actors saying and doing what they must.

He had always thought he was the main author, if not the sole one, of his life — as did most people. He had set the terrible events in motion when he chose to have sex with Jacintha's mother, a woman he had no love for, and then walked away, knowing she was pregnant. If only there had been an author and director with a better plot.

But then immediately he thought, *If there's a scriptwriting god, here is his plot for me: I abandon a pregnant woman, which results in me eventually almost sleeping with my own daughter.*

And here is Scriptwriter God's plot for most of the men who abandon a woman: they never hear from her or their child again, and if they do, it's all open and above board, and it's for uniting a family, or for medical or financial reasons.

Why is our hero singled out? Answer: *I'm not, because there is no omnipotent goddamned scriptwriter, and I'm no hero.* But couldn't Jacintha just as easily, in the vast world of possible endings, not have been bent on revenge?

Maybe the god who had stepped into his life was Eros, and not a scriptwriter but a rogue director, by turns mischievous, treacherous, enchanting, and punishing. "I'm ready for my heartbreak, Mr. Eros."

THIRTY-NINE

JACINTHA WAS VISITING Skitch in a farmhouse in the Fraser Valley, an hour's bus ride from Vancouver.

She hadn't seen him since the day after he attacked Richard, when he had told her how he'd found the DNA test result and lost his mind over her sexual relationship with her own father. She'd told him that day she had had no sexual relationship with Richard. And she'd told him about her revenge scheme and how it had changed, how she had fallen in love. She had been very angry with Skitch and he had begged for forgiveness.

"At least nobody died," Skitch had said.

"No, nobody died."

He asked if she was going to turn him in.

"No," she said. "For the same reason you are not going to put out gossip about this anonymously. It would harm Richard and his

family if information about me and him became known, and I don't
want that. It would harm me, too. And if I got you arrested, it would
probably come out in court. Besides, I don't want you to go to jail."

He had said how shitty he felt, especially about Beth, and asked
if she was okay.

"They'll both be all right. Physically," Jacintha said.

The next day, Skitch had apparently left the city.

Now, all these weeks later, he had phoned Jacintha and asked
if they could talk. She told him she was leaving the country and
would like to come and say goodbye to him in person, and could
she have his address.

"As long as you have forgiven me, at least a little," he said, with
a nervous laugh.

"A little," she said. "At first I hated you, and hated that I couldn't
punish you somehow, but ..."

"But you noticed revenge could bite you in the ass."

"Yes, fuckin' right on, my little Skitch."

He was quiet for a moment, then said softly and sadly, "I would
have lost you anyway. You were never going to tell him the truth,
were you?"

"No."

She had arrived with a suitcase, saying she planned to go straight
to the Vancouver airport later that day.

"Whose house is this?" she asked.

"My grandfather's. He died a couple of months ago, and my parents wanted a house-sitter while they get organized to sell the place."

"Sorry about your grandfather."

"We weren't close. He was a nasty old bastard. Good timing,
though. I needed a hideout."

"Not really."

"Well, I didn't want to run into Richard on some street." He
said *Richard* with a sneer. "He might have changed his mind about
having me arrested."

"I already told you why he wouldn't do that. And anyway, I'm pretty sure he takes full blame for what drove you to it, and I take full blame, too."

"And I stuck in the knife, so that's three full blames. Bad arithmetic."

"Geometry."

"What?"

"The triangle. Not intrinsically bad, but bad in this case. And I put you into it."

"There you go again with the big words."

"Don't play dumb."

They sat down to eat microwaved pizza and drink a passable cup of coffee made by Skitch. Jacintha avoided talking any more about the past over lunch. Not good for the digestion and, besides, she saw how vulnerable Skitch was. He had let his hair grow into short, soft spikes, and looked so young — a boy with too-pale skin and large, worried eyes.

"You look like a hedgehog," she said.

After a moment of confusion, Skitch smiled and patted his head.

"I'm worried about you, you know," he said.

"I'll be all right. I don't have another long-lost father to fall in love with," she said, and laughed.

"Jesus, don't joke about it."

"I worry about you, too. Promise me you will never do something so foolish and violent again."

"I promise. But listen, what if you stayed around and got to know your father in a different way? Shit, I'm assuming you aren't still with him."

"I'm not, but I can't stay."

"Why not?"

"Because I made him love me in the wrong way and he wants me out of his life. If I don't go, he might grow to hate me more than he hates me now."

"I don't think he hates you."

Jacintha said nothing, eyes downcast.

"Shit, what a screw-up. But fucking hell, Jacintha, what made you do it? Go after him like that, and then get so hung up on him?"

"Let me tell you about a woman from the southern U.S. that I met on my travels."

"Don't dodge the question."

"I'm not. Just listen. This woman told me that her teenaged son used to get into her bed and try it on with her. She said she just told him to get out every time. I asked her if that made her very upset, and she said — and here is the killer sentence — 'No, he was just a highly individualistic kid,' in her heavy drawl. *Haaaly individooolistic.* So can't you think of me as just a highly individualistic kid?"

"Shit, that's funny. But you are kind of dodging the question."

"There's a kernel of truth there that applies to me. And I can't cry all the time."

She let Skitch take her in his arms then. He held her close and said, "I love you."

"You'll find someone else," she said.

"I know, but why couldn't it have been you?"

"I don't know, but that is one of the saddest questions in the world."

"Don't cry," he said. "Do you have to go? You can stay here with me as long as you like."

"No, I have to keep moving," she said. "I need distractions. The Mexican sun. Hot food, hot music."

"And hot men."

"Yes, those, too. Could you please call me a taxi now to get me to the bus back to the airport?"

*   *   *

In the taxi, she opened her suitcase. She had packed lightly, not counting the things that were heavy with memory and loss. She took out her camera to look yet again at the photo of Richard she had taken in class when his attention was on another student who had asked a question. He looked so handsome, with a lively, engaged expression and a slight smile. She put the camera back into the suitcase, alongside her mother's photo taken in the pub, and Blake's *Songs of Innocence*, and lifted out a small towel in which nestled the clay dog she had stolen. She stroked its bristly back for a moment, then carefully wrapped it up again. Precious mementoes.

Maybe she would be less sad as time went on if she could think of Richard as a part of her, she herself a kind of memento. Flesh of his flesh. Never parted.

FORTY

"LET'S INVITE CAROL over for dinner on Friday night," Frances said. "She's ready to see you."

Frances had visited Carol a couple of times in the past week, but Carol had yet to visit Richard again.

"Oh, I don't know."

"She's been trying hard to understand what happened and says she sees you were more sinned against than sinning."

"Oh, Christ!"

"Richard, you'll have to join the real world sooner or later."

"You have no idea how real my world is."

"You know what I mean."

"Here's some good news. I actually cried when I saw a starving child on TV last night."

"You congratulate yourself for realizing that someone is worse off than you are?"

"No, of course not. I just mean the scar tissue has thinned a little, or the scab is cracking, letting in some air and light. Or some other cockamamie metaphor to say my self-pity eased up for a minute or two, that's all."

"That's all? It's better than nothing."

"It's minimal."

"How about it, then? Carol on Friday?"

"All right, but I fear it won't go well."

"You might be surprised."

"I'm a bit averse to surprises these days."

"Yes, I know. I meant pleasantly surprised."

They decided on a menu and then sat with their drinks, watching the fire in the fireplace as it spat and crackled.

"Green wood," Richard said.

"Just a bit damp, I think," Frances said. "Richard, why don't you have a look at Aubrey's books? That shelf just to your right has his philosophy collection."

"I find it hard to read these days. Can't concentrate."

Frances got up and took a book from the shelf. "Marcus Aurelius, *Meditations*," she said. "Aubrey loved this, read it frequently — to keep himself humble, he said. There's a lot about the futility of wanting fame, and Aubrey tended to want fame. But it has a lot of other wisdom, too."

She handed the book to Richard. He looked at the cover photo of a bust of Aurelius in bronze, or maybe gold. A sad face, it seemed to him. He opened the book and read silently: "One philosopher goes shirtless; another bookless; a third, only half-clad, says, 'Bread have I none, yet still I cleave to reason.'"

I'm bookless, he thought, *my books drowned like Prospero's, although Prospero chose to engage more fully with the world through reason, whereas I've turned away from the world and my reason is shaky.*

"What did you find?" Frances asked.

Richard read aloud the line about cleaving to reason.

"Good advice," Frances said.

"Unless you're half-mad."

"Don't dramatize. You're not mad at all. Only suffering."

Richard sipped his Scotch and savoured the rich, smoky taste — a moment or two without suffering.

On Friday morning, Richard made an apple pie using a frozen crust from the freezer. He couldn't do pastry, so it would have to be without a top crust or fancy latticing. Standing rib roast was as simple as could be. It was in the oven by four o'clock. Carol was arriving at six. He kept busy enough to hold his nervousness at bay, but by five o'clock he had begun to sweat and his hand shook as he poured himself a straight Scotch. He took the bottle and his glass upstairs and ran a deep bath. He was still in the tub, the hot water having been replenished several times, the Scotch not quite as often, when the doorbell rang.

Half-drunk, he had trouble dressing. Buttoned his shirt wrong, rebuttoned it, found he'd put on one grey sock and one black. Spent several minutes choosing between jacket and sweater, jeans and grey flannels. Was halfway downstairs in jeans and tweed jacket when he realized he hadn't combed his hair. Went back up.

He could hear Frances and Carol speaking softly in the kitchen. Smelled the meat and vegetables. Delicious. Nauseating.

He sat down in the living room.

"Richard, there you are," Frances said from the kitchen doorway. "Come in here and join us."

He sat down without looking at Carol. Looked at a plate of crudités.

Carol picked it up and held it out to him, an offering. "The dip Frances made for these is good," she said.

"No thanks." He looked into her eyes.

She kept holding the plate aloft.

"Oh, Richard," she said and set the plate down hard.

The clattering made Frances, who was fussing with something at the counter, jump and turn around. She turned away again, quickly.

"Richard," Carol said again, and started to cry.

"Don't," Richard said. "Don't."

But she kept on crying.

"Could we open that wine, Frances?" Richard asked.

Frances poured three glasses. "The roast needs to rest a while," she said, and left the room with her wine.

Carol shuddered, wiped her eyes on her sleeve, stared at him, her eyes too round. "How are you?"

"I don't know."

"You look quite well. Are you feeling a bit better?"

He wanted to scream at her effort at normality. "Yes. I guess. A bit."

"That's good."

In the silence that followed, Richard could hear the hundreds of unsaid words, cries, accusations, lamentations.

"This is so awful," Carol said at last. "I miss you. Won't you talk to me?"

"I don't know what to say. My vocabulary has become strangely inadequate."

"I know. I know. Don't worry. I can see I shouldn't push you. I'm glad I can just sit here with you for a while."

"I don't think I'll be able to eat anything," Richard said.

"Neither will I."

"Look, I'm sorry, I literally don't know what to say. Only, I'm sorry I hurt you." He heard his cold, matter-of-fact tone, but felt incapable of saying the words with feeling. "I think I need to lie down for a while. Will you excuse me? Sorry to be so formal. Absurd. Sorry." He stood up abruptly, almost knocking over his chair, walked clumsily from the room, his legs like lead. Upstairs, he lay on his bed, his heart pounding.

When he heard footsteps on the stairs, he prayed it wasn't Carol. From outside his closed door, Frances said, "She's gone. But she said she'll be back, maybe in a couple of days. She says she knows how hard it is for you."

Richard said nothing and Frances left. Then, with a sense of relief, he cried, not for himself this time, but for Carol.

FORTY-ONE

RICHARD SAT IN the dark cabin with his overcoat on, clutching a glass of Scotch and watching the sky lowering between the fir trees. It would rain soon.

Memories erupted painfully, as though they'd been lodged in his flesh — small, silent explosions. Or buzzed like bluebottles in his ear; swat and flail at one and another attacked. The faint, teasing whispers were the worst: bittersweet reminders of things never to come again.

He'd found the cabin on the Sunshine Coast — a misnomer for a place that seemed in winter as grey and wet as anywhere else in BC — in an online ad, met the owner for keys and directions, handed over a certified cheque, and was on the ferry the next day. He'd left a note for Frances saying he was going away for a while, not to worry, but didn't tell her where. He'd bolted to avoid Carol's imminent visit and the threatened visit from Gabe to discuss his "concerns."

The waters of the Georgia Strait were near but not near enough to see or hear. He'd thought of going to the west coast of Vancouver Island, but the trip was much longer, and also his memories of his honeymoon in Tofino with Carol might have added another level of pain.

The village, here by the less-primal waters, was only a mile away from the cabin, and would be easy to walk to when he needed to call a taxi to the ferry. The place was well equipped for off-season rental, but had no phone (he still had no cellphone) or TV or radio, which suited him fine. He'd brought along two bottles of wine, and one of Scotch. He'd had the taxi from the ferry wait at the village store while he picked up canned beans, tuna, sardines, soup, bread, butter, jam, honey, apples, eggs, coffee, and milk.

He drank until he fell asleep in the chair. When he woke, stiff and cold, he found the thermostat, turned on the furnace, ate some bread and cheese, undressed, and fell into bed. He dreamed terrible dreams, of which he couldn't remember the details in the morning — only that he'd been threatened and shamed in a kind of dim, confusing purgatory by people he thought he should know but couldn't place.

After a breakfast of toast, a fried egg, and coffee (plus Tylenol and two glasses of water for his hangover), he set out for the beach. When he arrived, he found that he and an elderly woman walking a dog were the only ones out there. There was always someone walking a dog. The woman wore the costume du jour: running shoes and a thick fleece hoodie. Her Lhasa Apso was off his leash and bounding ahead of her, rushing with mad enthusiasm at seagulls. Richard was glad to see the woman briskly following the dog. He didn't want to talk to anyone.

He sat on a log, watching the waves crash on the shore, over and over. A satisfying, heavy sound. Roar, swoosh, roar, swoosh.

His mind was blessedly empty for seconds at a time. Roar, swoosh, roar, swoosh.

He took a few deep breaths of the salty air. It was the first time he'd been to a beach since he was stabbed; he had been a bit nervous about how he might react, but it was all right. If it were dark, it would be different. He was pretty sure he couldn't face a beach after dark, but here, in the drizzly daylight with the tide going out and the solid log under him, and no one but the woman and the dog sharing the beach, he could almost relax.

Someone else was striding toward him. A man — medium height with a square, sturdy build, wearing jeans, a windbreaker, a toque. Panic overcame Richard and he ran back to the trail and was halfway to the road when he turned to see if anyone was behind him. No one. He walked swiftly back to the cabin, where he closed the curtains and locked the door.

He drank a glass of wine, sat still until his heart slowed down, and finally concluded that he'd been a fool and that he must guard against paranoia.

What had he really come here for? To try to escape. The crazed squirrel in the cage. He could understand how men ended up sleeping under dirty blankets in doorways. How many of them couldn't forgive themselves for some crime against their wives and children?

"You can't change the past, only how you think about it," was one of the current mantras. But how do you change your thinking about the unthinkable?

Maybe if he wrote some of his thoughts down. He found his notebook and a pen, thought a bit, but nothing came to him. Not a word.

He poured himself more wine, drank it down quickly, poured another glass, and drank half of that.

He dug into his duffle bag and found the Marcus Aurelius book. He'd grabbed it from a shelf just as he was leaving Frances's house. He needed some professional philosophy now. Stoical input.

Hell, yes. Now is the time for stoicism. He laughed, already a bit drunk.

He opened the book at random and read: "Accustom yourself to give careful attention to what others are saying, and try your best to enter into the mind of the speaker." Whose mind should he enter? Jacintha seemed the logical choice. She'd been saying a lot, and he remembered so much of it word for word. "It was the way I knew you would suffer the most." He wrote this down in his notebook.

She'd said, "We have to stay together. I'm flesh of your flesh." *Get inside her mind. She's happy believing she owns me, but I have to make her unhappy for her own good, to save her.*

"Our connection isn't really about sex; it's an expression of our deeper connection, a marriage of our souls," she'd said. "A kind of holy ritual."

If our bodies joined. Flesh of my flesh. No! I can't think about that.

He threw the notebook across the room.

Enough of this useless pondering. He needed a distraction. No damned radio. He had a newspaper. Might as well see what was happening in the crazy, fucked-up world at large. On most days there were hordes of the criminally insane roaming freely.

He decided to bypass the front-page articles, full of international tensions, wars, and local incidences of violence. Names and places changed, but little else.

Further inside the paper he saw a small item about a man in the U.S. who had thought, one night, that an intruder was on his porch. He shot first and looked afterward. He had killed his son, who was coming home late from a party.

Poor, stupid bastard.

And here was another one. A teenaged boy had beaten his sister for flirting with boys. "It was my duty," he said.

The next item Richard noticed was about a proposed form of birth control: go into space. It seemed that astronauts' sperm count went down. Laughing, he had a vision of thousands of criminals being shot into space to keep Earth's gene pool pure, a modern alternative to shipping them to Australia, as England did in the nineteenth century.

He turned a page and his eye was caught by the story of an unmarried woman being stoned to death for having an affair. He didn't go on reading.

"Shit, shit, shit," he said and threw the paper down.

When he finally fell into bed, he had a dream. He was locked in a closet the way his mother had locked him in once, as a punishment. In the dream he was his adult self and Jacintha, about six years old, was sitting beside him, crying. Some of her tears fell on his hand as he reached out for her cheek. Then heavy footsteps approached the door, a growl. "It's a bear — he'll get us," she said, so much fear in her voice. "No, we'll be all right," he said, but she didn't seem to hear him. "He'll get us," she said, and then was gone.

Someone was opening the closet door. His cry woke him up. His heart was pounding. He'd felt Jacintha's fear as though it were his own. He'd felt her terrible sadness. He hadn't been able to help her as a child, and he couldn't help her now.

He lay still for a while, letting his wretchedness engulf him. Maybe that was all he needed to do: sink into the pain, not try to avoid it or rationalize it. Stay with it, drown in it, let it take its course. Maybe it would end. Maybe it would never end.

She needed my protection, he thought. *She wanted my heart before she was born.*

He tossed all night with dreams and nightmares. When he woke, it was out of a dream of Emily, in which she'd been looking at him with pleading eyes. He couldn't help Jacintha, but he could help Emily. He *would* help her. He'd go back to Vancouver this morning and look for her.

He packed quickly, didn't bother about breakfast. He had a mission now and it gave him crazy hope, crazy because there were so many reasons to fail: he might not find her, and then might not find a way to help her. Still, he felt a buoyancy he hadn't felt for a very long time.

He left all the food and booze for the next tenant. A nice surprise — the expensive Cabernet and the Glenfiddich Scotch — and the thought of that added to his tentative feeling of good humour.

FORTY-TWO

RICHARD GOT OFF the bus from the ferry at Georgia and Granville, climbed onto a No. 4, Powell bus, stepped off at Carrall Street, then walked up to Hastings. His plan had been to walk the few blocks to Main Street on the off chance that Emily was among the crowd selling their wares — salvaged things, maybe some stolen things — on blankets on the sidewalk. Drug dealers, and blank-eyed users, and women who might or might not be hookers leaned against buildings or paced nervously back and forth.

But as soon as he stepped onto Hastings Street, he saw that a couple of blocks farther along the street had been cordoned off, and dozens of people, mostly women, were milling about, singing. Several women were drumming. As he got closer, he saw placards that read Our Sisters and Daughters Are Dying. Does Anybody

Care? and We Demand Action for First Nations Women, and many others along the same lines.

In spite of his sympathy for the cause, he couldn't face joining the rally, or even trying to make his way through it. He decided to backtrack and find a way down to Cordova, but as he was about to turn around, he saw a woman with shiny blond hair in the middle of the crowd. He couldn't see her face, but he could see she was wearing a sea-green jacket. And when she looked his way briefly, his heart jumped and he was almost sure it was Jacintha.

He walked quickly toward her, keeping to the sidewalk, which was less congested. Even so, he bumped into a woman, who yelled at him and hit him on his back, not too hard, thankfully, with her placard. He'd walked only a block but it had seemed to take forever.

He arrived breathless across from the blond woman, keeping himself shielded from her sight by the others standing near her. He breathed in sharply when he saw that it wasn't Jacintha. An attractive face, but not her face.

Shaken, he somehow got through the intersection at Main Street and continued eastward. What had he been thinking? He should have run in the other direction if he thought it was Jacintha. But the truth was he hadn't been thinking at all. What would he have done if it had been her? He had thought that her being far away was essential to his peace of mind. But was it peace of mind he wanted? More than seeing her once more?

But this was no time for wallowing in confusion. Emily was his mission now. He would go to Powell and Hawks, only a few blocks away, to the corner where he'd first met her. Maybe she was still working there.

She wasn't. The woman there now stood smoking, wearing a silver-sequined bolero over a tank top that revealed her ample breasts. She didn't speak, smiled weakly. He could see she was high on something.

"I'm looking for a young woman called Emily who used to be on this corner. Do you know her?"

"No."

"Are you sure? She's about eighteen, small, olive skinned, dark hair in a ponytail."

"Don't know her."

"How long have you been at this spot?"

"A month or so."

"And she hasn't been here?"

"No. Listen, I can give you what you want," she said, her words slurred.

"No, sorry. Thanks for talking to me."

She giggled and waved one hand limply, a gesture so pitiful that Richard wished she had cursed him instead.

Where could he go next? Other corners? There were places all the way from Main to Clark Drive. He'd seen a women's centre on Cordova. Near Gore? He'd go there first.

When he entered the centre, a dead silence greeted him. Several women stared at him, frozen as in a child's game of Statues. A pockmarked woman broke the silence, shouting, "Get out, asshole."

"Now, Crystal, there's no need for that," said a middle-aged woman, walking toward him. "Can I help you? I'm Joyce. I'm in charge today. Sorry, but men aren't really welcome here."

"I'm looking for a young woman called Emily. I helped her once when she was in trouble and I want to find out how she's doing. She used to work at the corner of Hawks and Powell."

An argument broke out at a table holding an array of soaps and shampoos and cosmetics. "Why the fuck can't I have two? Sometimes I'm in a pink mood and sometimes I'm in a god-damned red mood." The woman was waving two tubes of lipstick in the air, one in each hand.

"Because we have to ration them, so everyone can have one."

"What bullshit! Look. There's dozens in that box." She put the two lipsticks in a pocket and walked away.

"Please come back," the volunteer at the table said.

"Fuck off, fuckin' bitch."

"Wendy! Don't talk to Gina like that," Joyce called after her. "She's giving up her free time to help us out. And put one of those back."

"You fuck off, too," said Wendy, and left the building.

"Sorry about that. Most of our clients are grateful, but some have emotional problems, you know."

"Yes, I know," Richard said. "About Emily."

"Women! Does anyone know an Emily who used to work at Powell and Hawks?"

"Skinny broad?" a woman, very skinny herself, asked.

"Yes. About eighteen. Five feet tall. Olive skin."

"Yeah, I think her mom lives on Haida Gwaii. Haven't seen Emily for quite a while. She might have gone home. Or she might have left town with her asshole boyfriend. Or maybe some pervert killer has got her."

"Let's hope not," Joyce said. "Anyone else?"

Sullen murmurs.

"Why do you want to know?" the skinny woman asked.

"I want to see if she's all right. Help her if I can."

A couple of women hooted. "That'd be a change," one of them said.

"You could try the police," Joyce said.

Richard thanked them and left.

He was exhausted and couldn't face going to the police station. He'd go tomorrow. This part of town could drain you after a very short while. God help the people who lived here.

When he got to Frances's, Carol was there.

"Richard, where the hell have you been? We've been crazy with worry."

"Sechelt. Please, not now. I'm all right. I'll tell you about it later."

"No, let's talk now."

"I'll make some tea," Frances said. "Unless you prefer Scotch."

"No, Christ, I've had enough alcohol."

"What have you been doing?"

"Well, just now, I was in the Downtown Eastside, looking for Emily."

"Oh, Richard!" Carol looked so stricken, Richard was frightened.

"What? What's the matter?"

She started to cry. "She's dead, Richard. I was looking for her, too. She's dead."

"No. Oh god. How did it happen?"

"They found her dead of an overdose in a hotel room a month ago."

"Who found her?"

"The police."

"But you didn't even know her last name, how did you …? I mean, how do you know it was her?" Richard asked.

"I had a photo of her."

"Where the hell did you get it?"

"From Nick Wallinsky. Don't ask. I'll tell you about that another time."

"Shit!"

"She was eighteen," Carol said.

Richard wobbled like a marionette whose strings have loosened. He fell onto the couch, still wearing his coat. Richard moaned and said, "I should have looked for her earlier — months ago." Then he reached out and brushed away a tear rolling down Carol's cheek and started to cry himself, quietly at first, and then with loud, racking sobs, like the sea on a rocky shore, like a man drowning.

Carol put her arms around him, held him as they cried together.

After a while they drew apart, sat close but not touching.

In spite of the light in the room, Richard felt they were wrapped in a dark cocoon together, in a joint aura of exhaustion and surrender. And he realized, as he sat there in his strange, partial peace, that he had been crying not just about Emily and Jenny and Jacintha, *all the lost daughters*, but also about his own failures as a man and a father.

Carol, he thought, was not crying just about the lost ones, either (and maybe not for Jacintha at all), but mainly about her sins, real or imagined, and her wounded heart.

FORTY-THREE

RICHARD MOVED BACK in with Carol the next day. He walked for an hour or so every day and cooked and cleaned while Carol was at work.

They were awkward with each other. In the evenings, after dinner, they sat in different rooms, Carol preparing lessons or reading while Richard watched nature programs and other documentaries on TV. Sometimes Carol joined him, but his silence discouraged her, and she didn't stay long.

They'd been sleeping in separate rooms at Richard's request. "I need more time," he'd said, and Carol hadn't protested. The important thing was to have Richard with her. Still, she hungered to just embrace him, just touch him. He hadn't wanted to be touched since that brief handholding after they'd cried over Emily, and now, even if she merely brushed against him accidentally, he tensed and moved away.

After two weeks of meagre coexistence, Carol said, "We've got to do something to shake ourselves out of this state we're in."

"A good shake? If only it were as simple as that." His shoulders slumped, as they often did these days, and his face reminded her of a basset hound, and for a moment she wanted to slap him, but she breathed deeply and said, "I mean that a big change of scene might help. And seeing Imogen. How about we go to visit Imogen?"

Over the next few days they talked about when they'd go, and the things they'd have to do to get ready, and Carol was glad to see how much Richard was enjoying the whole process.

They put Carol's new phone on speaker and called Imogen. "Are you going to be staying in London for a while?" Richard asked. "We don't want to get there and find you're off to Argentina or somewhere."

"Yes, I'll be here for the foreseeable future."

"Good. We're planning to book a flight for early March. Carol is taking a leave of absence and I've resigned." Carol noticed his voice was a bit too upbeat as he slid quickly over the fact of his resignation.

"Oh, I'm sorry to hear you're not going to be teaching. Is it because of a health problem? Hasn't your wound healed properly?"

"No, the wound healed. I'm all right. Just need a break. Need to think about new directions. I'll tell you more when I get there."

"Well, I'll be very glad to see you. How long can you stay?"

"At least a couple of months. It's open ended at the moment. We'll rent an apartment, probably outside of London, where the prices are lower. Maybe you could keep your eyes open for something."

"Yes, of course. And you're welcome to stay with me for a while."

When they hung up, Carol said, "That was cheering, wasn't it? And now, when we're not shopping and packing and dreaming of London and Paris — we'll have to visit Paris — we need to be more ... more ..."

"And Venice," Richard said, and Carol's heart lurched.

"Yes, Venice, that would be wonderful," she said. "Anyway, what I was going to say was we need to be more *ordinary*."

"I forget what that is."

"It's doing things together, going for walks on the weekends and reading our books together in the evenings. Remember how we used to read interesting passages to each other? And we could go out to dinner or a movie. We've been just coexisting, wary of each other, too careful, as though we're made of glass. We're keeping too much to ourselves, definitely not talking enough."

"Sorry, I'll try to be more sociable."

"Oh, Richard. I know you're trying. It's not even what we do, so much. It's having pity on each other, being tender and more aware of each other's needs, even when we're in separate rooms. You know what I mean. You can feel those things through walls, I'm convinced of it. We're ordinary, pitiful human beings. That's always our state of being. It's just more obvious in a crisis. The only extraordinary thing we need to do is to remember how pitiful we are, every day, and try to be tender with each other."

Richard put on a mock frown, forehead creased, lower lip protruding. "Every day?" he asked.

"All right. Every other day. Did I just hear you laugh?"

"More of a gurgle."

"Close enough."

March 2012

Dear Carol,

I recall with pleasure and affection our reconciliation:
recounted above. I was so grateful for how tenderly
you treated me, how sweetly. We had some good times
in England, didn't we? For a while we were closer than
ever, almost like honeymooners.

I hope you remember it fondly, too.
Love,

Richard

(I received no reply.)

FORTY-FOUR

RICHARD HAD THOUGHT about going to visit Frances by himself before they left on their trip, to thank her for how she'd taken care of him, but in the end he felt he couldn't face any more of her frank assessments and probably probing questions about his "experience." With Carol along, Frances would be more discreet; at least, he hoped so.

The first thing they noticed after arriving for dinner was a huge, new painting above the fireplace. The bright red, blue, and gold shapes made Carol gasp. The piece was vibrant and strangely moving.

"Very few abstract painters move me," Carol said. "Mark Rothko is one. You've used Rothko's technique of blurred borders between the colours. It makes quite an impact. What's come over you, Mother? This is amazing. The last things I saw of yours were watercolours, lovely but sedate."

"I started using acrylics a while ago, while Richard was here. I find them more muscular, you know. I felt I needed to make larger gestures."

"Did you exorcize Dad's ghost? You said you were always content doing a few watercolours now and then because Dad was the great artist. I never believed in your contentment. And you know he never exactly encouraged me, either."

"I'm sorry if I ever made you believe he oppressed me. And I'm sorry he discouraged you, truly, but I think I used him as an excuse for not committing myself to my work. I seemed to need to believe I was of more use to him as his muse, as you so ably pointed out to me."

Over dinner they talked about Imogen and England, and afterward they went to Frances's studio and looked at two more of her remarkable paintings.

When Carol went to the bathroom before they left, Richard said, "Listen, Frances, I came here tonight expressly to thank you for looking after me so well when I was at my lowest, saving my life, and I haven't said a word about it all evening. I'm saying it now. Thank you." He pulled her into an awkward hug.

"I was happy to do it. You're my dear son-in-law and you always made Carol happy and I know you will again." Then her tone of voice became solemn. "You were thrown into a purifying fire, Richard, and you'll find you are changed in ways you can't imagine now. Profound ways. I'd bet on it."

"Can one bet against a philosopher queen?"

Frances laughed. "Good, take me down a peg or two."

"Please, Frances, as I've said before, don't make what happened into something it isn't."

"And I keep telling you to see it in a larger context, a spiritual one, for want of a better word." Frances looked into his eyes, held his gaze. "Something *has* changed, hasn't it?"

"Sometimes I feel a change, for a moment or two," he said, "a kind of shifting of my axis — occasional feelings of joy."

"Those moments will lengthen," Frances said, "and you'll go from shame to acceptance, maybe even a fragile sort of gratitude."

"I doubt that."

Frances hasn't seen the true nature of what I'm going through, Richard thought, *how ambiguous, how paradoxical it is. How dangerous it might be.*

As Richard pulled on his gloves, Frances said, "Those are so beautiful. Are they new?"

They were made of forest-green suede, so beautiful, so organic looking he was sometimes surprised they didn't smell of fir or pine. "Yes," he said, "I lost my old ones."

"He was never much of a shopper," Carol said, coming back into the room. "But he picked those out himself. Good taste, don't you think?"

Richard shook his head and looked away, walked closer to Frances's large painting as though to get a better look. In fact, the gloves were from Jacintha. He had been cleaning out his university office, packing up books, when he saw that the clay dog Imogen had made was missing. On the shelf where it had stood was a package wrapped in white tissue paper and tied with a red ribbon. He'd torn it open and found the gloves and a note that read, "Wear these and think of me. Love, Jacintha."

He turned back and forced himself to smile at the two women. He embraced Frances and kissed her on the cheek. "I'll miss you," he said.

"But you'll be back," Frances said.

"Yes, of course."

In the car on the way home, Carol said, "If we stay in England for any length of time, how are we going to support ourselves?"

"We'll cross that bridge later."

"No, really. I'm a little worried."

"I could busk."

"You can't sing."

"I can dance a little."

Carol laughed. "We will get through this, won't we?"

"One day at a time."

"Oh, I hope it won't be that … tentative."

"Life is tentative," Richard said.

"You'll go back to teaching, I think," Carol said.

"Maybe."

"I might teach a little, but I don't want to work full time. I want to paint. Mum has inspired me."

"That would be good," Richard said.

They were both silent for a minute, and then Carol said, "Last night on the radio I heard a writer say that it's more creative to love than to be loved."

"Isn't that a non sequitur in this conversation?"

"I don't think so."

"Well, the statement is open to more than one interpretation, and in any case, it's debatable," Richard said.

"Yes, it is, isn't it?"

AUTHOR'S NOTE

OBVIOUSLY, IN SPITE of Carol's pleas, I did publish. I took the chance. For one thing, I thought, since Imogen lives half a world away and now has a married name, it's unlikely she would be involved in any publicity should my real name be revealed. Also, I thought she *could* handle the facts of the story, as she's smart and compassionate and loves me and would respect my honesty and understand my motives. *And she would believe me.*

I live in the hope that all of the above is true.

And I devoutly hope that those who were very young will never be identified because they don't need to have these "events" trailing after them like hungry dogs. If it were only Carol and I (and Nick), we'd cope. As middle-aged adults, we would be able to survive tossing out a few bones with bits of flesh still clinging to them.

Some people might say — Carol isn't one of them — that I shouldn't have suffered so much, that I mainly just lusted after Jacintha, and anyway, I didn't know who she was. They might tell me to "man up" and stop moaning.

Even the almost saintly Jimmy Carter famously said, "I've committed adultery in my heart many times." (Who knew that U.S. presidents would delineate sexual parameters?)

The first agent I sent this book to declared that Richard did suffer too much and everyone was "so mean to him"; therefore, she couldn't market it. I told this to a friend, who said, "Wait until she reads Shakespeare!" I cherish that as a most excellent literary put-down.

I was recently thinking about all this in terms of an imaginary *Tempest* rewrite. Suppose Prospero had lived on the island alone and one day a young woman washed up on the shore half-drowned and he had lusted after her. More and more. Then, in Act IV, he found out she was his daughter. Shakespeare would surely have had Prospero undergo torments of the soul until he killed himself in Act V. And that for "only" lusting.

That said, let me emphasize that Jacintha was the one who truly suffered in all this. I suffer still, but mostly from remorse, which is of an entirely different and *lower* order.

I don't want anyone to feel sorry for me. Still, I like what Flaubert wrote: "Human speech is like a cracked kettle on which we beat out tunes for bears to dance to, when we long to move the stars to pity."

And I was grateful for the occasional exhalations of sympathy from Carol, the stars and their pity being out of my reach. Dancing bears, on the other hand, even in their clumsiness, like my dear wife thrown off balance, can offer significant solace.

So what now? My father died at sixty of heart failure. I used to worry that I'd suffer the same fate, and even though I still have a strong feeling that I will, I don't worry about it anymore. A chapter of my life has ended, and I don't know if I have the desire to write another one. There are points, I think, where many people make choices of whether to go on or not, following the loss of, say, a marriage or career, or, more seriously, following the news that they're suffering from a terminal illness or when dealing with the death of a loved one. But losing the will to live isn't always big and dramatic and doesn't necessarily result in the sudden blow of suicide. It can begin with something as soft and small as a sigh of resignation, and continue as a quiet sliding away.

What is the right amount of suffering?

AFTERWORD TO THE
SECOND EDITION OF
JACINTHA

By Carol Wilson

RICHARD DIED OF a heart attack shortly after the publication of his novel. He had only a few months to enjoy how well it was received. He was found two days after his death by his upstairs neighbour.

On the whole, time having given me a greater perspective, I like the book in terms of the personal story (in spite of my earlier, well-documented objections!). I ended up having more sympathy for Richard as a result of understanding more about his struggle. And I also admire it as a literary work.

Richard appointed me executor in his will, which he'd written only weeks before his death. His premonition must have been strong. He bequeathed his computer and his books to me. He owned very little else — nothing of value. The money in his bank account, several thousand dollars, he left to Imogen. He'd been working as a freelance editor.

He stipulated that any future income from sales of his novel be donated anonymously by his publisher to Doctors Without

Borders. (So now, in spirit, he is doing some of the "good works" overseas that he thought for a while he might do in the flesh.)

In his files I found several unfinished stories. In one, a man reconciles with a long-lost daughter and makes amends by helping her and her young children — quite boring — and in another, a man has a breakdown in Mexico that reads like a sad imitation of *Under the Volcano*, replete with hallucinations and DT's.

But what I want most to share with you here is a chapter he removed from the end of the book, maybe to spare my feelings, or maybe just because it was too close to the bone, too raw. I think he should have left it in because it is powerful and painful in its honesty and reminds me that we are all flawed, that nothing is black and white, and that most of us, if we've lived long enough, have a "what-if" or an "if only" of our own — not as terrible as Richard's, perhaps, but still haunting and full of regret.

Before we get to that chapter, I'd like to tell you one significant thing that he didn't mention. About a year after we moved to England, he had an affair with a young woman who looked uncannily like Jacintha. (They moved to France together, but she left him within a few months.) That was really the end of us, but I don't want to dwell on it. I don't hurt the way I used to. It was several years ago, after all, and I am happy with Nick. But sometimes, as Richard put it, the ghosts "press up against me," and require of me a certain amount of sadness.

Love itself is never *wrong*, but sometimes we have no choice but to turn away from the object of our love. Richard most certainly had to. Still, apropos of the chapter to follow, most of us know how both body and mind can continue to yearn, and how the heart rebels and refuses to harden, and how we can become more human for it.

Here is the previously unpublished chapter:

FORTY-FIVE

THREE DAYS BEFORE Richard and Carol were to leave for England, Richard received a letter from Jacintha. Trembling, he opened it.

The first thing he saw was a photo of Jacintha and a man who looked so much like him that at first he thought it was himself on some forgotten occasion. Or that he could be in two places at once. Or that he was losing his mind. He took a breath and looked more closely. The man had Richard's sandy hair, a nose like his, light eyes like his, and an expression that Richard had sometimes caught on his own face in the mirror. But, no, it wasn't him.

They were standing on a beach, a sparkling azure sea behind them. Jacintha wore a yellow halter top and a blue skirt, and her hair shone golden in the sun. He turned the photo over. *Me and Jonathan in Puerto Vallarta.* He read the letter.

Dear Richard,

Jonathan is a Brit I met here in Mexico. You'll have noticed he looks a lot like you and that pleases and comforts me a little, but he's not you, and that still pains me. But don't worry, I have let you go, as you asked. Jonathan is good to me and I love him in my fashion.

There's just one thing, one important thing that I haven't told you. (If I'd stayed with you, there would have been endless things to tell you.) Sorry, there I go again.

The thing I want to tell you is this: I was pretty sure you were my father for a while before I got the test result. I saw the three moles on your neck. I have three moles in the same place in the same inverted triangle. I thought it was a sign that we were twin souls, meant to be together, but that, tragically, has proved impossible. Dear Richard, dear Papa, I'll always cherish the time we had together. I'm not saying I'll never see you again, but I'll do nothing to make it happen — I'll leave it to the universe. I like to believe we'll never really escape each other because we belong to each other.

Beth says Carol is back with you and you're going to England to visit your daughter, the unsullied one. But remember, there are so many ways for a girl to be damaged in this world. But not by me. Or you. I didn't mean that.

I'm glad for you, truly I am. I wish you and yours all happiness. And all shall be well, and all manner of things shall be well.

All my love,
Jacintha

Richard shuddered. His heart raced and his head swam; he was gripped by a terrible thought.

She'd never worn her hair completely up. But once — oh, god, he remembered now. It was on Thanksgiving Day, when, hot from dancing, she'd lifted her hair from her neck for a moment. He was standing behind her, very close, and he had seen two of the moles, not large but very noticeable, velvety brown, one at the base of her neck, the other at an angle an inch or so above. It had never occurred to him that there might be a third.

A chill crawled up his spine. What if he had seen the third mole, had the same thought as Jacintha, and had decided it was too much of a coincidence? Or what if he had found out the truth another way, *before the knife came down*. Would he have run from her, escaped before it was too late?

Or would he have done the opposite? Taken her away with him. Run away with her and never looked back. Prayed if she knew who he was, she would never admit it. Could he have done such a thing? How strong would he have been, one way or the other?

He would never know. And that would be the worst part of his punishment.

ACKNOWLEDGEMENTS

FIRST OF ALL, I'd like to thank my family. Love always to my beautiful, wonderful daughters, my dear son-in-law, and my grandchildren. All of you are also beautiful and wonderful. Your love sustains me, lifts me up, and never lets me down.

I'm very grateful to the whole Dundurn team for their talents and hard work.

Thanks so much to Scott Fraser, publisher, who chose my book for publication and started this exciting adventure for me.

Thanks to Dominic Farrell, developmental editor, for your insightful and razor-sharp editing skills and your kindness.

Thank you, Victoria Bell, copy editor. Your astute insights into Jacintha (the character) — one comment in particular really pleased me.

Jenny McWha, project editor, gracious and efficient. It's been a pleasure working with you.

Laura Boyle, thanks for your beautiful cover design. "Stunning" was one of the comments I received.

Elham Ali, excellent and enthusiastic publicist. I'm enjoying working with you.

Thank you, freelancer Janice Zawerbny, for your insights early in this process.

Stephanie Sinclair, my agent at Transatlantic: You have been a rock, always believing in my novel and cheering me on. And finding a publisher! Thank you so much.

Special thanks to my first mentor, Shaena Lambert, novelist and short story writer extraordinaire. You gave me your friendship and the confidence, in those early days, to continue writing. I am so grateful.

Thank you, Zsuzsi Gartner, brilliant short story writer and now novelist, for your encouragement and editing skills, and your wonderful Writers Adventure Camp in Whistler.

Thanks to the many friends who have been there for me over the years, including some of the dearest ones: Lilia Petri, Liz Weis, Agi Rejto, and fellow writer Clare Gomez.

I can't say enough about you, my lovely friend Denise Wrathall. Your constant support and generosity in many areas, good times and bad, have meant so much to me. And your computer skills have saved me countless times!